THE MOST DIMINUTIVE OF BIRDS

*…for the poor wren
The most diminutive of birds, will fight,
Her young ones in her nest, against the owl."*

William Shakespeare—Macbeth

THE MOST DIMINUTIVE OF BIRDS

Carmen Lynne

Writers Club Press
San Jose   New York   Lincoln   Shanghai

The Most Diminutive of Birds

Writers Club Press
an imprint of iUniverse.com, Inc.

For information address:
iUniverse.com, Inc.
620 North 48th Street, Suite 201
Lincoln, NE   68504-3467
www.iuniverse.com

ISBN: 0-595-13074-7

Printed in the United States of America

For Simon

INTRODUCTION

TUESDAY MARCH 3rd, 1992

Billy knew how it felt to fly.

This was how it felt, rocketing downhill on skimming wheels with the frosty air whipping his cheeks. To his right, the lake shimmered in the morning sun and then sped by. The only sounds were the whisper of his tires along the ground and the cooing of wood pigeons in the trees.

A house appeared on his left. Billy slid to a halt outside it and paused a moment astride his bicycle, feeling his heart thump. It was impressive—like all the houses in this street—and stood detached in a large area of ground. Ivy crept over the walls and two turrets jutted incongruously into the London sky, like something out of an old horror movie. Sometimes Billy almost expected to see Boris Karloff lurching towards him with arms outstretched.

Today, however, that didn't seem possible. (Monsters are always asleep by dawn and shun the sunlight. They would be afraid to leave their coffins on such a perfect day as this.) A dusting of snow clung to blades of grass and formed a negative outline along the branches of trees. Billy liked the look of snow better than the feel of it in his fingers. Snowball fights didn't appeal, any more than shoveling up mounds of the stuff to make snowmen. Making footprints, though, on a virgin sheet of white, now there was pleasure.

But first there was work to do. Billy leaned his bike against the garden wall and took out the bundle of newspapers from his saddlebag. He had been doing the job long enough to know which newspaper each house wanted, but he made a cursory check on the numbers just to be sure. As he strode up the path to the front door, his thoughts meandered and came to dwell on the things most important to him. Two more weeks of school before the Easter holidays and by that time he would have enough money saved to buy the Raleigh Racer. He was early today—it was just before seven—and if he hurried he could finish the ten big houses in East Field Lane in time for a walk on the heath.

When he came out of number 21 and collected his bike to cross the road, he noticed a small brown dog cocking its leg against a tree about ten yards away. Billy encouraged the dog towards him and patted its head while it snuffled around his feet. It was a mangy little dog of indeterminate breed and seemed happy to have found company, for when Billy made his way to the heath side and on to the grass, it trotted beside him, looking up from time to time with hopeful eyes.

The heath was magnificent, a huge expanse of snow broken only by brittle, angular trees. Billy noticed a squirrel poke its head out of a hole, observe him in alarm, then shimmy up the tree trunk, disappearing amongst the tangle of branches at the top. Although almost blinded by the glare of sun and snow, his eyes came to rest on the outline of a tree some fifty yards distant. The trunk was arched in a curve like that of a ballerina and the two main branches forked upwards like a pair of arms reaching to the sky.

The dog had seen the tree too, and was careering towards it in wild expectation. On reaching the tree, it scrambled around the back and dropped out of sight for a few moments, before its wagging tail and hind legs reappeared to the side. The dog was making strange jerking movements with its body as if it were trying to pull something. It capered around to the front of the tree, gave a few short yelps and then resumed its struggling with the unseen object to the other side. It came to the front again and began to bark in earnest, pausing only to dart to the side and continue tugging at its discovery.

Intrigued, Billy followed the dog, looking down occasionally to check the impression his footprints were making in the snow. When he reached the tree, the dog was still tugging.

"What have you got there boy? What's all this fuss about?" said Billy, squatting down to see what the dog had found. With a last ferocious yank, the dog pulled at the thing and let it plop to the ground, then crouched staring at it with jaws hanging open.

It was a human hand.

*   *   *

Mrs. Donnelly distinguished her son on the horizon as he cycled down the road towards her. She had just been collecting the milk and was going to take it inside when some vague premonition held her on the doorstep. She waited till she saw Billy descend from his bike and run up the path towards her, and when she was close enough to see his face she knew her premonition had been correct.

"Billy, what's wrong darling?" she said as she reached out and clasped him in her arms. "What's wrong, what happened?"

For a few moments he couldn't speak and when he did his words gasped out in sobs. She stroked his hair as she listened, then guided him indoors, sat him in the armchair by the fire with a blanket over his knees and called the police station at Temple Green.

Story One

Chapter One

Detective Inspector Graham Brunswick stopped for a moment with his razor poised in mid-air, and contemplated the reflection that stared warily back at him from the mirror. It was what his mother would have called a "nice" face—a square jaw (covered at the moment in white foam), warm brown eyes without too many crows feet around them, unruly dark eyebrows that gave him an air of mystery, a broad expanse of forehead and a good crop of silvery gray hair. He surveyed the face as if it were that of a stranger he was encountering for the first time and trying vainly to comprehend. Closing his eyes fleetingly, he fought down the feelings of repugnance that a glimpse of his own image induced, then, with a shiver, applied himself once again to his shaving, taking more than usual care not to nick his chin.

He repeated to himself that his current state of mind was a product of his hormones, that there was a rational scientific reason for these unfamiliar feelings which surged abruptly through him disturbing his equilibrium. Hadn't Dr. Thacker said Graham's symptoms were classic examples of the male menopause? Graham felt rueful now at his cynicism over the doctor's explanation and the way he had scoffed that women go through the change of life but men just get older without getting wiser. Considering it now, he clung on to Thacker's definition like a drowning man to a branch, offering as it did the only proof that he wasn't going quietly mad.

So, who is this stranger? he asked himself as he wiped the foam from his face with a flannel. *Whose are those eyes filled with doubt and a kind of despair? They don't belong to me.*

Just then, Pat called up the stairs ordering him to breakfast, and the sound of her voice—wholesome and real—chased the demons, at least temporarily, from his mind. He slapped aftershave briskly on his cheeks and went downstairs to the kitchen.

The couple—each occupied with their own concerns—didn't bother speaking for a few minutes. Graham munched on the bran flakes in his bowl and pretended to be reading his copy of *The Times*, but his thoughts kept straying from the page to himself. He was on his second cup of tea but his body still felt as torpid and slow as if shaking off a sleeping drug. He remembered a time when he'd always been alert at this time of the morning, like a young tomcat ready for action. But now, the days seemed to wash into each other like colors in a badly dyed shirt, making the whole thing gray. Was it something to do with growing older, this feeling of stolidity and dullness, watching the years rush by as if they didn't have time for him any more? Or was he actually losing his grip? Superintendent McGivern obviously thought the latter, since the Hackett case anyway. He wondered if he should have left the Force, as he'd said he would then, in that first flush of battered idealism. At least he would have gone out with a bang, not a whimper. Well, there was no living that down now. What's done is done.

"Toast's done, dear." Pat turned from flipping her omelette and smiled, indicating a rack of toast on the table with her eyes. "It'll get cold."

She was still quite a good-looking woman for her years. Stout, of course, with too many laugh lines around the eyes and mouth. But that's what happens to the English rose in middle age. She had been a beauty once. Graham couldn't help a brief pang of pity—as he studied her back in the flowered kimono—for her and her dreary household life. And with the pity came guilt. Guilt at the knowledge that he no longer enjoyed her company—if he was really honest about it—but that he stayed with her anyway, for convenience. Their marriage felt like a sham and had done for quite a few months, and yet he carried on living the lie, pretending that everything was the same as ever. So where was his precious integrity that everyone admired him for? That famous honesty that had landed him in hot water with the Super on many an occasion? Had it been sacrificed on the altar of convenience?

"I didn't tell you, Gray", Pat said as she caught her husband looking at her. "Gemma rang last night when you were out. She says she's coming home for the weekend."

Graham hid his disappointment at missing the chance to speak to his daughter with a flippant remark: "Don't tell me, she's spent her grant money already?"

Pat—having misinterpreted Graham's humor—complained: "How can you be so cynical? I thought you'd be pleased to see her."

"I was only joking."

"Well, I wish you wouldn't"

"It'll be good to see Gemma, of course" Graham placated.

"I'm looking forward to it," said Pat meaningfully, "And it may be the last time she can get back for a while." Graham caught an accusing tone in her voice and guessed at the sub text to her words.

"Really?" He didn't rise to the bait but continued looking at the sports pages, scanning them to see if there was a good cricket match he could take Gemma to at the weekend for a treat outing. His head half-hidden in the test results, he appeared unconcerned with what Pat was saying.

Pat raised her voice slightly. "You know it's her finals in June. She'll have to give up all her time to studying."

"Yes, I imagine she will."

"She won't have time to visit us then. I'm sure visits to parents will be very much on the back burner."

Sometimes, Graham hated the way Pat spoke in cliches, and so pedantically, like something out of one of those women's magazines she was so fond of. She was right about Gemma, though. Gemma—he thought, not without pride—was the ambitious type who would work hard for what she wanted. And achieve it. He folded the newspaper into a neat oblong and began to butter a piece of toast. "I'm sure she'll pass with flying colors. And then what'll it be, Gemma Brunswick B.A. Honors, taran tara!"

"I hope so. But we mustn't assume…"

"Ah, she'll do all right. Our little girl's got a head on her shoulders." Graham reflected that his daughter resembled him at that age: sensible, bright, hardworking, reliable, unstoppable on the ladder to success. *But what does it matter if you get what you want?* he concluded with a touch of bitterness. *It doesn't always make you happy.*

"She's very lucky. She's had the benefit of an education" said Pat, gently lifting the omelette on to a plate.

She was harping on one of her well-worn themes. "Which not all of us had. Yes, I know." Graham imagined that Pat was referring to her own lack of an education, to the fact that she'd chosen to marry rather than go to university. Pat wasn't the sort to feel bitter about such things, but sometimes she let a little regretful comment slip.

"Which not all of us *have*, even. There's your omelette, dear."

"Thanks, it looks very edible." Graham began to eat. Then a thought occurred to him: "Have you taken some new fledgling under your wing at the hostel?"

"Why do you say that?" she demanded, taking the lid off the coffee jar, and looking slightly stunned as if her mind had been read.

Graham said nothing, but tapped his nose with his index finger in a knowing gesture and looked at his wife.

"Am I that predictable?" she asked. "Well all right, yes, in a way. A young girl was there for the first time last night. She's so young, hardly older than Gemma. Apparently, she's just lost her baby in a miscarriage and now her husband's left her. I just don't know how these people cope."

"Has she got somewhere to live?" he asked through a mouthful of omelette.

"I'm not sure. She left rather suddenly at the end of the meeting. I was going to write down our number and give it to her, just in case she—"

"For heaven's sake, Pat. I've told you before. Don't take the whole world on your shoulders. There are other people, professionals, who are trained to deal with that sort of thing."

Pat was going to reply, but the words died on her lips. It was too early in the day to start an argument. She wanted to tell Graham that her job meant more to her than he realized, that the more he ignored her the more she would be driven to seek solace in helping others. She almost burst out that she deserved more of his time, and that she was the person he should come to if he needed to talk. But she kept quiet and buried her face in her toast.

Having finished his omelette, Graham pushed back his chair and stood up. "Didn't *The Telegraph* come today?"

"I don't know. You could go and check."

Graham was glad to get out of the kitchen. His mind felt like a big ball of tangled string which he couldn't unravel. He went into the hall and said good morning to Serena in her cage. The parakeet waddled along her pole and nuzzled him with her beak in their little morning ritual, pushing aside the piece of yellow ribbon that had been tied to the bars by Graham's team-mates when presenting her to him on his promotion to Detective Inspector. A little card still dangled from the ribbon, and the message on it made Graham smile: *To D.I. Graham Brunswick from all at Temple Green. Tom said you fancied an exotic bird, so we got you Serena.* It had been a while since he'd let her out of her cage to fly about the room, since the last time she had disgraced herself by landing on the head of one of Pat's friends and scaring her half to death, much to Graham's secret amusement.

The telephone started to ring, and it was just at that moment that Graham got one of his heartburn attacks. The pain doubled him over for a moment and then was gone. Fortunately, by the time Pat came through the kitchen door intending to answer the phone, he had recovered and he pushed past her, saying: "It's all right. I'll get it."

"It's probably for you anyway." She retreated into the kitchen and Graham lunged to pick up the receiver.

"Hello, 2938."

"Good morning sir, we've got a call out for you, I'm afraid."

"Oh, can't they time these things better? O.K., I've got pen and paper ready."

"Right, there's been an incident at the bottom of East Field Lane…"

"What number?"

"No number, I think it's on the heath itself actually, sir. Anyway, we've got a couple of patrol cars out there at the moment, so if you'd like to make your way there as soon as possible…"

"Will do. Thanks Carson."

"See you later, sir."

Graham went into the downstairs bathroom and looked in the medicine cabinet for the antacid pills that he kept secreted in the back. He hadn't told Pat about his stomach problems, telling himself that he didn't want to worry her about something so trivial. Maybe he also didn't want to worry himself.

He could hear Pat's voice in the kitchen crooning *You've lost that loving feeling*. Her voice was sweet, if a little flat, and she sang the correct words with gusto, but Graham had never been enamored of her choice of music. To Graham, nothing could equal the beauty of a Vivaldi or a Corelli string concerto with its orderly melodies and its echoes of a world long gone where everything had a designated place.

He swung into the kitchen. Pat was pouring coffee into her Royal Wedding mug, and Graham grabbed the jacket he'd flung over his chair.

"I'll have to go."

"Oh—no time for…"

"Sorry. I'm called out to Hampstead."

"All right. Well, you won't forget tonight, will you?"

"Tonight?"

"I told you ages ago. The Rockwells are coming over for dinner."

"The Rockwells?"

"Those new people who've moved in across the street. I told you we ought to make friends with them, make them feel welcome."

"Oh yes, of course. I'll be there. See you later, then, love."

She followed him to the front door, holding his *Times*, and put her face out to be kissed. "Try not to be late."

When he pecked her, her cheek felt soft and downy, but it had an old woman's smell, of perfume too cloying. Graham took the paper from her hands and was gone.

*   *   *

The two girls giggled as they stumbled over the wet tiles and ran to the shallow end of the pool, their bare feet making a slapping sound on the floor. Gemma was in front and the first to descend the metal steps into the water. "God, the water's cold in here today!" she exclaimed, as she slithered into the pool, splashing her arms with water till she got used to the temperature. Karen hesitated on the first step, testing the water delicately with her toe and screwing up her face in a mock grimace: "I'm not coming in. It's too cold."

Gemma—now comfortably enveloped in the water—aimed a few splashes at her friend: "Come on, come on! If you don't get in, I'll pull you." She was laughing so hard that she took in a gulp of water, and the bleach stung the back of her throat and burned her nostrils. Karen covered her laughing mouth with her hand and remained on the steps till Gemma grabbed her by the ankle and yanked it hard, shouting "Scaredy cat" as she gasped for air. Screaming in part-genuine, part-feigned terror, Karen lost her balance and toppled backwards into the pool with an enormous splash. The two girls faced each other, both jumping gracefully from the bottom of the pool like ballet dancers doing restrained jetes. After a few moments they rained idle blows on each other, both now helpless with laughter, until Gemma submerged herself in the water, did a quick somersault and surfaced a few feet away from her friend. "Catch me if you can!" she hollered, waving her arms in the air.

"Oh!" Karen gasped. "I'm not coming after you. It's bloody freezing in here."

"It was your idea to come swimming" accused Gemma.

"No it wasn't" denied Karen. "You're the sporty one. When I said we needed exercise before lessons I was thinking more of a stroll over to the bar for a coffee."

"Well we're here now, so let's enjoy it."

"You're a masochist, you—"

"Just shut up and swim" exhorted Gemma. "It's the only way to get warm." She didn't wait for Karen to reply but shut her eyes tight and plunged into the water, swimming as fast as she could in a forceful crawl that had more energy than grace, all the way to the deep end without stopping to draw breath. Once there, she heaved herself up on to the edge with a strong lift of her arms and sat dangling her legs in the water, waiting for her friend to bring up the rear. Gemma noticed a young man standing by the edge of the pool and guessed that he was the lifeguard. He was tall and slim with wavy blonde hair, and he was staring at her with a friendly grin.

Gemma liked the look of him. She wondered why she hadn't seen him around the University campus before. "Are you trying to freeze us out, or what?" she called out to him, aware of her swimsuit clinging seductively, she hoped, to the contours of her body as she arched her back in a display of nonchalance.

"You'll have to get tougher than that, if you want to enter the swimming competition," he replied. He had a nice voice, with a hint of a Northern accent.

Gemma speculated as to whether he had a girlfriend. She'd seen the notices about the swimming competition, but it hadn't had much appeal before. Now it seemed like a golden opportunity. "I don't know how to dive" she hinted with a flirtatious smile.

"I could teach you I suppose." He smiled invitingly, and sauntered back to the shallow end, no doubt aware of the impression his tanned back made on the two girls.

"He's a bit of all right, isn't he" whispered Gemma to Karen, who had now joined her and was regarding the object of her interest.

"Who is he?"

"The lifeguard."

"I think he fancies you."

Gemma looked up and saw that he was eying her from the other end of the pool. She knew how strong and graceful her body looked as it pierced the water. She didn't reply to Karen but launched herself back into another crawl, even more energetic than the last one. Once submerged again, the water felt pleasantly warm, and she enjoyed the feeling of power in her muscles as she plunged in each arm. She didn't stop after her length of crawl, but did the breast stroke up to the deep end and then yelled to Karen, who was still floundering behind her, "Come on! Twenty four lengths to go". She stole a quick glance at the lifeguard to make sure he was still watching, before she set off again for a length of back stroke.

She was glad that she'd dragged Karen out for a swim before classes. The release of energy was exactly what she needed, after hours of sitting at the cramped desk in her room studying for her finals. And it offered an opportunity to forget recent events, forget the debating over whether to tell mum and dad, and just concentrate on sheer enjoyment.

She wasn't going to think about Julian. He'd got to stop pestering her, and that was that. She wasn't going to live with him, however many times he said *In view of what happened* and *You need protection* in that pompous way he had. She wasn't going to argue with him any more over her reasons for refusing to marry him. He was just going to have to accept that she didn't want to marry anybody. And it wasn't fair of him to blame her parents with all that pseudo-analytic babble about them being bad role models. What the hell did he know about it anyway?

The way he harped on about "the incident" only made her angry. Of course it was scary, being jumped on by a total stranger, and in the college grounds where she had thought she was safe. But she wasn't going to let what had happened stop her enjoying herself, whatever Julian said about *reasonable precautions.* He'd thought she was simply putting on a brave face when she'd said that only fear breeds fear, but she genuinely wasn't afraid of being attacked again. It was just a measure of the distance between them that he couldn't understand that.

Still, for his sake she would keep the *rape scream* he'd bought her in her pocket. There was no sense in taking foolish chances. But the main thing the event had taught her was that she no longer wanted to be with Julian.

She was still aggrieved at the way he'd muscled in and tried to organize her life. He always had to go poking his nose into her business and telling her what to do. If she didn't want to tell the police what had happened, that was up to her, wasn't it? It was obviously pointless, because there was virtually nothing to report. So for him to go threatening to call them himself was quite out of order.

If she'd felt she could trust him she might have told him about the nightmares she'd had recently where she'd seen the stranger's face—or what she had managed to glimpse of it—rising up out of the shadows of her imagination. But the thought of Julian clucking and fussing over her like a mother hen had made her keep quiet about her deepest fears.

She bobbed up and took the opportunity to look in the lifeguard's direction. He had his back to her and was ambling down the length of the pool. Gemma noticed how his feet turned out as he walked and she wondered if he found his job as a lifeguard boring and what else he did with his time. Her gaze made him turn his head and when he caught her looking at him he grinned as if unsurprised. Karen splashed towards Gemma doing an ungainly breast-stroke with her head poking out of the water like a turtle peering from its shell. Something about the sight of her made Gemma want to giggle, and she and the lifeguard exchanged a knowing glance. He certainly was dishy. The prospect of diving lessons suddenly seemed very attractive. Gemma made plans to come to the pool every morning from now on, and not just for the exercise. If Julian didn't like it, that was tough.

*   *   *

The air was chill and uninviting on Graham's cheeks as he stepped out of the car. With its usual English caprice, the sky had now gone a stubborn gray and the fresh breeze of an hour previously had become a harsh and insistent wind. Graham put up the collar of his coat and crossed the road to greet his colleagues in the patrol car.

"Good morning, sir" said DC Smart, leading Graham on to the heath, his young face as red as ever with the cold. Graham was glad to see Tom amidst the clutch of men. Tom was talking to Tyson, the Scene of Crimes officer, and his lean body was buffeted by the wind as he stood, legs splayed out like a scarecrow. The men were encircling a twisted, knotty tree that rose up conspicuously from the bleak whiteness of the heath. A flash of light to the right indicated that Curnow had started taking photographs.

Tom was the first to notice Graham approaching. "Morning mate. Nippy one, isn't it."

"Morning Tom, Mr. Tyson. I hear there's been an incident."

"There's been an incident, all right. Take a look at this."

Graham followed Tom round the back of the tree.

"Not a pretty sight, eh?"

"Jesus!" exclaimed Graham with an intake of breath.

"Newspaper boy found them. Sniffed up by his dog."

"Poor kid. Guess it'll put him off video nasties for a while."

"Now he's seen the real thing."

They evidently were, or had been, a man and a woman. The brightly-colored skirt of the female corpse was recognizable, although her face was not. She lay strewn on her back, her legs twisted unnaturally, like lumps of meat in a butcher's window. One high-heeled shoe still clung to the decaying foot and the other lay half-buried under snow on the ground nearby, as if she had stumbled and fallen. Her right arm was raised and Graham could see the purple bruises where she had probably been trying to ward off her assailant.

The man lay on his belly a foot or two away. Blood from his gashed head had seeped into the surrounding snow and spattered the tree trunk with dark clots. One cold and lifeless hand was clamped to the strap of a woman's handbag in a dead man's grip, the rest of the handbag being buried beneath newly fallen snow.

"Have you had a look in this, Tom?"

"For I.D.? No, not yet. Thought I'd leave that to you."

Graham checked with Curnow that he'd finished taking photographs, then brushed away the snow lightly with his fingertips. The rusted clasp was unyielding, but he managed to prize it open just enough to remove a leather wallet, surprisingly little damaged. What he saw inside gave him a jolt.

"Here Tom, look at this." Tom leaned over and peered at Graham's discovery. Normally impassive, he raised an eyebrow in surprise.

"Full of money—good God!"

"Untouched." Graham straightened himself and stood up with a sigh. "Well, we know who she was anyway. She doesn't look like the sort to make enemies, does she?" he mused, looking at her photograph on the travel card.

"No" Tom agreed, "but whoever did that to her wasn't exactly friendly."

Around the bodies, a crisscross of footprints had been sealed into the snow crust, although later snow had fallen powdery on top, leaving a thin layer. The sky was full and heavy with snow and a few flakes began to descend, dribbling on to Graham's neck and forehead. Tom had on the brown Trilby that Graham told him looked ridiculous, but he would have been glad of such a hat himself now. At moments like this, he sometimes wondered why he hadn't taken over the grocery shop, as his father had wanted. But oh no, he'd insisted on joining the police force. *To help people*—he'd said in his naivete—*to make sure justice is done.*

How ironic it was—he thought now—that the only effect his years on the police force had had on him was to make him immune to sights such as these, sights of destruction and death that would make any normal person's stomach turn, but which to him were par for the course. He didn't start thinking yet about who the murderer could be. But the bodies—lain as they were like mute offerings in that isolated spot—reminded him powerfully of another murder he'd seen, two years before. One of a chain that he'd been investigating for months, and which had come to have a sickening familiarity about them. He shook off the memory with a toss of his head.

"Come on then" he barked to D.C.s Smart and Fields, "let's get some casts made of these prints and bag up the evidence. We can't stand around here all day."

Chapter Two

After giving her hair and face a cursory check in the mirror, Ruth put her feet up on the dressing table and tipped her head back, massaging her neck lightly with her fingers. In this position, a postcard on the wall caught her eye. It was one that Graham had given her. The picture was of Degas' Blue Dancers, purchased at an exhibition during the first heady days of their romance, and it rekindled sweet memories. She remembered how she'd been so astonished to find that this big, blunt, ordinary-seeming policeman had a passion for the finer things of life such as art and classical music, demolishing at a stroke all her preconceptions about his profession and the people it might attract.

Truth to tell, what had attracted her at first—physically attracted her—was his very quality of ordinariness. There was something strong and large and wholesome about his body and the way he moved. Like a farmer, or a man in contact with the earth and the elemental forces of nature. And the way he talked, in that firm voice, without any flowery phrases or attempts at flattery or condescension. She could see that he was an honest man, one not given to outward shows of affection or demonstrative behavior, but honest nevertheless. And that was his finest quality, so far as Ruth was concerned.

"Miss Ramon to the set, please. Five minutes to the next item" came the announcement over the tannoy, calling Ruth back into the present and out of her dressing room with no time for reflections.

She poured herself a cup of spring water from the machine in the corridor as she passed by and took it with her to the presenter's corner, where she positioned herself on her chair and tried to block out the distracting noises around her. It reminded her of being in an airplane—where all around her people were issuing instructions and preparing for takeoff—with herself as the only passenger. She was glad she'd decided to wear her new yellow blouse—she considered the color flattering against her rather dark skin and jet black hair, and yet it wouldn't be too garish for the television cameras. She thought back to the time when she'd been so anxious to choose the right outfit for the program that she'd literally spent an hour staring at her wardrobe before going out in the morning. But these days, there were many other things to occupy her.

"Hey, Ruth, remember Mr. Dervish?" Tony Bolero leaned over the back of Ruth's chair and jutted his face into hers, assaulting her with his rancid garlicky breath. Ruth contemplated suggesting to him again that he freshen up with a mint or a gargle after lunching at the Italian restaurant, then decided it wasn't worth the bother.

"Pardon?" Ruth responded, after a beat. She kept her head bent over her notes and hoped Tony would get the hint that she didn't welcome interruptions.

But he soldiered on, oblivious: "Mr. Dervish. The fella we had on last week. With the T.V. repair shop."

Ruth gave an intake of breath and regarded Tony steadily. "Yes I remember, the man who—"

"The break-in, yeah. Well, they caught the kids that did it."

"Really?" she responded with interest, resting the notes on her lap.

Tony sat down opposite her with a satisfied grin, and spread his corpulent frame on the set sofa. "Yeah. He's been on the phone to me just now. Thanking me."

Ruth wondered what Dervish had really said, considering Tony's tendency to misquote people. "Thanking you? But I was the one who—"

"Yeah, yeah, you interviewed him. Thanking *us*, then, the program. For doing the reconstruction."

"That's great." said Ruth with genuine pleasure, thinking how rarely people took the trouble to show their gratitude.

"Yeah, we jogged a few memories. That's all it takes sometimes." He clapped his hands together in a gesture of finality. "Fate acompley. Just thought you might like to know."

"Thanks, Tony." She didn't invite conversation by saying more, and Tony slapped his hands on his thighs and heaved himself off the sofa. Ruth smiled at his retreating back as he sauntered across to his dressing room smoothing the crease of his immaculately pressed trousers, and mouthed the words Tony *Trousers,* recollecting the nickname the technicians had given him in recognition of his obsession with that crease. She remembered the Christmas party where they'd watched the out takes and everyone had remarked on how often Tony could be seen, off camera, running his hands down his trousers in a sort of neurotic, narcissistic gesture. Ruth wondered vaguely what he had to prove and whether he'd been a scruffy little boy at school.

She began to feel hot and shiny under the lights, and was aware of a buzz of activity around her, as cameras were swiveled into position. John approached her and, keeping his eyes averted from hers in an earnest gaze at her chest, fixed the radio microphone to her blouse, apologizing for his clumsy hands like a doctor doing an indelicate examination. He replaced the headphones over his ears and followed a length of cable back to his recording machine. Ruth breathed steadily, and filled her mind with the questions she was going to ask. She was glad when Sue approached with her tray, frowning a little as she did when something wasn't quite perfect, and removed a powder puff from a lower level sending a little cloud of dust into the air. "Can I just…" she began, dabbing Ruth's nose and forehead, then stroking her cheeks with a soft brush of red. "Yes, that's better."

"Thanks." said Ruth absentmindedly, as she absorbed her opening lines from the auto cue, so that they would appear to trip naturally off her tongue when she faced the cameras. Her stomach juddered slightly at the knowledge that soon she would be watched by thousands of people. She breathed in and out deeply and consciously willed her mind to calm. Then gently rolled her head from side to side to free her neck, stretched her back and eased down her shoulders. She checked her appearance in the television monitor on her right and saw a body poised and still and exuding relaxed confidence. She felt good. She was ready.

Ruth noticed Ewan regarding her preparations appreciatively. He was a tall man with a round cheerful face and a crop of sandy brown hair, now receding from the crown of his head and leaving a bare circular patch which resembled a monk's cap. He stood behind his camera, one hand placed protectively on the hard metal side as if caressing a fragile woman, and winked at Ruth. "Sock it to 'em!" he encouraged in his soft voice with the hint of a Scottish burr. The red light on Ewan's camera also began winking at Ruth and she angled her body to face it.

She smiled. "Sure."

Ruth winced slightly at some feedback from her ear piece, and then the producer came through, speaking in a determinedly calm voice: "Ready are you, love?"

"Sure, Maggie."

"Did Tanya give you the notes on the background?" The pitch was low, almost like a man's.

In reply, Ruth waved the A4 sheets at the producer's box, where she could see a few figures silhouetted black against the lights. "I only just got them, though. I haven't had much time to look them over."

"Sorry about that. I did try and get them typed up before lunch but the computers went down. I'm sure you'll cope—you're a professional" the voice concluded briskly.

"I'll do my best" said Ruth to the air, the producer by now having moved on to something else.

John gulped down the remnants of his coffee and flung his plastic cup into the bin, where it landed with a clatter. Ruth noticed how the glare of the lights accented his pasty, acne-spotted skin.

Tanya bustled over to the presenter's corner, anxiously clutching her clipboard, and shepherding a tall, gangly man in his thirties: "This is Mr. Ross. We're going to go with the music. Everything O.K.?" Not bothering to wait for a reply, she positioned the terrified interviewee in the chair opposite Ruth and hurried back to the producer's box.

He was a thickset man in his early thirties with cropped ginger hair which stood away from his head and pale, slightly bulging blue eyes.

"Is it your first time on television? Don't worry. You'll be a natural." Ruth gave him her warmest smile. His fear was almost palpable. He made Ruth think of a rabbit blinded by the headlights of an oncoming car. He didn't smile back at her or even look at her, but fidgeted with the cord of his radio microphone in a dazed manner until Ruth interrupted him. "You'd better not fiddle with that thing, Mr. Ross. The sound will register. Ready?" He nodded distractedly, then sat with his hands clamped on to his knees as if holding on to them for dear life.

Ruth could hear the last chords of the title music fade away, as she turned to Camera One and began: "Good evening and welcome to *Watch Out For Crime,* the series where you the viewer get a chance to help the Metropolitan Police. Tonight, we have with us in the studio, Mr. Terence Ross. Mr. Ross is a self-employed plasterer from Stratford, who has been married for six years. He and his wife Sandra have a son, Damon, aged five and a half. Last Tuesday, just over a week ago, both Sandra and Damon disappeared and haven't been seen since. We're appealing to you, the viewers, to contact us if you have any clues as to the whereabouts of Sandra and Damon Ross."

Ruth waited while a photograph of the mother and son—smiling happily, taken in the back garden—was briefly flashed on to the screen.

Turning her head to Mr. Ross and the Camera Two auto cue, Ruth continued: "Mr. Ross, can you tell us, when was the last time you saw your wife and son?"

"Er…last Tuesday." He cleared his throat, self-consciously.

"What sort of time was it? Morning? Evening?"

"It was in the morning, before I wen' off to work."

"Right, so that would have been about nine o'clock?"

"Something like that, yeah." He shifted a little in his chair and ran trembling fingers through his thatch of hair.

"So you said goodbye as you went off to work, and she gave you absolutely no indication at all that she intended to go anywhere unusual…?"

"No, everything was like normal. I says bye, see you later, and I leaves the house thinking nothing of it."

"What about Damon? Didn't your wife have to take him to school?"

"No, he was sick that day. It was…I dunno, flu or something, so he was staying at home, and Sandra said she was gonna stay in all day and look after him."

"So you got home at around…five o'clock, and found that they'd gone?"

"Yeah, they'd just disappeared. There was no note, nothing.

"What did you do then?"

"Well, I thought maybe she'd gone round her mum's house, so I calls her, but she doesn't know nothing, so then I calls all her mates, but they don't know nothing either, so then I calls the police, and I told 'em my wife and kid have gone."

Ruth stole a quick look at her notes and saw out of the corner of her eye: *Format of interview. Ask him to give background material briefly, then let him make his appeal to camera. Wind up.* The red light on the auto cue was flashing, meaning one minute to go. Winding up time. On impulse, Ruth threw in a final question. "Can you think of any reason why your wife would suddenly disappear like that? Had you had an argument or something recently?"

She hadn't expected much response and was very surprised at how the man's face suddenly darkened. "Argument? No, we never had no argument. What are you getting at?"

"I'm not getting at anything Mr. Ross. I was just trying to find out—"

"Look, we might have a go at each other now and then, but who doesn't? That's no reason for her to go off and leave me, is it? And take the kid. He's my kid as well you know." The man's tone was becoming increasingly indignant.

Making up her mind to finish, Ruth turned again to Camera One. "So, Sandra and Damon Ross are still at large, and if you have any idea of their whereabouts, please call us here at the studio. The lines are open now."

The cameras switched to Tony Bolero, ready on the other desk with the next item, and Ruth visibly relaxed. Terence Ross continued to glare at her. "Why d'you have to say that about an argument? I bet that's not in the script."

A slight smile played about Ruth's lips. "I don't have a *script*, Mr. Ross. I'm sorry if I embarrassed you. I just thought it may account for her sudden disappearance with the child."

Ross stood up. "And *I* was supposed to do the appeal to the public, wasn't I? I thought it was me doing the appeal."

"There wasn't time—"

"Everyone's gonna think I beat her up or something. You've made *me* look like the criminal" he said in a belligerent tone. "I'm gonna have words with your boss!" he added, waggling his finger at Ruth. "I'm gonna tell her what I think of you and your bloody questions!" With this threat, he stormed off in the direction of the producer's box, yanking his radio microphone violently from its cord and throwing it down in disgust.

"Go ahead", Ruth called after him. She couldn't imagine that he would make much impression on Maggie, an oaf like that. Ruth thought it would be evident to anyone that he *had* beaten his wife and she had touched on a raw nerve by inadvertently hitting at the truth. "Methinks he doth protest too much" she mused softly.

John came up and removed her microphone, having retrieved the other from the floor. This time he didn't apologize for his hands but gave Ruth a look she couldn't interpret. "His nose was a bit out of joint, wasn't it?"

She felt subtly wrong-footed. "He was quite a character. How long have I got?" she added, changing the subject quickly.

John glanced over at Tony, who was mid-spiel: "A good ten minutes, I should say. Enough time for a ciggie."

Ruth sighed: "*If* you smoke." She left the set gratefully and went back to the comparative peace of her dressing room.

Later on that afternoon, as Ruth shared coffee in the Green Room with the production staff at the end of shooting, Tanya was talking with barely-disguised pleasure about Terence Ross's complaints to the producer: "He was really in a state, you know. We tried to keep him out of the box but he insisted on talking to Maggie right away. Right in the middle of shooting Tony's bit it was."

"You mean, Maggie wasn't watching my bit?" interjected Tony, his eyes widening over his coffee cup.

"Yeah, course she was watching, but she also had this bloody mad angry punter giving her hell. He was going on and on about Ruth"—she turned to the object of her tale—"He kept saying you didn't know your job and that you made him look like a criminal."

"He doesn't need Ruth's help to do that" laughed Ewan.

"I didn't make him *look* anything that he isn't" added Ruth, wiping the sides of her lips with a tissue. "I'm sure he did beat up his wife, actually. The very fact that he was so incensed about it only goes to prove that" she declared.

"I'm sure he did, too" Ewan agreed, passing a packet of biscuits to John next to him.

"Well, whether he did or not, it's none of our business" replied Tanya. "That's what Maggie says."

"Isn't it our business? I thought we were supposed to be helping people here. I think that poor woman's frightened for her life" Ruth asserted.

"Don't be so melodramatic," said John, with a smirk. Ruth caught him giving a look towards Tony that seemed to say, *These women! What do they know?*.

"Anyway, Maggie wasn't happy about you upsetting him" continued Tanya.

"It wasn't her fault" commented Ewan, "He was a ding bat. I should forget it if I were you, Ruth."

"She wants to have a chat with you about it" Tanya persisted.

"Uh oh," John grinned, "Called in to see the big white chief? We all know what that means." Tony laughed and waited for Ruth's reaction.

"That's O.K." Ruth said calmly, "I'll just explain my position. I'm sure she'll understand. After all, who does she know better? Her employee who's been working for her for close on two years with no complaints, or some homicidal maniac she's never clapped eyes on before?"

"Whew!" said John, waving his hands as if to put out a fire.

"It doesn't matter whose fault it is," Tony chipped in, stuffing his mouth with chips. "The fact is, you upset one of the punters, and the customer's always right. This is television, my love, and you can't afford to go around upsetting our public. You'd better apologize."

"What for? Thinking on her feet?" asked Ewan.

"You know what Maggie's like. Just say sorry. Better than losing your job over it" said Tanya. Her face was all concern, but Ruth speculated that if she did lose her job, Tanya would be first in the running to take over.

"I shan't lose my job. But I shan't apologize for finding out the truth. I don't care if I made him look like a criminal. He *is* a criminal."

"Watch out. Ruth's on one of her crusades again!" Tony interposed, with a look towards John.

"I hope he doesn't find his wife. I don't want innocent people to suffer because of the program. If Maggie doesn't like the fact that I care about the people we represent, that's fine. I'm quite prepared to resign."

There was silence in the room. Nobody seemed to know what to say. Ruth picked up her large leather handbag and walked out with her head held high, feeling a lot less confident than she appeared.

Chapter Three

"I'm sorry if this is unpleasant for you, Mr. Hunt."

"No, I…I know you have to do your job, Inspector. It's just that…when I identified her body, I asked the pathologist how she'd died. He wouldn't tell me."

"Well, it was er, very sudden, she died very quickly—"

"You can tell me what happened, Inspector. I need to know, can you understand? It might help me accept what's happened."

Tom lit another cigarette. The conversation stagnated for a moment while Graham studied the man sitting opposite him. Hunt was a well-built man in his fifties with untidy gray hair and a ragged beard. His hands—placed purposefully on his thighs—were delicate like a woman's, and Graham guessed that beneath the bluff exterior lay more sensitivity than Hunt cared to admit.

"If you really want to know, it's up to you, of course" said Graham, carefully.

"Listen, I'm a writer, I write thrillers mainly. My daughter found them too gory I think. In my own way, I'm possibly as well acquainted with death as you are, Inspector."

Graham remained unconvinced by Hunt's apparent equanimity. Graham had been there when the news was broken to Hunt of his daughter's death, had seen the color drain from his face and his body begin to shake.

"I've spoken to the pathologist who conducted a post-mortem on your daughter's body. Although he hasn't made an official report yet, in his opinion she was dealt a fatal blow to the head with a blunt instrument. We discovered a large log on the ground close to the scene of the crime and some brownish stains were identified by our forensics department as human blood. They're checking the blood group against your daughter's at the moment, and if these tally we can confirm that the log was the murder weapon. Our hypothesis is that she collapsed unconscious after the attack and died several hours later from blood loss."

"You mean, if she'd been discovered earlier—"

"We can't possibly tell what might have happened. We can't even tell exactly when she died."

"You said about a week ago."

"Approximately, yes."

"The night she went out with James. I wish to God I hadn't let her go!" Hunt hid his face in his hands in a gesture of despair. Graham had seen this sort of reaction before, and he knew that the best thing to do was maintain his professional composure.

"When did you first realize your daughter was missing?"

"That night—last Wednesday—at about one o'clock. I telephoned the police. I knew something must have happened to her, she never stayed out beyond midnight without phoning."

"Where had she gone?"

"She said something about a film, but I had no idea which cinema. I thought she'd be all right with James to look after her. I trusted James to protect her. Oh God, why did I let her go with him?"

"He was killed too, you know" interjected Tom.

The man subsided and was quiet for a moment. "Yes, yes, of course. His parents must be upset too. He was a nice boy."

Graham paused for a moment to let Hunt regain his equanimity. Then he asked the question that was always the most difficult. "Mr. Hunt, can you think of anyone, anyone at all, who might have had a reason for killing your daughter?"

"Jenny…she made friends, not enemies. She was a popular girl. Everybody liked her."

Parents invariably said that. And yet they often didn't know everything about their children. Graham waited for a moment, his pen hovering over his notebook. "Could she have been in any trouble?"

"If she had been, she would have told me. We were very close, closer than most."

Graham's eyes flickered over the sleek velvet curtains drawn across French windows, the pine bookshelves, the open fireplace with its tiled surround, and then alighted on the photograph of a woman in a gold frame. It stood next to a head and shoulders shot of Jenny, her long black hair cascading over one shoulder, and there was a strong resemblance between the girl and her mother. Mr. Hunt read Graham's thoughts.

"My wife died just over a year ago, of cancer. We didn't have any more children after Jenny. Martha—my wife—found childbirth too painful. So we decided that one would be enough. Why do you think he did it?"

The question was unexpected and it hung on the air like an accusation. Graham drew in his breath quickly, before replying. "It's a complicated case. It's difficult to assess a motive for the killing."

"Difficult to assess. Of course it's difficult to assess, because there was none. There couldn't possibly have been a motive for killing Jenny." Hunt's tone was pugnacious now, as if he believed the police were deliberately concealing something from him. The truth was, people often thought the police knew more than they did. But in this case, Graham was as much in the dark as anyone.

When he replied, his tone was cautious and guarded. "You may be right. But we still don't have all the facts."

"Inspector…have you really told me everything you know? Was there anything else…of a perverted nature?…Anything to suggest that it was a psychopath, or…?"

"There was no evidence of any sexual assault, if that's what you mean" Graham reassured him quickly.

"Why did he do it then? He didn't want her money. So why did he do it?"

All these questions—thought Graham—*he should stop thinking about it, stop probing for answers, she's dead now, anyway.* But Graham knew what it was about the man's insistence that made him squirm: it was too near the knuckle, too close to his own situation How would he have reacted if Gemma…? Probably in exactly the same way, asking the same questions. *Why? Why me? Why her? She never did anything wrong, nothing to deserve a death like that.*

Graham didn't usually find himself getting so emotionally involved with cases: after all, nobody who suffered along with the victims could last long in the Force. But this had touched a raw nerve somewhere. He remembered how pleased he and Pat had been when Gemma had decided to live on campus at Sheffield University rather than in digs with people they didn't know. He had wondered at the time if he was being over protective, but the faces of girls came back to him—teenage girls killed for no reason, because they were vulnerable and alone and therefore easy targets—and he couldn't help wanting to stem the tide of evil against his own daughter. If there was a protective bubble to shield Gemma from danger he would have encased her in it, but the most he could do was offer guidance and pray for her safety. He found himself relieved that it was this man's daughter who had been killed, not his. And he mentally chastised himself for his selfishness.

He gave Mr. Hunt the only answer he could. But it was said with an earnest sincerity that surprised both listeners: "I really don't know why anyone would murder your daughter, Mr. Hunt. But believe me, I intend to find out."

*   *   *

Ruth always had difficulty remembering which way to turn at the end of the corridor for Maggie's office. Trusting her instinct, she turned right and pushed through heavy double doors to find herself in another long corridor with many doors leading from it.

As she passed a buxom black woman in overalls who was hovering over a trolley of cleaning implements, Ruth gave a quick nod and a smile of recognition and considered asking the woman the location of the room she was seeking, then decided not to bother. The massive BBC building was such a warren of little rooms and offices which all looked the same from the outside, it was unlikely that the cleaner would be able to distinguish one from the other.

Ruth twisted her head from side to side as she walked down the corridor, checking the name and number on each uniform door. All was silent apart from her soft footfalls on the carpet and some distant generator, throbbing like the building's heart.

Turning left into another corridor identical to the last one, Ruth gave her watch an anxious glance and began to walk more quickly. To her relief, a bronze plaque proclaiming *Maggie Tatler—Producer: Watch Out for Crime* appeared on the first door on the right, and Ruth gave it a soft tap with her knuckles and entered without waiting for a reply.

As she had anticipated, Maggie was at her desk and in the middle of a jovial telephone conversation. Ruth was greeted with a terse nod and a wave of the hands inviting her to take a seat on the chair opposite. "Won't be a minute" Maggie mouthed with emphasis to Ruth, as her caller's voice bludgeoned her ears.

Ruth occupied herself by looking around the small, cramped room which was crammed to overflowing with bursting filing cabinets; every desk surface covered with books, pictures, pens and ashtrays; two metal wastepaper baskets about to disgorge their contents of white plastic cups and screwed up paper on to the floor; every wall space canopied with photographs of actors, posters, certificates hung in frames, reminder notices scrawled in heavy blue ink and monthly planning charts hastily adapted.

"D'you want some tea, love?" asked Maggie as she put down the phone abruptly and reached into her desk drawer.

"No thanks."

"Oh, I forgot. You don't drink this muck, do you? Nothing else to offer you I'm afraid."

"That's O.K." replied Ruth, settling herself into her chair and waiting for Maggie to come to the point.

"Now where the hell did I put my...?" Maggie continued to rummage in the drawer with impatient fingers, her short bleached-blonde hair sticking up from her head in a sort of ruff. "Right—here we go." She extracted some chewing gum from a packet, offered some to Ruth who refused with a shake of her head, and popped a piece in her mouth before continuing. "I'm not going to beat about the bush, darling. I know you too well to give you any bullshit, right?"

Ruth nodded, and thought briefly and distractedly to herself how much more attractive Maggie's square face would be with some makeup.

"The fact is, I have to tell you that we've had complaints about you."

"From Mr. Ross?"

"Yes" said Maggie between chews. "I guess you got the message that you'd upset him. Thing is, I know you'll think I ought to take your side, but we have to take these sort of complaints seriously, right?"

"I really don't think his complaints were justified."

"Nor do I, love, of course not. I know the bloke was an idiot, it was written all over him. But you do get those types, I'm afraid, and you just have to deal with them."

"I'm aware of that" replied Ruth curtly.

"Look" said Maggie leaning forward, "It's not our job to judge these people, it's just our job to make programs."

"We can't stand back completely" asserted Ruth.

"Oh, but that's just where you're wrong" replied Maggie, with the air of someone reaching a desired message, "We *can* stand back, and that's what we should do. We don't make laws and we don't uphold justice, we just show the public what's going on. And sometimes we do a hell of a lot of good."

"Sometimes we do" admitted Ruth. "But sometimes we do harm as well." She was suddenly surprised at herself. She was voicing the very sentiments that Graham had expounded to her and to which she had vigorously objected during one argument.

"That's as maybe" Maggie continued. "We can't help what might happen as a consequence of the programs. In general, we get a lot of good feedback, and as you know the police are all in favor."

Ruth wondered if Maggie had forgotten the Charlie Hackett case, where the policeman concerned had definitely *not* been in favor, but she decided not to mention it.

"Did Tony tell you about Mr. Dervish?"

"Oh yes, he say that the boys had been caught—"

"So you see, most of the time we get it right and we do some good. We've a valuable role to play. You mustn't question that, Ruth." The sentences rolled off Maggie's tongue with the ease of long usage. She stretched back in her chair and regarded Ruth through slightly narrowed eyes. "It won't help anybody if you go getting people's backs up, will it?"

"It wasn't intentional."

"No, I'm sure it wasn't. But we have to be tactful with these people. It pays to remember that the customer is always right."

Ruth thought how like Tony Maggie was, so convinced of her own arguments and blind to any other points of view. And how unlike both of them *she* was, with her desperate searching after truth and morality. Neither Tony nor Maggie would ever understand how important it was to her that a thing was *right*. Recognizing this, Ruth resolved that further argument would be a waste of energy. "All right. I'll try and bear your comments in mind" she conceded.

Maggie seemed relieved to abandon the subject. "That's great. Now, I did want to have a brief word with you about next week's program while you're here. Hang on, I'll just get the notes on it." She left her desk, wrenched open the drawer of one of the filing cabinets and pulled out a slim green folder, extracting a typewritten page which she glanced at before handing it to Ruth. "We've just had this one in. It's about some bodies found on Hampstead Heath, last week I think. It's from the station at Temple Green—you dealt with that lot before, didn't you?"

With a little thrill, Ruth recognized the name of Graham's beat, but she replied calmly: "Yes, I did" and dipped her head over the paper she'd been given, skimming the words with her eyes.

"They want us to run a piece on it and do a reconstruction on next week's program. As you'll see from the notes, it happened on the Heath well away from the neighboring houses and at night so far as they know, but we might still be able to jog people's memories about seeing something unusual that evening. You never know, the murderer might have been loitering around for a while beforehand, that sort of thing, looking for likely victims."

Ruth shuddered at the casual way Maggie talked of the event. "Have you got an outline of the reconstruction?"

"Not yet. Tanya's getting some actors in to see me tomorrow, and then we'll firm up the script. But it'll be something like: seeing the young couple at the cinema—they went to the cinema first, apparently—walking home from the cinema, deciding on impulse to take a stroll through the Heath—then we'll see the murderer in the street watching them pass, stalking them on to the Heath, coming up behind them, but we won't see the actual murder taking place, that's not necessary."

"No" mused Ruth. "O.K. then. Do you want me to interview any of the police officers?" she added.

"No" responded Maggie, unaware of the anticipation in Ruth's face, "they've said they don't want any interviews, just a brief explanation to the viewers and the reconstruction."

"Fine" said Ruth trying to keep the disappointment out of her voice. "I'll have a look at this then" she said referring to the typewritten sheet.

"Great" replied Maggie, as the phone began to ring again. "I'll see you later." And as she started a conversation, Ruth picked up her briefcase and left the room, bumping into Tanya in the corridor.

"Hi" Tanya said brightly. "Someone's been trying to get hold of you."

"Oh. Who?"

"I don't know. It was Melanie took the call."

"Melanie?"

"I don't think you've met her yet, have you? She's that new researcher we took on last week to cover Jackie's maternity leave. Anyway, I don't know who it was. She just said it was a man and he rang several times."

"Oh—right" said Ruth with a shrug.

"Secret admirer?" asked Tanya flippantly, on her way into Maggie's office.

"I don't know" Ruth tossed back with a casual air. But secretly she thought of Graham, wondering if he was trying to get out of their date and why he was trying to contact her through a researcher when he knew her direct line.

*   *   *

Tom puffed on a cigarette and inhaled deeply, one gaunt arm resting on the rolled-down car window, watching the vehicles in front bump each other forward inch by inch. The air outside was stuffy and petrol-laden and thick clouds hung ponderously in the sky, threatening rain.

"Well mate, this could prove to be a tricky one."

"When have you not said that?" Graham replied, biting his lip in impatience. His stomach crawled and nagged with a pain that made him irritable and jumpy. He felt around on the dashboard for his indigestion tablets and, finding the packet empty, threw it into the car pocket with a mumbled curse.

"Oh I know I always look on the black side, but this time there's no other side to look on." Tom remarked with his customary mixture of pessimism and cheerfulness.

"I must admit," said Graham thoughtfully, "When Hunt was talking about psychopaths, I thought he'd been reading too many of his own novels, but..."

"He may have a point?"

Graham sighed, disinclined to reveal his gloomy feelings to Tom. Then, reflecting that the truth would out eventually, he admitted: "What have we got to go on? Sod all really. We've checked out all her friends, all her acquaintances, everyone who knew her or knew anything about her. *And* the boy. They're both totally clean, like blank sheets of paper. Unless there's something we've overlooked, I can't see any reason at all to kill either of them. What would a stranger get out of it, if he didn't want their money? And with the impulsive nature of the killing—a log, the nearest thing to hand—it *looks* like a stranger. Not a revenge attack, not a planned attack. Motive, method, opportunity. Unfortunately, motive comes first."

"If it *is* a psychopath, of course he won't stop at just one."

"Yes, *if* it's a psychopath" Graham repeated with a shudder.

"We know that once never satisfies them. They have to carry on. So, he'd be likely to be a serial killer..."

"Yeah, lock up your daughters. There'll be articles in the *Ham and High*, interviews on *Watch Out for Crime*, members of the public ringing us to see what we're doing about the 'Beast of the Heath'. And meanwhile, all this publicity's got the killer well on his guard, so when we finally manage to arrest the bugger, he's got a watertight alibi, and we haven't got enough evidence to convict him, even though we know...!"

Graham was fighting to control his anger: he didn't dare say anymore, but scowled out of the window, feeling his face grow hot.

Tom turned and looked at his friend, his expression a blend of reproach and sympathy. "Don't dwell, Graham. It happened a long time ago."

"Nine months isn't that long."

"Everyone else has forgotten about it, why can't you?"

Graham wished that the memory of Hackett wasn't so vivid in his mind. He could still see the puckered Welsh face with its almost comical grin and the childishly small feet in their holey shoes, could still smell the stink of filth from a thousand streets and alcohol from a thousand beer cans lingering on his clothes and his breath. If there was one person in the world Graham hated, it was that little man. He looked so harmless and pathetic in his ragged jacket and trousers. Yet Graham and the other policeman on his case knew that he had killed at least six times. And would probably kill again. And there was nothing they could do to stop him. Not without evidence.

Tom—noticing that the black clouds had gathered again over Graham's head—tried to cheer up his companion with a change of subject: "Talking of *Watch Out for Crime*, are you still seeing that T.V. presenter, what's her name?"

"Ruth Ramon."

"Ruth Ramon." Tom rolled the name about in his mouth as if it were a gob stopper, then he shot Graham one of his rare cynical smiles. "How do you do it, mate? She must be half your age. And quite a body on her, too." He shook his head slowly, in mock dismay. "I don't know, if I tried to pull a bird like that she'd never look twice at me. But you—what have you got that the rest of us haven't, an extra long dick or something?"

Graham laughed. Then was suddenly serious. "Look, Tom, I told you about Ruth in confidence. You haven't gone blabbing all over the station—?"

"No, no, course not."

"Because I wouldn't want Pat to get wind of—"

"Come on, mate. What d'you think I am?"

"It's not something I make a habit of—"

"No, I know."

But talking of Ruth had had the desired effect on Graham, and his voice was much brighter, as he divulged: "I'm seeing her tomorrow night. Taking her out to Darcy's in Kensington, which I like a fool offered to pay for, although she must make twice as much money—oh God!"

"What?"

"I just remembered. Pat said Gemma was coming home for the weekend. I'll have to get out of it."

"What, the dinner date or the prodigal daughter?"

"What do you think?"

"Knowing you? The dinner date." Tom winked at the air as he made this comment, stubbed out his cigarette under his shoe and threw the butt out of the window.

Chapter Four

▼

Pat had one hand on the oven door, tilting it open and squinting inside at the row of glistening tarts. She concluded that they were baked to perfection and withdrew the baking tray, carefully sliding it on to the kitchen table. She was so glad she had remembered to make Gemma's favorites, just before she came home. It was hard to find the time, these days, to keep track of everything she planned to do, what with the hostel never far from her mind.

It really had been a godsend, getting that voluntary job at the hostel. Her days now were filled with purpose and she felt useful and needed again—something she had missed after Gemma left home. Yes, life on the whole was very pleasant.

She only wished that Graham weren't so crabby and could snap out of his depression. Ever since his troubles over Charlie Hackett—and that was a few months ago now—he had been perverse and sullen, given to uneasy silences and frequently staying late at work. He was becoming absent-minded, too. She didn't like to nag him about the other night, but it had been quite embarrassing finding something to say to the Rockwells to explain Graham's absence. And then, when he finally did arrive—long after the Rockwells had departed with pitying smiles—no proper excuse, just "I'm sorry, I forgot."

Thinking of Graham reminded her that it was time to feed Serena. Pat was not fond of the bird but she fed it dutifully every day at four o'clock as Graham had enjoined her. She would have preferred a creature that you could pet and treat like a child, not this haughty madam with the imperious stare.

The bird was hiding her head under her wing when Pat reached up to toss some seed into the cage. At the sound, she swiveled and watched coldly through one unblinking yellow eye, then began to flex her talons and scrape them along the inside of her cage. Pat drew away and crossed the hall to the kitchen, humming softly to herself.

Just then, the front door banged shut suddenly, and Gemma breezed in, making her usual unceremonious entrance. "Hi mum!" she called from the hall, easing the heavy backpack from her shoulders on to the floor with a sigh of relief.

"Gemma!" Pat beamed, as she gave her daughter a floury hug. "You're home early, aren't you? I thought you said—"

"The train was early! Can you believe it? And then I was lucky with the tube from King's Cross. Oh mum—no need—I'll take that upstairs, it's full of books" said Gemma, as Pat tried to lift the backpack.

"Do you really need all these, dear?"

"Yes I do. I've got to study. I have got a present for you, though." Laughing gaily, Gemma pulled a plastic bag full of washing from the backpack, strewing a couple of mis-matched socks on to the floor as she did so.

"Thank you, dear" said Pat with ironic gratitude, as she took the bag. Something else had fallen out and she picked it up: a small black cylinder that Pat didn't recognize. "What on earth's this?"

"That?" said Gemma, as she turned away to hang up her duffel coat and woolly hat, "Oh—haven't you seen one of those before, mum? It's a rape scream."

"A what?"

"A rape scream. You know—you carry it about with you at night, when you're walking about the streets on your own or something—"

"I hope you don't go walking about the streets on your own—"

"Oh, I don't much—I mean, you have to sometimes. Anyway, you just press this button here, and it makes this terrible loud noise—"

"Oh, I see. And the person runs away, does he?"

"Yeah, hopefully. How about a cuppa, mum?"

"Of course, dear. I'll just put these in the machine."

Pat bustled into the kitchen with the washing and Gemma followed, slipping the small black object into her jeans pocket, and hoping that she'd successfully changed the subject. "Is dad going to be home tonight?" she asked, perching on the edge of the kitchen table and kicking her legs under her like a child.

"How should I know, dear? He never tells me about his work, you know that." Gemma thought she detected an edge of bitterness in her mother's voice, but she couldn't tell for sure how Pat felt, because her back was turned and she was bent over the washing machine. Gemma hoped her father *would* be home in time for dinner. Then she could pretend that they were a family again, a tight little unit who shared everything.

"He must be working on something pretty big" said Gemma thoughtfully, twirling one of the coasters on the table. It had a picture of Hever Castle on it, that dad had taken on one of their holidays and mum had had made into six coasters for one of his Christmas presents.

"Why do you say that?" replied her mother, glancing round at her with a wary look.

"Just that he seems to be out a lot. He's always out when I phone" said Gemma. "Or perhaps he's avoiding me" she added flippantly.

"You are the last person he would want to avoid" said her mother, straightening her back with a little grunt. "Don't sit on the table, dear. I've told you before. You'll have the whole thing over."

Gemma placed herself in a chair with an obedient sigh. "Well if I was married—which I'm sure I never will be—I'd make sure my husband told me everything about his work, just everything. And if he didn't, there'd be hell to pay."

"It's not always as easy as that, dear" said Pat resignedly, withdrawing her tarts from the oven and scooping them on to a plate.

Gemma wrinkled her nose and grabbed a tart from the plate before her mother could restrain her. "They smell fabulous. God, I'm starving." She let the delicious hot pastry melt on her tongue with undisguised pleasure. "We never get grub this good at Uni."

Pat gave Gemma's hand a gentle slap. "Don't talk with your mouth full."

Gemma ignored the instruction and stretched out her hand again. "Can I have another one?" Before Pat had a chance to reply, the tart disappeared whole into Gemma's open mouth to be relished with lip-smacking appreciation.

Pat sighed: "Just the one, greedy guts. They're not all for you."

Gemma made a disappointed noise. "Who else are they for? How dare you make tarts for anyone but me?" She went up to her mother and hugged her round the waist in an impulsive gesture of affection.

"They're mostly for you, of course. But I'm going to take some of them down to the hostel with me tonight."

"You're going tonight?"

"Just for a little while. I go every night. Don't worry, there'll be plenty of time for me to cook your dinner."

"Why do you have to go every single night?"

"Because if I don't go, those people wouldn't get anything to eat at all."

"But why do *you* have to go?"

"Well, there isn't anyone else, is there?"

Gemma regarded her mother in silence for a minute or two. *She really seems to like sacrificing herself*—she thought—*But it's stupid. She'd be much better off with a proper job that pays money.* Suddenly, Pat was reverting to an earlier subject: "So where did you get that thing…that rape thing? You don't buy them in the shops, do you?" Gemma considered that her mother had an annoying habit of harping on about things—once started on a subject, she was like a terrier that could never let it go completely.

"I dunno if they sell them in the shops. Julian gave me it."

"Julian, that's the boy you're friendly with at college?"

"He used to be my boyfriend" admonished Gemma, tutting and raising her eyebrows to heaven.

"I'd like to meet this Julian."

"No you wouldn't."

Pat let this comment go. "Why did he think you would need a thing like that?"

"Honestly, mum, everybody has them, it's just a precaution." Pat might have been satisfied with that reason, but now Gemma decided to continue. She knew it would come out sooner or later. "I had a bit of a…"

"What, dear?" said Pat, with an overly-anxious look, putting Gemma's cup of tea on the table in front of her.

"Oh, it was just…" Gemma—relieved that her mother was too busy sifting flour for her pastry to be actually looking at her—spilled the beans as quickly as she could, keeping her voice unnaturally casual. "I was walking home from college one night, it was about eleven o'clock—"

"That's rather late, isn't it?"

"I'd been in the bar with some friends. Anyway, there's quite a long driveway from the college before you reach the main road, and this man jumped out of the bushes—"

"What!" Pat turned with a horror-stricken look.

"He didn't do anything, mum, he didn't have time. I shouted at him to leave me alone, and I ran away. It was just a shock, that's all."

"Did he come after you?"

"No. At least I don't think so, I didn't look behind me, just kept running till I got to the road. Then I was lucky, because a bus came up just at that moment, and I jumped on it."

"You might not have been lucky. Oh, I do wish you'd be more careful."

The anxious whine in her mother's voice irritated Gemma: "I *am* careful. That's why I've got that rape scream."

"But you shouldn't go walking about on your own. Couldn't Julian walk you home?"

"Oh mum, I can't ask Julian to escort me everywhere. I don't even think I like him any more. And anyway, I'm a grown woman!"

Pat had been going to chide Gemma, but when she looked at her daughter—sitting there at the table trying to maintain her haughty, grown-up air—she could feel nothing but maternal affection and concern. Gemma always seemed at her most vulnerable when asserting how independent she was. Maybe she'd inherited her stubborn strong will from her father or maybe it was just her age, but Pat knew that, however difficult it was, she would have to let her little bird fly.

*　　　*　　　*

Graham shared an open-plan office with another detective inspector and two detective sergeants on the ground floor of Temple Green police station, on the windowless side facing Green Street. Across a narrow passageway lay the interview room and on his right a glass-panelled door led to an ante-room—the 'closet' as Tom called it—where the secretaries worked.

Graham winced as he looked at the pictures of the girl and boy on the wall in the color snapshots donated by their parents, with their young faces full of expectant optimism. The images formed a disquieting contrast to some black and white photographs of their corpses taken by Curnow on the Heath, the bodies lying lifelessly in the snow like rag dolls after a child's playtime, with blood hardened into dark grooves around the neck and head.

"Who would want to do that?" he brooded aloud to nobody in particular, then felt the air move near his head and turned to see Tom next to him with his angular profile pointed in the same direction.

Tom offered no explanation, but put a bony hand on his colleague's shoulder: "Carson's come up with the computer printouts of likely suspects. Thought you'd want to see them first." He pushed a piece of paper into Graham's hand, to which the older man grunted in thanks. Flinging himself into the nearest swivel chair, Graham scanned the sheet avidly.

During the silence that followed, Tom sucked thoughtfully on a cigarette while contemplating the photographs on the wall. Suddenly he was startled by the crack of Graham's fist as it slammed a desktop.

"Have you looked at this?" Graham exclaimed.

Tom shrugged by way of a negative reply.

"It's completely bloody useless." Graham paused to let his irritation register. "Why do they waste my time with this crap? Half the people on here don't even operate in London, so what's the point of listing them?"

Tom moved towards Graham and propped his weight on the desk with one hand as he skimmed the paper over Graham's shoulder. Running a forefinger down the typed list of names, he paused at one and mumbled thoughtfully: "George Baines—he's an East End lad isn't he?"

"Still in the nick for a few years unless he's done a bunk we've not heard about."

Tom nodded and hesitated by another name which already had a pencil mark beside it: "Slick Sylvester, eh." He grunted in recognition. "I'll bet he's glad to see he's still in our thoughts, looking down on us from heaven or hell or wherever he's gone to."

Graham echoed Tom's grunt in response, and added: "There's only one more name on here that's halfway possible".

"Charlie Hackett" Tom mused as he came to a name at the bottom of the list which had been underlined in red. "They've got this in the wrong order, haven't they— shouldn't H be before S?"

Graham didn't reply but stared at the list with a furrowed brow as he chewed one thumbnail in concentration.

"It's odd, you know. I was just thinking about him the other day when we talked about the case." Tom stubbed out his cigarette and ground it underneath his foot. "I was thinking he'd been keeping his nose clean for too long. Always gives me the willies when they do that, like they're plotting something really big or something."

Graham shook his head. "Doesn't this all seem a bit obvious to you?"

"P'rhaps he's been keeping a low profile, hoping we'll forget about him" suggested Tom.

"You'd think Charlie would cover his tracks better." Graham pursed his lips in thought and stroked a non-existent beard with his thumb and forefinger.

"He's not exactly Mr. Brain of Britain, is he?" asserted Tom.

Graham made no rejoinder but, rising from his chair, picked up a nearby phone and dialed an internal number:

"Jane, bring me Charlie Hackett's file would you?" There was a pause. "It's in the Cases Closed cabinet, under H. You should know where that is. Soon as you can, please Jane." Graham threw down the receiver and raised his eyes to heaven, to which his friend gave a snort of laughter in appreciation of its meaning. "Any forensics reports in yet?" Graham inquired.

"No. They're still at the lab."

"They would help a lot. I'm stumbling in the dark here."

"Got any ideas on the m.o.?" asked Tom.

"I had a chat with Sturgeon this morning" Graham replied. "Off the record, he reckons the assailant must have been short because of the angle at which the log hit the head."

"Heads" corrected Tom. "How many blows?"

"No more than a couple in either case."

"Must have been a pretty powerful swing, then" guessed Tom. Extracting a plastic ruler from the pen holder on top of a nearby computer, he tested his theory, with the object taking the place of an imaginary log aimed with playful force at Graham's head.

Graham ducked and warned: "Careful with that thing."

"Just doing a reconstruction, mate." Tom took up a sitting position on the edge of one of the desks, his long legs stretched out in front of him and crossed at the ankles. "It was quite a big log. If you swung it backwards first and got enough momentum going, you wouldn't need to be a strong man to deal a hefty blow."

"I suppose one crack could be fatal, if it knocked them out cold for long enough" Graham added, seating himself in a chair opposite Tom. "One wonders how he managed to kill both of them so easily. Surely the other one would have put up a fight."

"All right, imagine this" Tom said, standing up and demonstrating as he spoke. "The couple are walking along in the dark, holding each other's hands or with their arms linked or whatever. The killer approaches from behind, so softly that they don't hear him at all."

"You're assuming that he must have been following them—" interjected Graham.

"Or lying in wait. How can we know?"

"What if they just happened to cross his path at some point? It was just bad luck, bad timing."

"You mean, he was just on the Heath, peacefully going about his own business until—bam—somebody crosses his path who shouldn't be there and that pisses him off so much he just has to kill them?" Tom said with an ironic tone to his voice. "Hmm, unlikely if you ask me."

"Your idea that he followed them, or lay in wait, pre-supposes that he had the intention to kill them already in his mind, that he had something against *them* in particu-lar, maybe even that he knew they'd be walking that way. But I don't think that's true."

"We don't know—"

"No, we don't *know* but we have to conjecture. Surely if there'd been any premeditation he'd have brought the weapon with him."

Tom paused and took an intake of breath. "If you're right, what the hell's the motive? That's what I don't get."

Graham grunted. "People like Hackett don't *need* a motive. It's human, it's alive, let's kill it. That's all they know. He's just like an animal."

"We've got no evidence against Hackett yet" replied Tom, with an odd glance at his friend.

"No, I know. I was just…Go on with your reconstruction" encouraged Graham.

"I think he sneaked up on them quietly" Tom continued. "He moves in for the kill, grabs the log and swings it at the girl's head, she goes down immediately without even knowing what's hit her. The boy turns around and only just has time to register what's happened before the assailant strikes again. Maybe the boy tries to ward off the blow with his arms, or maybe backs off a little—"

"I don't think he moved away at all. The bodies were lying so close together, only a foot or so apart" interjected Graham.

"O.K., so the killer comes after him with the log before he even has time to get away. One blow to his skull and he's down as well. It wouldn't take much with a log that size."

"Then the log's thrown down and the killer runs away" said Graham, completing the story. "You know what the interesting thing is? There's no malice there."

"What—that's not malicious, to hit two perfectly innocent people over the head with a heavy log?" snorted Tom.

"No, I mean, once he'd done the job—that is, killed them—he ran off. He didn't stay to smash their faces in with the log, or to molest them or do anything perverted with the corpses—"

"Well, you're right there" agreed Tom. "In fact, he didn't even bother disposing of the bodies. Why d'you reckon that is? Caught in the act?"

"Don't think so. It would have been reported to us, surely" said Graham. "No, I think he guessed—rightly as it happens—that it would take a while for the bodies to be discovered in such an isolated spot, especially in the middle of winter when not many people go wandering about on the Heath. And while we're collecting enough evidence to locate the killer, he can make himself scarce."

"Have you checked whether Charlie's still at the same address?" Tom asked.

"Why d'you think I asked for the file?" replied Graham.

As if on cue, Jane Cherrill entered clutching a manila folder, her wide eyes expecting approval. She was a chubby little girl with a permanent smile who had wormed her way into the job with more charm than qualifications. "Is this the right one?" she gasped, handing the folder to Graham.

He nodded and raised his eyebrows in surprise. "Well done".

Jane—having received a metaphorical pat on the back—smiled at both men and left the room with a customary wiggle of her rather oversized hips.

Tom smirked to himself, maintaining his position on the edge of the desk, and lit another cigarette.

"It's very peculiar, you know" Graham ruminated as he turned over the pages in the folder, his eyes skimming each one. "As I said, it looks like an unpremeditated affair with the murder weapon being the first thing to hand, so he doesn't set out to kill them, it's done on impulse. And yet, it's almost businesslike in that once he's done the job he leaves. Every psychopath I've ever come across gets a perverted pleasure out of the killing, not just because of the killing itself but because of the other sick stuff he does to the victim, either before or after."

"Of course he might have intended to do something, but got frightened off before he had the chance" Tom opined.

"I suppose that's possible. If so, there's a great witness out there somewhere. I only hope they come to us before someone gets to them."

"Any useful info on the file?" asked Tom with a nod to the folder.

"I was just trying to refresh my memory on Charlie's modus operandi. Some of it tallies with this case and some doesn't."

"He always killed them outside, didn't he?" Tom recalled.

"I think he did, yes. And he always disfigured the faces afterwards, do you remember? There was no attempt to do that here."

"Perhaps, as I said, he was surprised. You know who'd be the person to ask, though, about Hackett's m.o.— Ronnie Plowright."

"Ronnie Plowright?" Graham repeated with a puzzled frown.

"You've got a memory like a sieve, haven't you. The forensic psychologist on Hackett's case. You thought quite highly of her at the time. Didn't you even ask her out for a drink once?" said Tom, leaning in and winking at his friend.

"God, yes" Graham replied, cringing in recollection. "Got my head bitten off for my pains."

"I could have told you. Anyway, she wouldn't be my idea of a good night out."

"She's a very bright lady" said Graham defensively.

"More brains than beauty, that's for sure. Well—give her a ring. Maybe she's forgiven your little indiscretion."

Graham didn't reply but began rummaging through the folder with a distracted air.

"You won't find her home number in there, she wouldn't give it out. Try Camden Hospital."

"What?" asked Graham, looking up.

"That's where she works" Tom smirked.

Graham compressed his lips and barked a little more harshly than he'd intended: "Right—well, while I'm at it, you might get the boys to check up on Hackett and make sure he's still contactable. Since he's the only halfway decent suspect we've got, I might pull him in for questioning." He reached immediately for the phone as Tom made his way out of the room.

A few minutes later, Graham was connected to the right number. "Hello. Veronica Plowright? Oh hello, Dr. Plowright, it's D.I. Graham Brunswick here from Temple Green Police Station. I just wanted to ask you a few questions about the Charlie Hackett case which you worked on with us last year."

"Go on" the voice fired in his ear like a bullet.

"I don't know if you remember much about the case—" Graham began.

"I certainly do. It's very fresh in my mind having given a lecture about the Hackett personality type only a couple of days ago. So, how can I help you?"

Graham felt his face grow hot but he continued politely. "I'm working on a homicide at the moment which seems to bear some resemblance...to have some things in common with Charlie Hackett's methods, but other aspects of it are unclear."

"Tell me about the case" ordered the voice. Graham explained as clearly as he could the main points of the Hampstead Heath murder.

When she had listened, the woman paused for a few seconds to consider before replying. "One of my main observations about Charlie when interviewing him was that he is a creature of habit. Rather bizarre and perverted habits, you may say, but to him these little rituals are important, if not vital. He is driven to perform certain acts again and again, in a very precise and organized manner. In my opinion, his modus operandi would not alter, because it constitutes his entire reason for killing. To my mind, the fact that these bodies did not have the usual disfigurements to the face can only mean one of two things: either the killer is not Charlie Hackett, or Charlie was intending to carry out his usual routine and was disturbed while doing so."

Graham scratched his head in thought. "Do you think it's *possible* that the killer is Hackett?"

"Oh yes, it's possible. I wouldn't rule it out. But I'd need some further evidence to make a firm judgment."

"I see. Thank you very much for your help." Graham rang off with a certain amount of relief and put down the receiver. Looking up, he saw Tom standing in the doorway.

"It's lunchtime, mate. Coming down the pub?" offered Tom.

"No, it's O.K." Graham replied. "I brought sandwiches."

"Made you a packed lunch, did she?" asked Tom, as his head disappeared back into the corridor. Graham sat for a few moments, lost in thought.

On the other side of the door, Tom slapped his colleague Bernie Carson on the back. "It's just you and me, mate" he said, grabbing his coat from a stand.

"Greta Garbo not coming then?" asked Bernie. He was a slightly tubby sergeant whose uniform jacket always seemed to want to burst free of its buttons.

"He often works through lunch" Tom replied, shepherding his companion through the front door and out into the street.

"Isn't he a little, you know, glum to work with?" asked Bernie. "I don't think I've ever seen him crack a smile."

Tom grinned. "Still waters run deep with our Graham. He may not be Les Dawson, but he's the best copper I know. I wouldn't partner him if I didn't think so."

*   *   *

The thwack that Gemma gave the ball with her racket sent it flying so high up into the air that it sailed over the top of the tennis court and out into the bushes of the park beyond. "Bloody hell, girl!" called Graham—who had made a gallant effort to run backwards at the same speed as the ball before accepting that he hadn't a hope, and who now stood panting and glaring at his daughter—"I said hit it hard, not kill it."

Laughing, her face pink with exertion, Gemma skipped up to the net. "You'll have to go and find it, dad."

"Why me? *You* knocked it out." Graham bent over and rested his hands on his knees, blowing out gasps of air.

"I found the one *you* hit out of the court."

"Oh, come on, that was only just—"

"Go on" Gemma exhorted, putting her hands on her hips and her head to one side. "You know it's your turn."

Graham threw down his racket in feigned vexation. "This is too much for me. I'm an old man. Why didn't we go and watch a cricket match?"

"Because they got rained off" Gemma replied to his retreating back, as he swung open the gate to the court and plunged into the shrubbery. Gemma—who lay down on the hard ground with her knees up to snatch a welcome breather—was surprised when her father came back in a few moments with the ball and bounced it near her head.

"It hadn't gone that far after all" he explained.

"Lucky old you" said Gemma, springing to her feet. "Right. I'm ready for another bout."

"Tell you what" suggested Graham, throwing the ball up in the air and catching it, "Why don't we call it a day? I'm knackered."

"Oooh" Gemma complained. "Just because you're winning."

"Isn't two hours long enough for you? Honestly, I'm whacked."

"Just one more game" pleaded Gemma. "I've got to even up the score a bit."

"All right" sighed Graham, unable to resist his daughter's demands. "But let's stop for a coke first. I'm thirsty."

"O.K." Gemma ran over to their knapsack and took out a can, pulled off the ring and passed it to her father to drink first.

After taking a swig, Graham passed it back. "Why did you do that to your hair?" he inquired, referring to Gemma's sandy red mane, which she'd had layered and permed, making her moon face seem even rounder.

"Oh, dad. Because it's fashionable, that's why."

"It doesn't suit you."

"I knew you'd say that. *I* like it."

"Well, as long as you do. What did mum say?"

"She didn't mention it."

"Didn't dare criticize, I expect."

Gemma didn't grace her father with a reply. She took a gulp of coke, stared into space for a moment and then said: "Mum's in a funny mood, isn't she."

"Why do you say that?" Graham replied after a beat.

"Oh, I don't know, she just…When I asked her if you would be home at the weekend she said *I don't know*, as if *He never tells me anything*. D'you know what I mean?"

Graham looked down in thought. "She gets jealous of my work sometimes. Because I'm often out in the evenings and she forgets that it's a policeman's wife's lot. And she's still smarting because I forgot about some dinner date we had with neighbors and she was embarrassed."

"She gets so upset about little things, doesn't she? I mean, the fuss she made when I told her about that bloke at college." Gemma made a grimace to her father, finished the coke and squeezed the can in her hand till it buckled.

"What—you mean Julian?"

"No, you know, the night I was walking down the drive and that man—"

"You shouldn't make light of that" Graham chided. "She was right to be upset. It's a very worrying thing to find out about."

"Oh dad—" began Gemma in a whining tone.

"No, really. You know mum and I have always worried about you being in another town on your own. That's why we were so pleased when you decided to stay on campus."

"Dad—" Gemma turned her head away from the nagging and scuffed her toe along the side of the wire mesh of the court.

"If I'd known you were going to go walking up driveways on your own in the dead of night—"

"Stop being so paranoid," sighed Gemma. "I'm seventeen! I can look after myself. I'm a big girl now."

"Not all that big" Graham teased, giving her waist a playful squeeze.

"You know what I mean."

"I'll have to start giving you self-defence lessons."

"That would be useful" nodded Gemma.

"Or how about a car?"

"A what?"

"A car—you know, one of those big metal things with wheels." Nobody laughed at Graham's jokes like his daughter, throwing her head back and guffawing till her permed curls shook. "Dad—you're a loon!"

"Seriously, though. If you drove to college and back every day, you wouldn't have to go walking about after dark."

"I couldn't do that."

"Why not? I paid all that money for you to have lessons—"

"I don't believe in cars, they pollute the environment by releasing toxic gases into the atmosphere. Do you know that carbon monoxide is the single biggest cause of the hole in the ozone layer?"

"Stop talking like a pamphlet, for God's sake."

Gemma gave her father an impulsive hug. "I know you just want me to be safe. But I will be. I'm careful, honestly I am. I've got a rape scream now and I won't walk up that driveway again on my own. I mean, I'm not stupid am I?"

"No, you're certainly not" admitted Graham with a smile at her.

"You just worry about me more than most dads, because you see lots of awful things in your job so you're aware of them. And mum mixes with all those down and outs at the hostel, so she sees the seedy side of life as well. But you know, 99.9 per cent of the time bad things don't happen, it's just that you only see the bad times."

Graham was sometimes surprised at Gemma's insight. It was true what Pat said about her having an old head on young shoulders. He kissed her on the forehead. "Are you ready for another game?"

"Sure am" Gemma replied, racing to get her racket.

"And we could hire a video this evening, if you like" proposed Graham. "How about *Father of the Bride*?"

Chapter Five

▼

Graham kept the top of his steel gray desk reasonably well-ordered, despite the plethora of paperwork which invariably built up during the day. His prize ornament was a stone paperweight which Gemma had made for him at school: bright blobs of yellow and blue poster paint depicted her version of a canary. Next to it stood a pewter ashtray with the inscription, 'To my dearest husband', given to him by Pat on their twentieth anniversary and now used mainly by Tom, since Graham had given up smoking. Graham loved this room, not just because he knew it so well, but because of the memories that lingered on the air like the scent of cigars.

He sat behind reception, listening with half an ear as Carson, the desk sergeant that day, conversed with a female member of the public. It was late in the day and the normally thronged room was still and quiet.

The glass door swung open and Jane emerged, a little breathless. She had been struggling to complete the reports Graham had given her to type that morning.

"I'm ready to take some dictation now, sir" she said, hovering uncertainly in the doorway.

"Fine. Just pop in for a minute, would you?"

She positioned herself on the swivel chair, smoothing the hem of her denim skirt and poising a biro over her note pad with pudgy fingers. Graham often wondered how she managed to type at all with nails of such decorative length. He knew for a fact—partly because he'd overheard station gossip and partly because he had an observant eye—that Jane had slept with several of his fellow officers (had "been through the men here like a knife through butter" as Tom would put it). Graham secretly disapproved of this sort of behavior, though he felt a hypocrite in view of his recent indiscretions. He found himself wanting to nag her to smarten up or to take care but, realizing that his intrusions would not be welcome, he restrained the impulse.

He was halfway through the dictation when the phone interrupted. "Hello. Brunswick" Graham snapped.

"Ah, Inspector Brunswick, I wonder if you could spare me five minutes of your time. My name is Tony Frimpton and I'm calling from the Hampstead and Highgate Express. We'd like to run a short article about the recent murder on Hampstead Heath and we believe you are dealing with the case."

"Yes, I am dealing with the case, but I'm afraid I can't give you any information at the moment. Why don't you talk to our Press Liaison Officer?"

"Couldn't you just tell us something about it? Do you have any suspects so far? I understand this was quite an unusual murder—"

"Look Mr. Shrimpton—"

"Frimpton."

"I suggest you attend the inquest on Thursday. Until then, there's really very little I can tell you. Now, if you'll excuse me, I'm extremely busy." Graham slammed down the receiver before the voice could persuade him to say more.

Jane was still scribbling, having taken the opportunity to catch up with her shorthand. She sucked the end of her biro as Graham prepared his next sentence.

"Footprint casts were made of three separate sets of prints. Prints believed to be those of the assailant indicate a shoe size of approximately 38 or 39; ridge patterns made with the sole suggest sneakers or sports shoes; weight of assailant calculated from depth of print is fairly light, estimated at 50-60 kilos. Foreign clothing fibers were found at the site; these were wool, possibly mohair from a garment such as a jumper or cardigan. Two head hairs were found at the site, measuring roughly 10 centimeters; fine, pale in color, believed to belong to the assailant. Fingerprint evidence from the murder weapon has proved inconclusive.

In conclusion, projected scenario taking into account the Coroner's report following autopsy, location of footprints, position of bodies and other evidence found at the site: the assailant approached without warning from behind, stunning victims with a single and fatal blow to the head in each case. Death occurred possibly some hours later from blood loss."

Jane looked up with relief to find that Graham had finished speaking. "Is that it, sir?"

"Yes, that's fine. Quite enough for you to be getting on with, hm?"

She flashed him one of her charming smiles in reply and exited so hurriedly that her biro lay forgotten on Graham's desk, like a memento.

Graham's eyes rested for the hundredth time on the paperweight Gemma had made him, and with the thought of his daughter he recalled a dream from the previous night. In his dream, Gemma was waving and calling to him from the banks of a river, it could have been the Thames. After a time he became aware that her cries were screams for help and the water threatened to engulf her. He staggered to the water's edge but could go no further, his legs had become soft and gelatinous. He had the sensation of helplessness so often experienced in dreams, as he watched his daughter drown and was unable to save her.

The alarm had jolted him awake and he had lain for a few moments, dimly aware of something unpleasant. When Pat asked him what the matter was as she brought him a cup of tea, he couldn't reveal his feelings to her. The dream made no sense to him anyway.

The sound of an ambulance siren outside brought Graham back to the present with a jolt. He remembered that there was someone he had meant to call. Knowing the number, he dialed it quickly, his heart beating slightly faster than normal.

"Good afternoon, Ruth Ramon speaking."

He was always surprised how her warm, slightly husky voice on the phone could arouse him. "Hullo gorgeous. How are you?"

"Graham! Perfect timing. I've just managed to grab my first cup of coffee today. Mike and Tanya have gone off to check locations…"

"So you're on your own? So am I."

"Did you call me the other day?"

"The other day? When?"

"Oh, I don't know. A few days ago. Somebody called me at work and spoke to one of the researchers. I thought it might have been you."

"No, it wasn't me. I wouldn't have called you on the general office number."

"Yes, I thought it was odd. Oh well, it must be someone else then. How was your weekend?"

"Listen, I am sorry about that. It was really unavoidable—"

"No problem, I understand totally. You've only one daughter." Was there a hint of sarcasm in her voice? Graham couldn't tell.

"I do miss her, now she's away from home so much. But there's nothing like seeing you, Ruth."

"The feeling's mutual."

He could almost hear her smile. Somewhere in the background a modern telephone chirped and a word processor commenced its alternate purr and bleep, purr and bleep. He hated the feeling those sounds gave him, that she was not alone and had a life independent from his. It was her independence that made her attractive, yet it frightened him. These snatched telephone conversations were always slightly embarrassing, the pauses between sentences rather too long, as he struggled to put his feelings into words. Much easier to talk face to face, when a gesture or a look were sometimes all that was necessary.

"What are you working on this month?" he inquired, in order to fill the silence.

"You're not going to be happy about this. I'm covering the Hampstead Heath murder. I heard on the grapevine that you'd been put on the case. I suppose you've no comment, as usual?"

"Well, I've already told you why."

"Yes. All my fault, of course."

"No, no. It's nothing personal. But there's something a bit…morbid…about stirring up the public's interest in true crimes, a bit like public hangings, I suppose."

"The program's not meant to be sensationalist."

Graham didn't want to put her on the defensive. "No, I know it's not."

"We're actually on the same side as you. If the program jogs people's memories about someone or something they've seen that could be relevant to the case, surely that's of some use, isn't it?"

"It could work against us. The murderer himself could be watching."

"You know what I like about you, Graham? You're an honorable man, I know that, otherwise you wouldn't have felt so badly about what happened over—"

"Could we not talk about that, please."

"Why do you always clam up when I—?"

"I'm not clamming up. I just don't want to talk about that right now, O.K.?"

"O.K." Ruth sighed. Graham could envisage her flicking back her hair with a single toss, as she always did. "We'll never resolve this, will we?"

"There's nothing to resolve."

"Yes there is. You think that people making programs like ours are just interfering in stuff that's none of their business. And I think the public have a right to know, and to be given the chance to help, even if sometimes we take the risk of doing more harm than good if the criminal himself is a member of the watching public, but that was a very unusual and isolated case. You must admit that it was, even if you're biased because of your personal involvement. I mean, we've never had that happen, before or since."

"We're just going to have to agree to differ" Graham said with an air of putting an end to the conversation.

Ruth laughed. "Well, you've put me in my place now, haven't you? I should have known not to go on about it if you didn't want to. But you know me and my Jewish stubbornness, I just can't take no for an answer."

"Well—if you'd believed me when I said I didn't want an involvement with you…" Graham left the rest unsaid.

Ruth, expressing it for him, replied: "So, Mr. Policeman, if I hadn't pursued you we might never have got together, is that what you're saying? I just hope you're glad we did."

"Of course I am." Why did he suddenly feel such a strong desire for her? She frightened him sometimes, with her perception and her confidence. But she evoked in him some kind of passion that had long since evaporated from his married life. "When can I see you?" he asked.

Now, her voice was brisk and efficient, as if she were dealing with a client: "Next weekend's out, I'm afraid, because I'm going to a conference in Swindon. Something about the 'Role of Television in Social Awareness'. The weekend after I'm going up to Hull to visit Pa, and taking a long weekend off work. I could come home early and invite you round to dinner—"

"You mean I'll have to wait nearly two weeks? That's unjust punishment for letting you down over Gemma."

She laughed. "All right then. I am going to a concert on Wednesday night at the Royal Festival Hall. And I was sent two tickets by the organizers, I suppose they think I'm some kind of VIP because I work in television. I was going to take a girlfriend, but—"

"Is it something I'd like?"

"Yes, I think so."

"Then I'll meet you there. Usual time?"

"Yes."

Graham looked up to see that Jane had entered and was standing by his desk in embarrassment. He wondered how long she had been there. She shifted from one fat little leg to the other and uttered something to Graham in a voice too low to be audible.

"What is it, Jane?"

"Sorry to disturb you, sir, but there's a call on the other line from Detective Constable Smart. He says it's rather urgent."

"O.K. thanks, put it through to me in a second, would you?"

He made sure she had left the room before resuming his conversation with Ruth. "Sorry, I'm going to have to go. Thanks for the invitation. I'd love to come."

"No excuses this time?"

"Oh Ruthy, I have apologized—"

She laughed. "Just kidding. I'll see you the day after tomorrow. Be a good boy."

Her tone was flippant. Had she really dismissed last weekend's broken engagement from her mind, or was she playing hard to get? Graham had wanted to end the phone call with a kiss or endearment, but there wasn't time and she had hung up too abruptly. He didn't understand Ruth:

she didn't seem to want the things women are supposed to want, yet he sensed that she was discontented with things as they were. So different from Pat in every way. But that was what he wanted.

The bell sounded and he grasped the receiver. "Hello Smart, what have you got to tell me?"

The young police constable sounded excited and a bit breathless. "Hello sir. I'm here in East Field Lane doing house to house enquiries and I've been talking to a Mrs. Cavendish at number 19. She claims to have seen somebody hanging about near her house on the 25th February. She says she noticed him at about 8 o'clock that night when she arrived home after visiting a friend and when she looked out of her window a couple of hours later he was still there. She didn't think to contact the police at the time, but the incident stuck in her mind."

"O.K. that might be very interesting, Smart. Could you ask her to come down to the station?"

"Certainly sir."

Graham glanced at his watch and saw that it was half past five. It was going to be another long night.

*   *   *

Ruth had succeeded in positioning herself at the front of the multitude of people and on the very edge of the platform. She could feel their weight thrusting her forward and she imagined herself slipping and falling on to the tracks into the path of an oncoming train. Her profession, perhaps, encouraged such morbid thoughts or maybe she simply enjoyed taunting herself with the idea of danger.

Afloat on a sea of anonymous faces, she became reflective. She loved the chaos and the drama of London. It was in precisely this atmosphere that she flourished.

But if she flourished there were many others who didn't, she mused as she saw a harassed mother with a screaming infant and a teenage boy with face as pale as death who sat crouched in a corner begging for alms. Was it fair that such people should exist and she be unwilling to help them? She'd been given everything in life: money, doting family, education, good looks. She'd tried to convince herself that her job as a T.V. presenter did help the disadvantaged, by helping to solve crimes, but sometimes her arguments seemed hollow and self-serving, and the money she gave to beggars in the street was the only way she could assuage her guilt.

A point of light flickered in the dark mouth of the tunnel, signaling the approach of a tube train. Ruth could feel the pressure of anxiety building up behind her, as a hundred commuters prepared to fling themselves through the doors. The train juddered to a halt, displaying faces squashed like flies against the glass. It waited a teasing moment, before the throng's collective impatience willed the stubborn doors to open. Ruth barely needed to move, carried as she was on a wave of bodies which streamed into the train.

Once moving, she closed her eyes and relaxed. It had been a good day: she had finally managed to get hold of the elusive double-glazing salesman in the Islington fraud case and had persuaded him to do an interview for the program. Maggie had obviously decided to forget about the Ross incident and had praised her for her "sensitive" handling of the battered baby story. And she had heard from Graham again.

She was never quite sure how seriously he regarded their relationship, and whenever he claimed to have a prior domestic arrangement, she wondered if it was a preliminary to a polite goodbye. Strange how her mind—once it had dealt with the business filing—always reverted to Graham, like a tune she couldn't stop humming. She knew from experience that she was foolish to get involved with a married man, she hadn't really deluded herself into thinking he would leave his wife and daughter for her. But she hadn't the strength to break it off. So far, she had managed to maintain her poise and her self-respect, but she didn't know how long that would last. She had convinced Graham, and maybe herself, that she was happy, but deep down, she knew there was something missing. Sometime—pretty soon—she would have to start demanding more, or get out altogether. When she had first met him he had seemed so solid and dependable, and that was the attraction. But she realized now that it was his very solidity and dependability that would make him loyal to his family. So what did that leave for her?

What could she say to Pa next weekend when he asked the inevitable question? Previously, she'd been able to get away with tales about the pressure of work and having no time for social life. But Pa wasn't going to buy that for ever. He wasn't stupid, just desperate that she should be happier than he had been. She couldn't bear to tell him that she was still seeing an older, married man.

All at once, the train stopped abruptly. A groan of disappointment emanated from the crowd as they realized they hadn't yet reached a station, then there was a breathless hush of anticipation, before the train mustered itself with a sigh and shuffled unwillingly on. Ruth put away her thoughts and opened her *Guardian* to the crossword page.

*   *   *

Mrs. Cavendish looked distinctly out of place at Temple Green Police Station in her expensively tailored lilac suit and her fur coat which Graham guessed was real. She made herself as comfortable as she could on one of the hard chairs in the interview room—dusting it first with a white handkerchief—and declined tea or coffee with the air of one expecting better things. She regarded Graham and Smart—the young constable who perched on a stool in the corner with a notebook in his hand— with a resigned demeanor, as she waited for the interview to commence. She had draped her coat over her knees, having refused to see it hung up on a hook with others, and she crossed her arms demurely over it, her posture erect and expectant.

"Now, I know you've already explained to DC Smart what you saw, but I'd like you to tell me again, if you wouldn't mind" began Graham.

"It was on the evening of the 25th February," commenced Mrs. Cavendish in a high-pitched nasal voice with an accent that made Graham think of fox-hunting and lavish debutante's balls. "I remember very clearly because I'd been visiting a friend of mine at the Royal Free Hospital—she was waiting for a heart bypass operation and I'd taken her some chocolates to cheer her up and visiting hours finished at seven, which means that I must have arrived home at around eight, after crawling through the traffic on Heath street. I put my car in the garage and I walked up the driveway to my house—I was walking quite slowly because there was a lot of snow on the path and I didn't want to slip." As she spoke, she swung one of her crossed legs up and down with the foot flexed. Graham noted her immaculately polished high-heeled shoes and speculated whether she had been wearing something similar on the night in question. "I noticed a young man standing on the street almost directly outside my house, in fact he noticed me too because he saw me looking at him. I wanted to ask him what he was doing outside my house but I thought better of it, one never knows what these people might do if you accost them—"

"Hang on just a moment" interrupted Graham. "Could you describe the young man for me?"

"Oh yes, I got a good look at him even though it was dark because my pathway lights were full on. They come on automatically whenever someone approaches." Graham sighed inwardly, wishing she would get to the point. DC Smart had his head down and was scribbling furiously into his notebook. "He was a young black man, about twenty-five years of age, although it's hard to tell with black people isn't it, and he had lots of sticking out black hair. He was quite short, only a little taller than me I should say, and slim."

"Can you remember what he was wearing?" Graham asked casually.

"What he was wearing" Mrs. Cavendish repeated to herself, pursing her lips and tilting her head to one side in an effort to remember.

"Anything unusual at all?" Graham had a sudden thought. "Was he wearing a jacket or a coat?"

"Well actually, yes, now you mention it. He was wearing a rather extraordinary jacket."

Graham cupped his chin in his hand and leaned in to her, his eyes on her face. "In what way extraordinary?" he asked with interest.

"A sort of denim material I should say, but when he'd looked at me and turned his back I could see that it had a lot of sort of designs on the back. Quite unusual, not the sort of thing you'd buy in a shop so maybe he'd done them himself or someone had done them for him. Pictures of, I can't say exactly but very colorful, people entwined around each other like snakes and faces and eyes peering out, that sort of thing."

"I see." Graham gave a nod to Smart, who scrawled something on his paper. "So you noticed him there at eight o'clock you say. And was he doing anything in particular?"

"Oh no, just standing there."

"Did you notice him again later?"

"Yes, it must have been a couple of hours later because I'd been in the back living room watching television with my husband, and I went to shut the curtains in the front room which overlooks the street. I remember I was surprised that the pathway lights were still on, because they should have gone off you know when I came in, and then I saw the reason why. It was because he was still standing there in exactly the same position. I watched him for a little while because I wondered what he was doing there, and he seemed to be looking up and down the street as if he were waiting for someone and he was shifting from foot to foot you know, like you do when it's cold. In point of fact,

I did mention it to my husband and even suggested that he go out there and ask the young man what he was doing, but he said I was being nosy and should stay out of other people's business." She broke off abruptly and compressed her lips. Graham guessed this might be a comment that Mr. Cavendish made frequently.

"Is there anything else you'd like to tell us?" asked Graham.

"No, not really. I didn't see the young man again, and in fact I'd forgotten all about it until your constable came to call. I don't know whether it will have any bearing on your case at all, but I thought I'd better inform you just in case." She had a self-righteous expression as if congratulating herself for her public spirited behavior.

Graham rose from his seat. "Thank you very much for coming in to see us, Mrs. Cavendish. DC Smart there will get your information typed up into a statement and then he'll ask you to sign it. I hope we haven't taken up too much of your time." He shook her hand.

"Not at all, it was a pleasure" she replied with a tight-lipped smile.

Graham left the room and went back to the Crimes Office, where he encountered Tom. "I've just been given a perfect description of Booker Mulholland" he informed his colleague.

"Who by?" asked Tom, squinting through cigarette smoke.

"A lady who lives in East Field Lane. He was lurking outside her house for a couple of hours on the night of the Heath murder. We'd better bring him in for questioning."

"Yep. I can't imagine him doing it, though. It's not his type of thing at all."

"Neither can I. But you never know, there may be a connection. He was obviously waiting for someone. Maybe there's a hidden agenda to this murder that we're not clocking."

"What d'you think? The kids were involved in some kind of drugs racket?" suggested Tom, frowning.

"Who knows?" Graham replied with a sigh. "It all sounds a bit grand for our Booker, but perhaps he's got hidden depths."

"I'll radio through to Tarrant and Doyle to bring him in. They're out on patrol now" said Tom, picking up a phone.

"Right. Oh, and Tom" said Graham remembering something on his way to the door, "Once they've brought Booker in, get them to sit outside Charlie Hackett's for a bit, would you? I want to see what his movements are."

"You want Hackett watched?" Tom asked, looking up. "You know what the Super will say."

"He'll say I'm wasting my time—"

"*Police* time—and money" warned Tom.

"He'll have to think what he likes. If Hackett's not up to his old tricks then we'll know soon enough and we can forget him. But I have a feeling he's behind this somewhere."

▼

Pat just managed to squeeze in her little hatchback between a Transit van and a glossy J-reg sports car that she suspected belonged to Eric Tideman, the hostel manager. She was parked on a single yellow line, but as it was 6.20 in the evening, she decided she could risk a ticket. The day had been overcast and gloomy and the evening darkness had already descended, making the gray buildings in the street seem even more somber. As she got out of the car, she could see that the hostel lights were on but the curtains hadn't yet been drawn. A few figures moved around the bare room—black silhouettes like puppets in a shadow play—and she felt worried at the thought that they might have been waiting for her, as well as guilty for being later than she'd intended.

She opened the boot of her car and squinted inside, pondering on the best way to remove the television set which had been jammed tightly in with a couple of blankets and an eiderdown. As she made a few tentative attempts to lever it out, she heard footsteps approaching and a voice behind her: "Need any help?"

It was Sarah, the other volunteer at the hostel, who only worked some evenings because of her family commitments. She was a bulky woman in her late forties with broken teeth and untidy hair. She never smiled or seemed to take pleasure in anything, and she made Pat uncomfortable with her direct manner. Pat often wondered why Sarah bothered to help at the hostel when she didn't seem to like people very much—then she would feel ashamed of her ingratitude. Sarah was one of the few helpers who always showed up on time.

"Yes, I wouldn't mind actually" Pat admitted. "It was quite difficult getting it in, and even more difficult getting it out I'm afraid." She gave a little nervous laugh, trying to make light of the situation, to which Sarah didn't respond.

"Here, leave it to me." The large woman heaved the television out with the minimum of fuss and began walking up the driveway with it, leaving Pat to bring up the rear with the blankets and eiderdown. In her haste to catch up with Sarah, she stumbled and almost tripped up on the edge of a blanket which she hadn't gathered up sufficiently into her bundle.

"Thank you so much."

"Why've you brought this in, then?" asked Sarah, as she pushed open the hostel door with her back.

"Some of the young ones asked me to. They said there wasn't anything to do here."

"I could give them something to do" responded Sarah, meaningfully, as if she considered that all the occupants of the hostel were wastrels and layabouts.

"Well, it was no skin off my nose" Pat gasped, struggling with the exertion of getting through the door with her arms full of blankets, "After all, we've already got two color televisions in the house and we never use this portable one. It was just sitting up in the attic, so I thought I might as well let someone else get some use out of it."

"You'll need to get a new license, won't you? Suppose you've ordered one."

"Oh yes" Pat lied, not wishing to admit she hadn't thought of that.

"Of course, you could try and get your money back off tightarse Tideman, but you'd be lucky. S'not him who'd be here if they come knocking at the door, is it?"

"No" Pat agreed hazily, anxious about her negligence.

"And the blankets? Those spares too?" Now, Sarah was regarding Pat with a cynical air, as if she thought her a silly little woman with more material possessions than she knew what to do with.

"Yes" Pat replied, not knowing what else to say.

Sarah dumped the television set on the little low table which sat in the corner of the room underneath the window and which was usually used for card games. She withdrew into the kitchen without another word. Pat said hello to some of the faces she recognized, threw the bedclothes on to the old worn settee, and hunted around for a socket in which to plug the television. Having found one, she turned the set on and fiddled with the aerial and knobs until it was tuned reasonably successfully to the evening news. Then she drew the curtains with a brisk swish. A few of the faces that had looked at her rather vacantly before brightened up at the prospect of something other than each other to look at, and turned their attention to the new attraction. But it wasn't long before desultory arguments broke out over which channel to watch. Pat left the dining room and took her blankets into the bedrooms, depositing them on the beds where she knew they were most needed—Midge Ellis who had a permanent cold, and Debbie Brown, who had begged for a spare blanket so she could let her dog sleep on the floor beside her.

Pat advanced into the kitchen and discovered Sarah stirring a huge aluminum pot of what looked like soup. Being familiar with the routine, Pat proceeded to get the dinner plates from the cupboard and stack them in a pile on the hatch, ready for serving. People were already lining up into an orderly if ragged queue outside the hatch. It was strange how, even in this place where what might be regarded as the dregs of society gathered, routine and ritual predominated. The most dominant man was always first, the boy who was perpetually hungry but who didn't dare to usurp the leader was always second, the girl who was consistently asleep when dinner was called was always last. Here was a little microcosm of the world, with its own unchanging hierarchy and social order.

"Vultures hovering, are they?" muttered Sarah, still stirring vigorously.

Pat didn't like the way Sarah referred to the people in the hostel, but was too polite to say so. So she contented herself with: "They're being very well behaved."

A few minutes later, Sarah decanted the contents of her pot into a large tureen by Pat's side and Pat began serving out the dinner.

"What've we got tonight, missis?" It was Daniel—the old tramp with the missing front teeth and the overcoat that stank of dust and grime—holding out his chipped china plate.

"Lancashire hot-pot with green beans" Pat replied, taking the plate from his filthy hand.

"Forget the beans, just gimme the hotch potch."

Pat didn't argue, but gave him an extra large portion. She'd tried to tell him before that vegetables were good for him, but he'd only made a scene. She liked him, despite, or perhaps because of, his lack of grace.

He didn't thank her, just grabbed the dish of food and shuffled away with it to a faraway corner, where he sat hunched over his plate and shoveling food into his mouth, every now and then glancing about him warily.

Pat remembered a time when all the people who came to the hostel were like him, old and decrepit, looking as if they'd spent a lifetime on the streets and had ceased to think of themselves as part of "civilized" society. Now the clientele had changed: the hostel was full of the homeless young, teenagers who'd come to London from the provinces looking for work or escaping from brutal families, kids Gemma's age and less, who slept in cardboard boxes on Waterloo station. Pat looked around her at the dingy walls of the prefabricated canteen, and pitied the people who had sunk so low that this place was their only haven.

"Pat! Pat!" She was jolted out of her reverie by hearing her name called in strident male tones. "Can I have another?" A young lad in a tattered leather jacket, who people referred to as Spic, stood before her holding out his plate.

"I'm sorry, you're only allowed one—"

"S'not for me. For 'er." He pointed to a young girl, standing shyly by the front door. "She don't wanna come in."

Pat studied the girl, standing alone in the door frame like a lost child. "I'll take her some" she said, taking Spic's dirty plate and putting it in the washing up bowl, "On a clean plate."

The girl was about twenty. She was small and very pale, with long blonde hair tied back in a pony tail. "Hello, my dear. I'm Pat. Do you remember? I saw you here the other day." Pat gave her a welcoming smile, as she handed over the plate of food. The girl nodded silently.

"Why don't you come inside? It would be warmer."

"No, it's OK, I'm OK out here" she asserted, in a frightened whisper.

"If you like" said Pat, giving her another encouraging smile, "You're welcome anyway, if you change your mind." She wanted to say more but there didn't seem to be any more to say.

Pat went back to serving the others, a little disturbed by her encounter. The girl was obviously in need of some help but was too afraid to ask for it. A few days ago Pat had managed to win her trust enough to find out about her miscarriage, but now the girl appeared to have forgotten her. Why did she have that lost, isolated air, as if she inhabited some other world?

About an hour later, most of the people had eaten and Sarah had departed for the evening. Pat was washing dishes in the small kitchen, feeling as she always did a sense of achievement that hungry people had been fed and a pride in the way she succeeded in keeping the kitchen spotless (although it habitually had a fresh coat of dirt every evening on her return). She had forgotten all about the girl in the doorway, and when she felt a tentative hand pluck her cardigan, she turned around in surprise to see her handing back her plate.

"Thank you. I was hungry." A little smile hovered about her mouth, as if unsure whether it was safe to come out. She didn't move out of the kitchen, but stood on the spot, looking at Pat as if she had more to say.

Pat was pleased that the girl seemed to trust her, and had maybe come to her for support. "Are you feeling a bit better now?" she inquired. The girl looked puzzled. "You said you weren't very well the last time you came. You'd just lost your baby?"

"No." The girl shook her head with a look of dismay.

Pat was astonished by this denial. The girl had been quite open before, and had volunteered to Pat the information about the miscarriage. Pat had conjectured that the girl had no one else to talk to and had flattered herself that she had been selected as a sort of mother confessor. She was expecting the girl to reveal some more of her story this time, and possibly tell why her husband left her. "But you told me—"

"No…I never had a baby…never had…" She started to back out of the room.

"Oh, I'm sorry. I didn't mean to upset you. It's all right."

A terrified look had come into the girl's eyes. She reminded Pat of a deer that has just seen the hunter's gun, and is wondering which way to run.

Pat was instantly regretful that she had been so pushy. She stepped forward, intending to placate the girl and win back her trust. "Don't be frightened. I just wanted to help."

But by this time, she was talking to thin air. The girl had fled. And Pat was left alone and confused, wringing her tea towel in her hand.

Chapter Seven

Graham and Tom's feet crunched over the gravel as they walked back to their car. It was a beautiful fresh day with a scent of Spring, and the Crown Court building towered majestically over the grounds, its windows glimmering in the sunshine, its old stones holding the secrets of justice meted out over many years. A young barrister scurried from the huge front door to the Modern Wing, his black coat flapping in the breeze, wig pulled slightly askew in his haste.

Graham's head was lowered, watching his feet as if they were the only interesting things to look at, his hands stuffed aggressively into his pockets. "A fat lot of good that was" he grumbled.

"I had a feeling Booker would be a dead end" replied Tom, taking this opportunity to light the dog end of a cigarette which had been hiding in his pocket throughout their time indoors. He inhaled the smoke of his first puff with a slight cough.

"It wasn't that I expected him to say, *Oh yes, I was waiting outside Mrs. Cavendish's house for the murderer, shall I tell you who it is?* but something a bit more interesting than that his girlfriend stood him up" continued Graham.

"Do you believe him?"

"I can't imagine Booker waiting around in the cold for any girl. I bet it was some drugs deal that got cocked up."

"I thought he wasn't a pusher" said Tom, his eyes on a pretty young solicitor's clerk deep in conversation with her superior as they walked up the drive.

"He may be" Graham mumbled. "Just because we've never been able to pin anything on him doesn't mean he hasn't got more than a few joints stashed around his flat."

"So there's no link with the murder" stated Tom.

"It was a long shot. I don't think those kids were feeding a habit. And even if they were, Booker was hardly their style—they'd be going in for the posh stuff, not Booker's little marijuana racket. Like you say, it's a dead end."

"Especially if his alibi holds firm" Tom commented.

"Oh, I think it will" said Graham. "Even if he wasn't home by 10.30 and in all night like he says, his girlfriend'll back up his story. Plus, I reckon that's the one part we *can* believe. After waiting two hours in the cold for some abortive drugs deal, Booker would be far too pissed off to hang around another hour or so to murder a couple of teenagers. He'd be off back home."

"Kids like him make me depressed" said Tom, as he stubbed out his cigarette and unlocked the passenger door of the car.

"Like who? Booker?" Graham asked, as he got into the driver's side.

"Yeah. Why can't he get his act together and realize that this drugs shit is just a vicious circle that always ends with him in there." He nodded towards the Crown Court building.

"Oh, it's not such a bad life" quipped Graham. "When he's not in the nick he's probably enjoying himself more than most kids on the dole." He turned the key in the ignition. "It's not Booker *I* feel sorry for. It's kids like Jenny and James, murdered in cold blood when they had everything to live for. If our society's sick, *they're* the real victims. Aren't they?"

*   *   *

It was about seven o'clock in the evening when Graham let himself into his front door. He turned on the hall light, hung up his coat, checked the ansaphone for messages and ran his fingers along the bars of Serena's cage by way of greeting. The house was silent and undisturbed. He proceeded into the front room, felt the radiators to make sure the central heating was on, poured himself a glass of sherry and threw himself on to the sofa grabbing the latest copy of the *Hampstead and Highgate Express* to flick through. A minute later, to his surprise, a thump sounded from upstairs. After a few moments the door opened and Pat bustled through on her way to the kitchen. She noticed Graham with a shock: "Good heavens! I didn't hear you come in."

Graham put his paper down and cleared his throat, putting an edgy hand on his neck. "I thought you'd be at the hostel."

"Yes, I was just on my way there actually. I start later on Wednesdays, because Sarah does the early shift. But, if you're going to be at home this evening I could stay in—"

"Oh—no, it's all right…erm…I've got to go out myself anyway."

"Oh." Pat paused for a long moment. "I see." She regarded Graham for a second or two as if about to say something, then changed her mind and passed into the kitchen. A few minutes later, she came back into the room clutching her handbag. "Is it work?" she asked a little too casually.

"What?" said Graham, looking up from the paper.

"Where you're going tonight—is it something to do with work?"

"Oh, yes, it's er…one of those staff functions, you know. One of the lads is being transferred and we're giving him a good send off in the pub."

"Really? Anyone I know?"

"No. You wouldn't know him."

"That's unusual for you, isn't it? You don't usually like pubs" asserted Pat, still observing her husband while fumbling with the catch of her handbag.

Graham kept his gaze averted. "Well, you know, I can't let him down so I'll put aside my prejudices just for once." He looked at Pat with a blank face. "You're going to be late. Hadn't you better be going?"

Pat regarded her hands. "Yes." She paused. "I saw that girl again last night" she said with the air of someone making conversation.

"What girl?"

"The one at the hostel. You know—she had a miscarriage."

"Oh yes" Graham replied without interest.

"At least, she told me before that she'd had a miscarriage but now she's denying any knowledge of it. She really is a strange person."

Graham was silent, his eyes scanning the paper without taking in any of the printed words.

"I was just thinking, Graham."

"Hmm?"

"It's been a long time since we spent any time together, hasn't it? Perhaps, one of these days, when you're not too busy, we could go out for a meal or something."

Graham considered his wife, not quite knowing what to say. "Yes. I suppose we could" he agreed at last.

"You...haven't been yourself for a while" continued Pat hesitantly, "And I just thought it would be nice to have a chat."

"Not myself? How?"

"You've just been rather...distracted...distant, not yourself anyway. Even Gemma's noticed it."

"She didn't say anything to me."

"Well, she wouldn't, would she?"

Graham put down his paper, went up to his wife and gave her a brief hug and a peck on the cheek. "I'm sorry. There's nothing wrong. I've just been working too hard. This case is...very difficult, and I can't seem to put it out of my mind."

Pat breathed a sigh of relief. "Yes, I thought that was it." She seemed noticeably brighter, as she added: "I really had better be going. Enjoy yourself tonight, dear."

"I will" Graham replied as he watched her leave the room. And he fought down the guilt at his too facile lies.

*   *   *

A couple of hours later, Graham sat in a large concert hall with Ruth by his side, exquisite music washing over him in soothing waves. He had his eyes closed to avoid the prosaic sight of musicians toiling over their instruments which might have distracted him from the soaring notes of violin and cello. Ruth's left hand was held in his right and from time to time he pressed on it lightly. He was aware of her body next to his—poised and still, with her attention entirely focused on the music—and he anticipated the time when he could embrace her. Her long black hair fell down in a cascading mane around her neck, and he could feel the weight of it resting on his right shoulder like a caress.

The air in the hall was chilly, but Graham was unaware of anything but the music. In fact, he was so lost in a daydream that when the concert finished and the audience began to applaud, he was brought out of his reverie with a jolt. He joined in the applause and clapped until his hands were sore and the musicians had taken countless bows.

As the performers left the stage and the audience members began struggling from their seats, Graham looked at Ruth and smiled. Judging from her expression what she'd thought of the concert, he kissed her on the neck and rose, taking her long woolen coat from the back of the seat in front and draping it over her shoulders. The couple shuffled behind a single file of people until they were out of the auditorium and in the foyer.

"Shall we grab a coffee?" proposed Graham.

"Yes, that would be nice. I'm gasping" declared Ruth.

Ruth located a couple of unoccupied chairs and a table and waited for Graham as he queued for their coffee. Her face down to study the program they had bought, she failed to notice the occasional glance that he threw her over his shoulder.

There was another person in the foyer that she didn't notice. This person was also watching her, but his gaze was hostile. He was not in the queue for refreshments, but had hidden himself amongst a group of Japanese tourists who were chattering noisily at the other end of the room. In his drab gray overcoat he sank into the background making little impression and he scrutinized Ruth without fear of discovery. His small body was hunched over a bag of peanuts, from which he would from time to time extract a nut, popping it into his mouth without diverting his stare from Ruth.

Graham finished at the line and approached Ruth with a tray bearing two coffee cups. "Here we are" he said, putting the cups on the table. "Sorry, they only had cream."

"That's O.K." said Ruth. "These program notes are really interesting. I never knew all that about Rossini's background." She paused as she ripped the lid from the cream container and poured the liquid into her cup. "Well—did the concert live up to your expectations?"

Graham nodded. "And more so. The musicians were wonderful. I've got the record at home of course, but it's totally different hearing it live."

"Like the difference between real and plastic flowers?" Ruth suggested. "Or the difference between tinned peaches and fresh?"

Graham gave a short laugh. "I wouldn't have put it that way, but...yes, I suppose so." He took a gulp of coffee. "Thanks again for inviting me."

"It was a pleasure. I don't think Judith would have enjoyed it nearly as much as you, anyway."

"And would you have enjoyed her company as much as mine?" Graham flirted.

"Of course not" Ruth admitted with a grin.

"I could never do anything like this with Pat" mused Graham. "I'm afraid Barry Manilow is more her scene." He slurped his coffee and regarded a poster on the wall which advertised the next concert.

Ruth hesitated for a moment, then changed the subject. "I don't mean to talk shop, but can I just ask you a little about the murder case you're working on?"

"You sound like a journalist now" replied Graham, turning his head back to her. "Yes, all right. What do you want to know?"

"Just whether you've come up with any suspects. We're doing the reconstruction tomorrow and I need to know all the facts. Tanya said she rang your office today and got rather short shrift from the officer she spoke to."

Graham made a wry face. "It's not that we're being obstructive. Just that we genuinely don't have a good idea ourselves about it." He sighed, unwilling to continue, but a glance at Ruth's eager face egged him on. "The murder seems motiveless and random, and yet certain things don't tie in with the murderer being a psychopath. No…sexual assault, no mutilation of the bodies. Do we have to talk about this now?"

Ruth ignored his plea. "Dare I ask whether you're considering anybody like Charlie Hackett as a likely suspect?"

"Yes, of course we're considering him. He lives in the area and he fits some of the forensic evidence, though nothing's conclusive. But Ruth—don't go blabbing about any of this on your program, will you?"

"Of course not" she declared with conviction. "Don't you think I've learnt my lesson?"

Graham smiled and didn't reply. "Let's not talk any more about business." He leant towards her and put his arm round her shoulder, kissing her hair. "I wish I could spend the night with you, but it's impossible this evening" he said softly into her ear. "Pat was in when I got home and she looked at me askance when I told her I was going out again."

"Never mind. There'll be another time." Ruth's smile seemed forced, and yet her hand was gentle as she stroked Graham's cheek with her finger.

"Perhaps at the weekend?"

"I told you, this weekend I'm away and next weekend I'm going to visit Pa in Hull."

"When will you get back from your father's?"

"I could come back Sunday afternoon. Tell you what, why not come over Sunday night for dinner—about eight?"

Graham nodded and kissed her on the lips. From previous experience, he knew that Ruth's dinners were generally a non-event. But it wasn't the meal he hungered after.

About half an hour later, the couple walked out of the building arm in arm. And the man who had been watching them followed at a safe distance, keeping them always in his sights. He continued to observe as Graham and Ruth made their way to the car park, got into Graham's car and drove away. Then, pulling up the collar of his old coat and holding it tight around his ears, he shambled to the bus stop across the street and positioned himself among the others waiting in the queue.

*   *   *

The face of the man sitting opposite him was almost as familiar to Graham as his own, having appeared so often in his nightmares. The man had dirty blonde hair which hung in a matted clump to his shoulders. From inside the hair peeked an urchin's face, scored with deep lines ingrained with dirt and with beady dark eyes which darted suspiciously about like a cunning bird. Charlie was wearing a denim jacket several sizes too big for his diminutive frame—probably stolen, Graham thought—baggy brown trousers with frayed bottoms, and a pair of worn trainers that had faded from blue to dingy gray and had holes in the toes.

Tom sat alongside Graham with a notebook ready. He knocked out a cigarette from his packet with practiced flair and began sucking thoughtfully on it. When Charlie saw the packet being produced from Tom's jacket, he grabbed for a cigarette with greedy fingers, but Tom slapped his hand. "Not till you're a good boy and answer some questions." The hand was retracted and Charlie scratched the side of his face with a mucky finger, the corners of his mouth curled up in a representation of a smile.

"Where are you living now, Charlie?" asked Graham, looking at him from a sideways angle.

"Same place" replied Charlie.

"That squat in Camden?"

"Not a squat. Belongs to my auntie, see." The eyes darted from Tom to Graham and back to Tom, then to the cigarette packet lying temptingly just within reach.

Graham ignored the lie he had heard before, put an elbow on the table and rested his chin on his left hand. "You were going to try and get a job last time I saw you, weren't you, Charlie? Any success on that front?"

"Been working." His mouth worked nervously. "Laboring, that's what I does."

Tom greeted this with a derisive snort and wrote something in his notebook.

"So you haven't had time to hang around in public places then, and go following people?" demanded Graham.

"What you mean?" Tom noticed that the hands in Charlie's lap were twitching almost uncontrollably. No wonder he was so desperate for a cigarette.

"Don't waste my time" said Graham loudly. "You know exactly what I mean. Following people is your trademark, it's what you do, isn't it? At least, it was last time. You admitted that much."

"Don't shout." Charlie winced and drew back. "Hurts my ears."

Graham leaned in over the table. "Following people. And then killing them."

"No. Told you before. Never killed nobody." His body was shaking, whether with anger or fear Tom couldn't tell.

"That's what *you* say. I don't think I believe you. I think you've killed lots of people. Six at least."

"You got no right" Charlie protested. "I was let off. You never proved nothing. I was let off, wasn't I?"

"On a technicality" muttered Tom.

"I was let off" Charlie repeated. "Can I have a ciggie now?" The hand reached again and Tom slapped it away. "Not yet."

Graham decided to change tack. "Where were you on February 25th?" he asked casually, leaning back in his chair and tapping a biro on the edge of the table.

"When was that then?"

"Friday before last. In the evening. What were you up to?"

Charlie made a face. "Can't remember. What you ask me that for?"

"Make an effort, Charlie" said Tom, pointing to the cigarette packet on the table.

"I dunno. At home, I suppose."

"Got anybody to back up your story?" asked Graham.

"Eh?"

"Anybody who can give you an alibi for that evening. You see, I don't think I believe you that you were at home. You could have been anywhere, for all I know." Graham was still tapping out a rhythm on the table with his pen, and the constant sound made Charlie squirm in his seat.

"Don't need no alibi, see. You got no proof" Charlie asserted without conviction, glancing at Tom.

"You don't know that" replied Tom, proffering at last the desired cigarette.

"Two people were killed that night" said Graham, stopping his tapping and leaning in again. "A boy and a girl. Sounds like quite your style, Charlie."

The little man didn't reply but puffed gratefully on the cigarette.

"And we've got some evidence which could easily point to you" continued Graham. "Hairs your color and length found on the murder weapon, the coroner said the killer was short, about your height, the footprints left in the snow were from someone with small feet, wearing trainers." Graham looked down at Charlie's feet significantly. "So you see, we could easily make the assumption that this killer was you. We might even be able to hold you in custody—"

"You couldn't—" Charlie began.

"Unless you can come up with a strong alibi to prove that you weren't in the vicinity when the crime was committed."

"You can't harass me, see. I done nothing" Charlie gabbled. "I going to get my solicitor on to you."

"I don't think she'd be much help" said Graham calmly. "Not if you can't supply us with any proof that you were at home all evening, as you say."

Charlie seemed to digest this for a few moments. Then he blurted: "I was at the pub."

"Which pub?" asked Tom.

"Yes. Friday night wasn't it. I would have been at the pub."

"You've got the money to go drinking, Charlie, have you?" said Graham.

"With my friends. They bought me a drink."

"One drink to last the whole evening?" said Tom incredulously. "What time did you leave?"

"Can't remember. Past midnight. Pub in Camden Town. Can't remember the name of it."

"Any of these friends able to corroborate your story?" asked Graham.

"Eh?"

"Can they tell us for sure you were there" explained Tom.

"Yeah" said Charlie uncertainly.

"Good then" replied Tom, closing his notebook. "You can give their names to the desk sergeant."

When Tom had left the room and Graham was showing Charlie out, the little man suddenly turned on him—the stink of his breath making Graham recoil in disgust—and hissed through clenched teeth: "You're gonna pay for this."

Graham snorted. "What with, your precious solicitor?"

"You're not Mr. Squeaky Clean" Charlie snarled in retort. "I seen you with your woman."

"What the hell are you talking about?" demanded Graham.

"I'm not following no boy and girl. It's you I'm watching—you and that woman."

Charlie pushed past Graham in the doorway without another word and hobbled away down the corridor. Graham watched the retreating back with loathing and felt his blood run cold.

CHAPTER EIGHT

"Our next story happened two weeks ago, on a cold Friday night in North West London." Ruth addressed the camera with a grave face full of solicitude. "A young couple—Jenny Hunt and James Anderson—were walking home from the Everyman Cinema in Hampstead, where they had been to watch a film. It was about eleven or eleven thirty at night when they must have taken a route from the cinema down East Field Lane, which skirts the Heath, on their way back to Jenny's home in Cricklewood."

Ruth moistened her lips with her tongue. She turned her head and waited for the camera to pan across to the large screen on which was projected a film of two actors portraying the couple. Ruth watched them reenacting the events she'd just described, as did the television audience at home. She was gratified that Maggie had chosen two actors who bore a strong resemblance to the actual couple, of whom Ruth had seen photographs. The young man was about 5'10" tall, of medium build and with short dark curly hair. The girl was a bit shorter than him and slim, with a lot of black curly hair which hung over her shoulders. Ruth discerned a similarity to her own hair as she dallied with a strand of it on her forefinger.

Following the couple, the camera mimicked someone stalking them as they walked laughingly away from the cinema and down the deserted street, turning promptly into a narrow path which led into East Field Lane. Ruth smiled to herself, remembering what Tanya had told her of the problems they'd encountered filming this sequence to keep members of the public—who were milling around even at that late hour—out of the shot.

After the couple passed by the house on East Field Lane that Mrs. Cavendish occupied, the film ended and the camera swung back to Ruth. "For some reason, the couple decided to take a detour by walking across the Heath itself. Perhaps they saw something that interested them or perhaps they just wanted to enjoy each other's company for a few more moments and take a romantic stroll in the moonlight. At any rate, it was a decision they would regret."

The camera swiveled back to the screen, and Ruth and the viewers watched the couple, now arm in arm on the Heath as they walked through the snow. Powerful lights had been used to simulate moonlight on the dark night of filming.

"Forensic evidence suggests their attacker was somebody short wearing sneakers. Maybe he followed them from the cinema, or perhaps he was already lurking on the Heath. We don't know for sure." A short actor in a hooded coat was seen from behind, lit darkly so that his face was almost invisible, then a close up showed his feet crunching through the snow.

"It's possible that he'd seen them coming out of the cinema, or that he'd been waiting for them along East Field Lane. If *you* saw anybody hanging around in any of these areas—on Heath Street or any of the streets leading from it or in East Field Lane—call our phone lines now. If you went to the cinema yourself that night and saw anybody suspicious outside, do call. Here's the number, flashing on to your screens. Don't forget. It's very important that the police are informed about anybody suspicious lurking around the vicinity on that night. This person has killed, possibly more than once, and he may well kill again. If you have any useful information at all, we're waiting to hear from you."

Ruth smiled warmly at the camera. "Thanks for helping us here at *Watch Out for Crime*. After the break, it will be over to Tony for a less gruesome item." The theme tune was played as the camera zoomed out.

Ruth's spot was over and she knew she wouldn't be needed again till the closing credits, so she decided to nip into the researchers' office to see if any interesting calls were coming in. The studio was quite a long walk from the office, and it was during the time lag between Ruth's departure from the first location and her arrival at the second that the following incident took place:

On the fifth floor of the BBC building, a phone commenced ringing from the desk of the most junior researcher with the *Watch Out for Crime* team. Observing her three more experienced colleagues answer their phones with alacrity, Melanie had been longing for an opportunity to prove her mettle with her first live call. "Watch Out for Crime office" she announced brightly. "Melanie speaking. How can I help you?"

"I got some information" a voice crackled.

"Could I have your name, please, sir?"

"No. No name. Tell you in confidence."

A bit thrown, Melanie hesitated, pondering how important it was to follow the next part of the script. "Oh. Very well then. Can you tell me what your information is concerning?"

"Concerning?" the voice questioned.

"Which item in the program?" Melanie's confidence was ebbing away, but she tried to keep her voice bright.

"It was on just now."

"Just now. I see. You mean the item about the couple on Hampstead Heath?" Melanie did her best to sound persuasive and encouraging.

"That's right."

"What information do you have? Were you in the area on the night in question? Did you see anybody suspicious?"

Hearing the silence that greeted this, Melanie fretted that she might have bombarded her caller with too many questions.

But after a long pause he responded, "I want to talk to her about it."

"Who do you mean?"

"Her" he repeated. "The presenter. Ruth Ramon."

Melanie started to explain. "What happens is that I take down all the information that comes in and then if anything seems really significant Miss Ramon calls you back to ask you more questions, or maybe puts you directly in contact with the police. I'm afraid we don't let people talk immediately to the presenter, or she'd have no time to do the program. We get an awful lot of calls."

Believing that she'd been really clear and reasonable, Melanie felt aggrieved when her caller didn't appear to get the message.

"Want to talk to her" he insisted. "Not going to tell you. Get her to call me back."

"I'm afraid I'd have to take some details from you myself first. I'd need your phone number, in any case—" But before she'd finished her sentence, the caller rang off.

Melanie stared at her phone for a moment or two, feeling a fool. She asked herself if she could have handled the situation any better, and wondered how a more experienced researcher might have coped. Looking up, she saw to her relief that the others were mid-conversation, unaware of her rebuff. She pondered whether to tell Ruth about the caller, who she was now certain had called before with the same request. While she sat and brooded, the phone rang again. Undaunted, she rekindled her enthusiasm and answered as brightly as before.

*   *   *

Graham generally enjoyed working the late shift. Tonight, however, as he floundered to his car through the punishing rain, he was gratified to be on his way home at last. It was raining so hard that water was gushing in two narrow rivers down either side of the street. On reaching the blue Metro, Graham fumbled in his pocket for his car keys and dropped them in the gutter, mouthing a silent curse as he bent down to retrieve them. Friday 13th was not his lucky night—he thought—as he hurled his sodden bulk into the driver's seat with a grunt of relief. Fortunately, the car started first time and, as he weaved up the street, his body tingled in anticipation at the prospect of a hot bath and a hotter cup of tea. He estimated that he would be home in about fifteen minutes.

Ten minutes later, a call came through on the car radio. He was needed urgently at a student discotheque in Camden Town.

*   *   *

PC Doyle was surveying the pimple on the side of his nose in the passenger's wing mirror, when the sound of a slamming door caught his attention. To his disappointment, the noise had come not from the house he and PC Tarrant were watching but the one next to it. A girl in jeans and a leather jacket tripped down the steps in front of the house, got astride a motorbike parked outside, kick-started it and tore away down the street.

"Wish that was me" muttered Doyle.

"What?" responded Tarrant, who'd been trying to read a paper by the light of a torch so as not to run down the car battery.

"That girl on the bike. I used to ride a bike, you know."

"Doesn't surprise me. That's all you Northerners do, isn't it, tear around council estates on motorbikes" said Tarrant dryly, giving up on his paper. He removed a squashed chocolate bar from his pocket and peeled off the wrapping.

"You know, before I became a copper, that's what I thought it would be like. Out on the road on your bike, picking up traffic offenses or chasing criminals. Dead exciting like. Not this boring rubbish." Doyle gave the house opposite them a baleful glare.

"Not all glamor, you're right there. Want some sustenance?" Tarrant proffered the chocolate bar. Doyle took a bite then passed it back.

"Bloody cold, isn't it?" grumbled Doyle. "Can we put a cassette on? I could do with some music."

"Are you joking? He'd hear us."

"What's the difference? I don't think he's in there anyway."

"He might be. We don't know."

"In total darkness?" said Doyle incredulously.

"He's probably got no lights. No electricity."

"Don't be daft" scoffed Doyle.

"Look at the windows—they're all either boarded up or broken" said Tarrant, indicating them with his forefinger. "I've been in these squats. You wouldn't believe how these people live. No running water, some of 'em. No flushing lav. He's probably got to shit in the back garden."

Doyle chuckled. "I don't envy him in this weather."

"You could keep your window wound up. That'd help" recommended Tarrant.

There was a pause while both men munched their chocolate in reflective silence.

"What are we doing here, anyway? What does the D.I. expect us to find?" Doyle inquired of his older companion, after a minute or two.

"Could be anything. Nothing would surprise me" Tarrant replied.

"Who is this bloke, anyway? Why's Brunswick so interested in him?"

"You don't mean to tell me you haven't heard about the Hackett case?"

"Why should I have? I was in Liverpool, remember."

"It made the national papers. Television coverage, too" said Tarrant.

"When was this?"

Tarrant pondered for a moment and scratched his forehead with a sticky finger. "Last summer. No—spring, round about May or June time. That's when they were reporting it, anyway, because the bodies had been discovered and Hackett was in custody. We were just about to bring him to trial, or the D.I. was rather."

"How many bodies?" asked Doyle with interest.

"Six." Tarrant shook his head in doleful reminiscence. "They were gruesome murders. All the bodies were dumped outside, all in North West London. It was like bloody Madame Tussaud's House of Horror or something. Never seen anything like it."

Doyle grimaced. "Why'd he do it?"

Tarrant just gave him a quizzical look, as if to say *If I knew that I wouldn't be in this job.*

"Is he queer?" asked Doyle, after a moment's contemplation.

"What's that got to do with it?"

"You know, like Dennis Nilsen, sort of luring young men back to his place and having his way with them and then killing them."

Tarrant laughed at the enthusiasm with which Doyle had delivered this suggestion. "No, nothing like that. For a start, some were girls. And he never sexually molested them. But there was a pattern."

Tarrant got some gum out of a packet and popped it into his mouth, chewing for an infuriatingly long time before continuing his story. Doyle waited with an open mouth, urging his colleague with eager eyes.

"They were all students at college or university, all teenagers. And he did stuff to the faces afterwards, with a knife."

"What sort of stuff?" prodded Doyle.

"Some weird kind of markings. I don't know what they were supposed to mean, but they meant something to him. We found the same knife markings on all the bodies."

Doyle shivered. "Creepy bugger. So what the hell's he doing out of jail?"

"We never got a conviction."

"Terrific" Doyle said ironically. "Why not?"

"Do you really want to hear this?" said Tarrant wearily. "It's a long story."

"We've got nothing better to do."

"O.K." Tarrant sighed. He chewed his gum for a while before commencing. "Brunswick was leading the investigation, and he had a DC on the case called Driscoll who was Brunswick's blue-eyed boy, a good copper but ambitious—you know the type. There was an informant, a chap called—I can't remember the name. Anyway, he knew Hackett quite well—I think he used to work with him or something—and he'd witnessed one of the attacks. Hackett was our prime suspect. We'd got some good forensic evidence against him, although nothing clinching. Our main ace in the pack was the informant. With his evidence, we had a good case. Anyway, we needed to find Hackett and nobody knew where he was, so Brunswick went on that television program—"

"Where they do the reconstructions?"

Tarrant nodded. "Brunswick was interviewed by the presenter and they did an appeal to the public to come forward if they had any information on a bloke called Charlie and they showed a photo fit picture of him. Some people rang in and we traced Hackett quite quickly. He was living here as it happens. And we were all saying how brilliant the program was for helping us find him and that."

"I've always thought it was a good idea" said Doyle.

"No, but keep listening. We changed our minds about that, especially the D.I." Tarrant took a deep breath. "We pulled in Hackett for questioning and we were all sure he'd done it, but we knew our evidence wasn't strong enough for a conviction. We needed our informant to testify against him in Court. The case was all resting on that. We had Hackett in custody for weeks and he kept saying he was innocent. He had this solicitor who was a real hard-nosed bitch—God knows how he got hold of her, he can't have been paying her anything so maybe she thought he was a good cause or something because she's Welsh too—and she really gave us a hard time and complained about us keeping him in with no evidence. Eventually, we had to let him go. But even then, we weren't so worried. The trial date was fixed, Hackett couldn't go anywhere and we were confident we'd convict him with the evidence of the informant." Tarrant took the chewing gum out of his mouth and wrapped it in paper before stowing it in the driver's seat pocket. "Anyway" he continued, "not long after we released Hackett our informant disappeared, nobody knew where. He just vanished off the face of the earth."

"Very convenient for Hackett" remarked Doyle.

"Exactly" Tarrant replied. "It was obvious to all of us that the informant had been nobbled. And we were all angry about it. But none more so than Brunswick, and his protege, Driscoll. Anyway, so the D.I. brings Hackett in for questioning again, and this time he and Driscoll start to get really heavy with him. Driscoll was an impatient man—he could see promotion in sight if he nailed Hackett—and I suppose he thought he could just beat a confession out of him. But Hackett was cleverer than anyone imagined. Not only did he not confess, he got his solicitor on to us for physically abusing her client."

"Did the case come to trial?" asked Doyle.

"Oh yes, it came to trial. It would have been better for us if it hadn't. Not only had we lost our key witness, which meant that our other evidence looked laughably thin, but Driscoll was up for malpractice. Brunswick had to testify against him and admit that he'd seen his favorite junior officer beating up the defendant. I suppose he could have lied to save face but that wouldn't have been in character. The case was thrown out of Court, Hackett went free and Driscoll got the sack."

"Whew!" said Doyle.

"And that's not the end of it" added Tarrant. "Driscoll was just a young bloke and being a copper was the only thing he'd ever wanted. I suppose being sacked was too much for him. He hung himself a few days later."

"You're kidding!" said Doyle, horrified. "No wonder the D.I. nearly resigned."

"To tell you the truth, a lot of us were surprised when he decided to stay on."

"I'm glad he did" said Doyle. "He's a good copper. Shame to quit over something that's not your fault."

"You're right."

Suddenly, Tarrant noticed something. "God, it's him! Keep your head down."

Doyle ducked and peered up through the glass. A man was approaching the house. The two officers watched as a small figure in a worn raincoat shuffled up to the front door, kicked it with one foot till the door swung open on its hinges and hobbled inside.

"Is that Hackett?" whispered Doyle.

Tarrant nodded. "What time is it? You've got the watch."

"10.24." Doyle consulted the illuminated dials of the timepiece on his wrist. "Had I better make a note of it?"

"Yes. We'll let the D.I. know when he rings in."

"Does that mean we can leave now?" asked Doyle hopefully.

"Of course not, you idiot. We're here till midnight. We'd better keep watching in case he goes out again."

Doyle gave an enormous sigh, stretched up his arms and leaned back against the headrest. "Excitement over for the evening, then. You got any more of that chocolate?"

*   *   *

The hall was thick with bodies and smoke. Now that the discotheque's multicolored lights had been turned off, glaring neons emphasized the squalor of the room with its drab walls, floor swimming in spilt beer and cigarette butts and debris of discarded pamphlets.

The boy at the door greeted Graham with a hostile stare. "Another cop?" he complained.

The inspector nodded. It always enraged him to find his profession so despised by these youngsters. His own daughter was one of them, for Christ's sake!

Students loitered at the bar craving a tumbler of beer, huddled in disconsolate bands around low tables or slumped miserably on plastic chairs. DC Smart—forever eager for promotion—was the first person to approach Graham.

"There's been an attack, sir" he disclosed, "One of the students here has been knifed."

"Is he dead?"

"Believe so, yes sir. The paramedics have just left. We decided not to move the body, as it seems to be a murder and there's no more we can do for him. Dr. Sturgeon is taking a look at the body now, sir. Myself and Fields are taking statements from the other students at the moment, sir."

"It'll take you all night to get through this lot" observed Graham, surveying the room, which surely contained over a hundred people. The constable merely smiled, showing gapped teeth.

"All right Smart, keep up the good work. I'll proceed with my investigations, if you'd like to show me round." Smart piloted Graham through the hall and up the dingy stairs to the ladies lavatory on the first landing. The corpse lay at the far end of the narrow room by the radiator and Dr. Sturgeon was bent over it, checking his thermometer. He looked up when he heard Graham arrive and gave him a cursory nod.

"Evening, Inspector. It's not good news, I'm afraid. The boy died a few minutes ago from loss of blood. An ambulance was called immediately, I believe, but it took them half an hour to get here through the traffic. He was dead by the time they arrived."

"I see. Have you been able to establish anything about the cause of death?"

"You see this bruise here at the front of the skull" he said, showing Graham a livid stain on the boy's forehead, "I would say that was a contre-coup head wound. The impact of a moving head against a hard, stationary surface—such as this wall—causes damage to occur on the opposite side of the brain to the impact point."

"You're saying he concussed himself?"

"There are some stab wounds here, as you can see, where the clothing has been slit" the doctor continued, waving his hand over three small gashes just below the neck, "but I don't think they would have been enough to kill him. Here, you see, there's a good deal of water on the floor—leaked from the sink most likely—and it's quite slippery." He demonstrated, sliding his fingers over the tiled surface. "My guess is the boy staggered backwards in the struggle, lost his balance and hit this window ledge where it juts out." The doctor pointed to a protruding ledge, with a small patch of red discernible on the lip. The sash window was tightly shut and locked with a key.

"Our murderer was in quite a hurry to go, wasn't he? He hasn't even bothered to take his knife" Graham quipped, indicating the black handle of the blade embedded in the boy's chest.

Dr. Sturgeon shook his head sadly. "Peculiar. He must have slipped out of here pretty damn quickly because nobody saw him go."

"Somebody must have" asserted Graham. He turned swiftly to find Constable Smart standing to attention in the doorway. "What's the dead lad's name, Smart?" he asked, removing a notebook from his pocket.

"Mark Winstanley, sir."

"Right." He scribbled down the name. "And who was the last person to see him alive?"

"That would be his girlfriend, sir. Annette Payne. She was with him when the incident occurred."

She was not pretty—her nose was too wide and her eyes were small and of a nondescript color—but she had a head of hair that many a prettier girl would have envied. Graham was reminded suddenly of Ruth and how her black mane shone under the lamp when she stepped out of the shower. He pushed the memory away with an effort and introduced himself to the girl.

"Can you tell me what happened tonight, Annette?" he inquired.

"I already told that other cop."

"Yes I know, but I'd like to hear for myself what you saw."

She sighed and compressed her lips. "I was dancing with Mark. I told him I had to go to the toilet. He followed me upstairs, we were stood in the lav. for a bit having a kiss. Then, you know, I was desperate so I went into a cubicle for a pee. Mark was saying he'd spilt beer on his t-shirt. I could hear him washing his hands. Then…" She frowned, trying to remember.

"Then?" Graham prompted.

"It was…I could hear Mark talking to someone." She halted.

"Someone had come into the lavatory?"

"Yeah, they must have done."

"What was he saying? Could you hear the other person?"

"No, I didn't hear them say anything. I just heard Mark scream."

"And what did you do then?"

"I didn't do nothing. I was terrified. I thought they might come after me next, whoever it was, you know." She glanced at Graham for support.

"When did you come out of the cubicle?"

"I heard them fighting and the noise like I said and then it all went quiet. I thought whoever it was might be lying in wait for me, waiting for me to come out, then I thought, they probably don't even know I'm in here. So I opened the door really slowly and looked out and there wasn't anyone there, no one but Mark. I saw him lying there under the window and his mouth was open and his eyes staring and that knife in his chest. I couldn't believe it. I just had to get out of there, you know?" She shook her head from side to side, as if trying to dislodge the memory.

"All right, Annette." Graham tried to put a hand on her thin shoulder, but she shrugged it off like a fly. "Can you think of anyone who might have had a motive for killing Mark? Was there anyone who had a grudge against him? Did he have any enemies at the college that you knew about?"

"Nah." She shook her head. "I'm not saying he was everybody's best mate, but no one to do nothink like that. It wasn't no one he knew. I'm sure. Otherwise, he would have, like, said hello to 'em wouldn't he?"

"Someone he didn't know but who had some kind of vendetta against him?" Graham suggested gently.

She lowered her head and shook it more forcefully, her pale face almost completely shrouded by hair. "I feel sick. I need a drink" she muttered.

"One last question," he begged, "did you see anyone suspicious when you left the toilet, anyone on the stairs, or—"

"I wasn't in no fit state. Anyway, it was dark out there. Listen, you want to speak to Gareth. He was on the door all night, taking tickets. I mean, there's only one door into this place, you know."

"Thanks for your help. We'll probably need you at the station later on for further questioning, but that'll do for now."

Graham made his way to the bar, feeling that he needed fortification. He fingered the final pages of his notebook, which were crammed with lines of microscopic writing, interspersed with question marks and arrows, then replaced the book in his pocket. While ordering a cup of coffee, his hand accidentally brushed against a paper plate carrying two dry sausage rolls and a wrinkled tomato. He was eying them hungrily, wondering if they were still edible, when he noticed a knife on the plate and something about its black handle seemed familiar.

Graham motioned to DC Fields, who was interviewing a turbanned Asian boy at a nearby table, and held up the knife: "Would you go upstairs and compare this knife with the murder weapon. These letters on the handle here— NLC—refer to the college probably. Check if that knife's got the same letters."

Graham decided to ignore the sausage rolls, but he collected his coffee and took it to the door, where the surly boy still sat. This time a dialogue was in progress—or more precisely a monologue—between a garrulous black youth, whose lithe body danced to the rhythm of his words, and the silent Gareth, who regarded him with life-less eyes.

Graham asked both of them if they had let anyone in that night without a student I.D. card. Gareth gave a firm denial, but his friend nudged him and smirked.

"Come on Gaz, do us a favor. What about that blonde chick? Tell the nice Inspector, man."

Gareth grimaced and murmured, "That was your fault. I wasn't going to let her in."

"It was just the one bird on her own, Inspector. Good-looking piece. Gaz wanted to get off with her, that's what he told me anyway."

Gareth simply shrugged and shrunk further into his chair while the black boy laughed at his friend's discomfort. Graham was about to ask if they could point the girl out to him, when he felt somebody tap his shoulder. He looked round to see DC Fields holding out the black-handled knife.

"I've had a look sir, and yes it is the same. Same letters and everything" he said, handing the knife back to Graham respectfully. Graham turned the knife over and over in his hands and wondered.

What had Mark Winstanley done to provoke such an assault? If his girlfriend was telling the truth, the assailant had been a total stranger to him—after all, according to Annette, they had hardly spoken. And Mark certainly hadn't anticipated the assault, or he would have called for help or made some attempt to escape. Graham wondered if interviewing the other students at the disco would throw any light on the reasons behind the knifing. The attacker had entered the disco, stabbed Mark for no apparent reason and then vanished into thin air. Could it have been a fellow student, with a motive as yet unclear? That would account for his entry and his necessarily quick departure inviting no suspicion.

Perhaps—Graham pondered—something *would* come to light when the statements from Mark's friends and acquaintances were taken. Something Annette had overlooked or didn't know. Perhaps, after all, Mark *had* known his assailant and had even been expecting him. It was so difficult to judge anything when all you had to go on was some noises heard from behind a toilet door. And Annette had not impressed him as the most reliable of witnesses, being vague and noncommittal, and with glazed eyes that suggested she was half stoned.

The proximity in time of the other murder on Hampstead Heath meant that Graham couldn't help comparing the two, tossing them about in his mind like a pair of juggling balls. Certain things stood out as being similar, although there could hardly be said to be a definite pattern. Jenny and James had also been students, also teenagers. Hackett always seemed to go for students. Did he have some resentment buried in his subconscious about his lack of education, some middle-class intellectual who had wronged him, so that he had to wreak revenge on the whole student population? It was something Graham had neglected to ask Veronica Plowright. That was the way a psychopath's mind worked, wasn't it: illogical, irrational and entirely self-obsessed.

But could Hackett have slipped into a disco such as this without anybody noticing? Wouldn't someone like Gareth have wondered what an "old man" was doing there and pointed this out to Graham? Also, Hackett's victims had always been killed in the open air—it was one of the hallmarks of his spate of killings the year before. Was he capable of changing his modus operandi, perhaps in order to confuse the police, to deliberately distort the pattern and throw them off the trail? Then there was the possibility that another psychopath was at work in North London, someone Graham as yet knew nothing about, and who would start the whole gruesome nightmare all over again.

He felt depressed and confused. It was not often he had to deal with two seemingly random attacks in the short space of a couple of weeks. And both involving teenagers, which inevitably made him worry about his daughter. Graham knew of many instances where a policeman in his position had had their nearest and dearest threatened by a criminal carrying out a personal vendetta. So he was glad that Gemma was in Sheffield and a long way away from Charlie Hackett.

It was still raining when Graham finally stepped out of the building and found his car on the dark corner where he'd left it. As he drove home, he contacted Tarrant and Doyle over the radio: "Has Hackett been at home this evening?" he asked Tarrant.

"No, most of the time he was out, sir. He came in at— when was it, Doyle?—10.24 pm."

"And he's been in since then?"

"That's right, sir."

"No other movements?"

"No, nothing else to report, sir."

"All right then. Good work. You lads can go home now."

"Thank you, sir."

Tarrant sounded grateful. Graham felt sorry for them, waiting outside in the cold for what seem to them like no reason. But it was interesting to know Hackett had been out until 10.30. That certainly put him in line for the knife attack on Mark Winstanley, which must have happened at about ten o'clock. Hackett could easily have got home in half an hour.

Graham thought it was worth bringing Hackett in again for questioning—as long as he kept his cool—because if Hackett was the killer, he was determined to get a conviction this time.

Story Two

Chapter One

JULY 1991

Set apart, on the corner of Bellevue Close and The Promenade, with one blue wall facing the beach, stands Coral Cottage. It was built—slightly later than the row of houses adjacent—in the 1920's, in a spot calculated to give splendid views over the North Sea and about fifty yards from the great arch made from a whale's jawbone, which is said to have been set there by Captain Cook. The Promenade runs along the cliff top, winding down into the small town of Whitby past souvenir shops selling shell boxes and sepia photographs of ships in ornamental frames and calling at tiny fishermen's cafes with low wooden doors through which a person of average height has to stoop. Then it climbs steeply upwards past the abbey in which Caedmon dreamt that God taught him to sing, and becomes at last a muddy footpath which meanders over the cliffs all the way to Robin Hood's Bay, ten miles to the South.

Susanne picked up the breakfast tray in both hands and braced herself to back through the swing doors into the front room. Rays of white sunlight pierced the net curtains, throwing a pattern of light and shadow on to the empty table by the bay window. The Donaldsons had finished and gone, leaving only the Flynns, still seated at the other table and looking as if they wished they were anywhere but on holiday together. Mr. Flynn had abandoned most of his cereal and was halfway through a cigarette, which he dragged on between coughs. A plume of smoke ascended into the air and assailed Susanne's nostrils as she drew near to the doleful threesome.

Mrs. Flynn nudged the child at her side with the sharp point of an elbow, making him wince. "You mustn't leave that, Kyle. Hurry up and finish your cereal. Mrs. Martin wants to clear away now, don't you?" she said in a lilting half-whisper, turning conspiratorially to Susanne as if defying her to take sides. Susanne studied the boy, whose face was sullenly averted, and felt an impulse to stroke his pale hair. Instead she offered him a plate of bacon and eggs and removed his half-empty bowl.

Mr. Flynn examined his hostess, screwing up his mouth around the cigarette. He reminded Susanne of the mouse she'd seen one night in the kitchen. She frequently awoke restless in the small hours, and on this occasion had been making Ovaltine when the creature had darted out from behind the biscuit tin, scowled at her with tiny red eyes and disappeared into the wall. Susanne quelled an involuntary shudder.

"Mr. Martin goes out early doesn't he" Flynn stated rather than asked, fixing his rodent's eyes on her.

Not wanting to betray herself with her reaction, Susanne struggled between affability and disdain and fell somewhere in the middle. "Oh it's just…sometimes…he has business, you know." Her right hand quivered slightly as she piled the used plates on to her tray.

"Only that I heard the door slam" he continued, extinguishing his cigarette on the rim of his saucer, which already contained three stubs. "About six o'clock, I think. Woke me up" he said, with an air of interest rather than criticism.

Susanne felt grateful for the strands of hair which fell over her eyes and screened her face from his scrutiny. She hurried into the kitchen, catching the edge of the carpet with her slippers where it was slightly worn in the corner. A week ago she'd begged Jeff to fix it. One day, she'd explained, especially if she had one of her dizzy spells, she could slip and fall, scald herself with hot tea or worse.

Once in the sanctuary of her kitchen, she put the tray of dirty plates on the draining board and warmed the teapot, then sank into one of the pine wooden chairs by the table. The radio was tuned to *Seaside Sounds* with the volume low, so that the soft patter of the disc jockey announcing the next record hardly reached her ears. She wondered how much Mr. Flynn had meant by his allusion to Jeff. Had he only become aware of Jeff's absence that morning? Or had he noticed Jeff's early departure on several occasions and been storing up the information till now? The kettle screamed for attention like a demanding child and Susanne made tea, almost unaware of her actions, so preoccupied was she with misgivings.

It was later on that morning, while she was in the garden cutting roses to take her mother, that the phone rang. She was feeling jumpy—having gathered all her courage to face the neighbor's tomcat, who was stalking the bird table—and the noise made her heart race. Once more she longed for a job that didn't involve telephones. Of course she knew what she wanted to do, but there was no hope of changing things now. After the tenth ring she decided that answering it was the only way to stop the racket, and ran into the hall. Lifting up the receiver, she was at first too out of breath to speak.

"Hello Susie, is that you?"

"Yes." Susanne was briefly nonplused. The voice was familiar but she couldn't picture its owner.

"It's me, Denise. You don't recognize me, do you?"

"Oh! No…"

"You great clown—fancy forgettin' me! Once seen never forgotten, me mam says" bubbled the voice, spluttering with laughter. "How you been anyway? Hey, it was the wedding wasn't it, last time I saw you? Bloody hell, that was when I was carrying Jason, must a' looked a right sight. What's it like being married, then?"

"Oh it's O.K.….it's good…great."

"Yeah? Any little Jeff's on the way?"

"Well no, not yet."

"That's right, you take your time kiddo. Enjoy yourself. I sometimes think our Jason's more trouble than he's worth—ah no, but it's easier when you've got a man to look after you."

"Yeah, but I want children. It's just that Jeff…"

"Don't he want none?" asked Denise in amazement.

"Well, yes, later on. But he says we can't afford it now."

"Bloody hell, how's he think I afford it?" She brayed so loudly that Susanne was forced to move the receiver away from her ear.

"Are you still working at St. Mary's?" ventured Susanne, when her friend had quietened.

"Yeah, I'm doing' night shifts in the geriatrics ward. Me mam looks after Jason when I'm not home. You know that Mr. Wilkins in the end bed, the one with Parkinson's Disease, he never stops goin' on about you, how he misses you. He told me he wished you'd never got married, selfish old bugger!"

The insolence made Susanne giggle. "It's all right. I like being missed."

"But you like bein' married better, huh?" Susanne was relieved that Denise gave her no time for a truthful reply. "Sister Morley told me they've got a vacancy in the children's ward anyway, if you ever feel like comin' back. Wouldn't blame you if you didn't, though. It's a right hole. But listen, I've gotta give Jason his bottle before he goes down, so I better stop gabbing. You look after yourself and give Jeff a big sloppy kiss from me." She rang off mid-guffaw.

Susanne replaced the receiver and stood for a moment smiling at it. As she turned to go, she caught sight of her face in the mirror and smiled again, this time at herself. A young girl smiled back. She had a delicate, small-boned face framed by blonde hair, so fine as to be almost transparent, large eyes which oscillated between gray and blue and a slim, graceful neck. Even her mother had to admit she was pretty. Gazing at her image, she felt almost happy. But she had somehow lost Jeff's love, like a glove carelessly dropped in the street. The question still hounded her: where was he?

*　　　　*　　　　*

Susanne took the number fifteen bus to Hazelmere, which fortunately stopped right outside Fairbanks Rest Home. The mid-afternoon heat was enervating. She'd put on her white cotton frock with the high neckline in lace of which her mother approved, and carried the roses in wrapping paper with damp cotton wool round the stems to stop them drying out. It was only a half-hour journey on the bus but the roses had already begun to fade and Susanne hoped that it wouldn't be commented upon.

As she walked up the drive, she scanned the porch for the silhouette of her mother, sitting in her deck chair. Today, however, she wasn't there. The nurse at the door was a new girl who didn't recognize Susanne, but she nodded when she heard the name.

"Mrs. Gray? Of course. I'll take you to her."

A man who looked old enough to have had his telegram from the Queen intercepted them in the door- way and grinned at Susanne through toothless gums. He groaned some sort of greeting and began to sway on his ancient, slippered feet. The nurse helped him to an arm- chair then took Susanne in the lift—which was big enough to house at least three pensioners in wheel- chairs—up to the first floor. Susanne accompanied the nurse down the straight, narrow corridor, following the wooden handrail to room 204.

At first Mrs. Gray didn't remember her daughter and merely stared at her in frank bewilderment.

"Her eyesight's failing, I'm afraid" whispered the nurse to Susanne, before scurrying away to more pressing duties.

"Who's that? Who's that? Come over here then, and let me see you. Is it Agnes? Is that you, Mabel?" Her sister

Agnes had been dead ten years and Mabel had moved to London, but they were always the first names on her lips.

"It's Susanne" her daughter said, rather too softly.

"Susanne? Susanne…" An idea came to her. "Do you know, I heard from her the other day, she sent me a postcard from America, there it is on the mantelpiece, lovely picture of…New York I think, isn't it?"

"No mum, it's Connie who's in America, you showed me the postcard last time. I'm Susanne, I've come to see you." She moved towards the shriveled figure in the armchair and sat opposite her on a low stool, which was the only other piece of furniture aside from the bed and the wardrobe.

"Oh—Oh—Oh!" the old woman exclaimed in three little gasps, preceded by gulps of air. Unable to progress to a full sentence, Mrs. Gray sent fluttering hands to caress her cheeks like a pair of startled birds.

"It's all right, mum." Susanne noticed that her mother had shrunk again. Each stroke seemed to diminish her further. Maybe one day she would simply evaporate and hang, like some ghost, on the air.

"What's this?" She plucked at Susanne's parcel with a withered hand.

"A present for you, mum." Susanne unwrapped the roses and laid them gently in her mother's lap.

Mrs. Gray regarded them in dismay, without touching them. "Oh yes, flowers, pink roses. But they're the wrong color, aren't they. I need yellow ones for this room. Couldn't you have brought me yellow ones? To go with the walls."

Susanne looked around her at the walls, which were quite white. She took the flowers back and began to enclose them again in the paper. "I'll try and bring you yellow ones next time."

"Well, as long as you've brought them, dear…" Mrs. Gray seemed suddenly to recollect who she was talking to and her vague expression was replaced by one of malice. "I hope you're looking after the house all right, Sannie."

Susanne interpreted the use of her pet name as a bad sign: "Yes, I'm trying to, mum." Her voice was unintentionally plaintive.

"And what about that boy you married? He never comes to see me." Mrs. Gray had always refused to refer to Jeff as a man. "I don't suppose he helps you much."

"He's very…busy at the moment…hasn't got the time." Susanne realized the feebleness of her excuse, but too late. She regarded her mother's stony face with its contemptuous expression and wished fervently that she could just be gone. In an effort to change the subject, she added, "Denise rang me today. You know, the girl I used to work with at St. Mary's? I haven't heard from her for ages."

"Oh, you mean that coarse girl from Filey. I never knew what you saw in her. I'm glad you're not working at that dreadful hospital any more, dear. I was always sure you'd pick up germs."

Susanne carried bravely on, trying to make her tone conversational: "Denise told me they were looking for a part-time nurse to work in the children's ward. I thought maybe—"

"You don't have the time, dear. Your guest house is the priority, now that I can't be there. You've got enough to do with that."

Susanne started the sentence that was always on her lips at this point, but it died unspoken as usual. *Mother, if only you'd understand*—she longed to say—*I've always hated the guest house. I always wanted to be a nurse.*

There was a soft rap on the door and Miss Johnson, the manageress, inclined her head into the room. "Everything all right?" she inquired, beaming. "Nice to see you, Mrs. Martin. I hope you're keeping well. Sorry to disturb you both, but the gong has sounded and I didn't think your mother would want to miss her tea." She whisked over to Mrs. Gray and started helping her out of the chair.

The old lady protested. "But I never eat tea. I'm not hungry, thank you." at the same time struggling into her white cardigan. The last stroke had paralyzed her right side, leaving it virtually useless. A vacant glaze covered her eyes again and she appeared once more to be nothing but a harmless old lady, shrunken prematurely by illness.

"She says that every day, but she eats more than anybody" said Miss Johnson to Susanne in a smiling undertone. Susanne was amused and could have laughed with relief that teatime had arrived.

*   *   *

It was quarter past six in the evening and Jeff stood in the doorway, holding a bunch of yellow roses.

"Surprise!" he said, handing them to Susanne. "Sorry I left you alone today, love. I just had to get out of the house for a while. Everything all right?" Cupping her chin in his hand, he bent down and kissed her lightly on the mouth. A faint smell of beer still clung to his moustache. Susanne's head was level with his chest and she could see the reddish patch of skin which had been burnt by the sun.

He loped past her and into the front room. Susanne trailed after, clutching her flowers, and stood silently behind him. She watched as he switched on the television and flicked through the stations, giving a small tut of disapproval at each picture that he saw. He had brought something with him wrapped in newspaper and was holding it in his left hand. Susanne came close and prodded the package lightly with her fingertips.

"What's that?" she asked.

"What? Oh that. I got something special for tea, from the fishmonger's down High Street. Do you want to cook it up for us, love? I'm starving. And better put those flowers in water, eh?" Having found snooker on BBC 2, he spread himself on the sofa, loosened his belt a notch and put his head back and slightly to one side. Susanne exited to the kitchen.

Laying the table for dinner, she got out the wine glasses that had been a wedding present from Jeff's brother, the silver-plated cutlery that had been handed down from her grandparents and the blue and white linen tablecloth with a picture of a windmill that they had bought during their honeymoon in Amsterdam. The centerpiece became the yellow roses, arranged in a many-sided cut glass vase that was Susanne's favorite.

"Well, this is something!" Jeff declared as they sat down to eat. "What's the occasion?"

Susanne simply smiled and said, "I've made trout with almonds, your favorite. And there's chips."

They ate mostly in silence. Jeff had left the television on and he turned to it occasionally, pausing from his meal to remark on the stupidity of a certain actor or the attractiveness of the girl in a new shampoo commercial.

From time to time Susanne gazed at him. Her eyes traveled lovingly from the top of his golden head over his firm neck to his broad shoulders reddened by the sun and down to the long hairs on his forearms and his bigger-than-average hands with the clublike thumbs jutting out. She felt exactly the same devotion, looking at him now, as before they had married. The first place she'd seen Jeff was the Falcon Pub, where she went on Sundays to watch talent night. He was playing the fruit machine, laughing and parading before his two friends as the money came juddering out. Denise noticed her staring at him, nudged her and grinned, mischievously licking her lips, and two minutes later Jeff sauntered over and asked if he could spend his winnings on a drink for her, ignoring the other girls in her group. She had felt proud to be the chosen one and he had impressed her with his tales of being a professional footballer. It was only much later—by which time she was already hopelessly in love—that she had discovered his footballing career was merely a dream he nursed from behind the counter at the local chemist's where he worked.

After washing up the dishes, Susanne joined Jeff in the front room. He had flung out his left arm over the back of the sofa and she sat beside him, wishing that he would encircle her with his arm and press her to him, but he sat resolutely still. After *Bill Barney's Chat Show*, Jeff channel-hopped with the remote control, but found nothing to please him. He strode out of the room in a fit of pique, leaving Susanne watching the new situation comedy, *Mum's The Word!*.

'Laugh till you cry' promised the blurb in the T.V. Times, but when Jeff left for the pub five minutes later, Susanne couldn't have felt less inclined to laugh. Only one bit of the 'comedy' filtered through to her. The middle-aged and fairly well-known actress playing mum, whose name Susanne couldn't recall, announced to a gale of canned laughter that she was going to join her teenage sons at the local disco.

Susanne decided to join Jeff in the pub. Before they'd married, they had always gone to the pub together, but lately he'd stopped asking. She remembered how Madame Theresa, the clairvoyant on the sea front, had predicted the previous summer: *Within a month, you will meet a tall, handsome blond man who will mean a lot to you.* It was only two months later that Susanne had met Jeff.

She guessed he'd be at the Falcon in Ellerby Road, not from any sentimental attachment to the pub, but because Paul and Bill would be there and they could team up with one of the regulars to play darts or pool. Susanne didn't like pub games, but she liked being recognized by the locals as Jeff's wife and she enjoyed the admiring looks passed over her by Paul and Bill.

From her wardrobe she selected a pale blue t-shirt dress with a plunging neckline, which she bunched up over a wide leather belt, and high heeled white sandals which pinched her feet. To this she added gold dangling earrings, a metal hair slide in the shape of a heart and some pale pink lipstick.

Five minutes later she found herself outside the Falcon pub. Although nervous about being out so late on her own, she hesitated at the door of the saloon bar, listening to the blurred sounds of voices and laughter and the ping of the till as it slammed home. Now that she was actually there, she asked herself if it had really been a good idea to follow Jeff. She took her hand away from the door marked push and had almost turned back into the street, when a man approached from the other direction. The overhead gas lamp illuminated his face and he gave Susanne a smile, half kindly half perplexed.

"Are you going in, love?" he said, holding the door open for her. Susanne had no choice but to thank him and enter.

Inside, she plunged through the thicket of bodies to the right of her, trying not to look lost. The air was sticky and drenched with sweat and noise and she felt like an outsider. She started to wish that Jeff wouldn't be there and she could slide out again unnoticed. But once trapped in the writhing jungle of people, she couldn't go back, and was forced to travel around the outskirts of the central, circular bar.

She was pushed unwillingly up to the bar, and hovered there uncertainly, looking around for Jeff. His face wasn't among the laughing, animated faces, and neither was Paul's or Bill's. She was wondering if the three friends had decided on some whim to choose another pub this evening, when the bar man thrust his face before hers and demanded what she wanted to drink. In embarrassment, she stammered the first thing she could think of—"A coke, please"—even though a drink was the last thing she wanted. He came back with her order and she paid him, she clutched the cold glass in her hand and took small sips of the liquid, but they only seemed to sting her throat.

She decided that she couldn't stay there, being elbowed and nudged by other people who wanted to get near the bar, so she headed for the far corner of the room, from where she could hear music—an electric piano, loud and rather too strident, and a girl's voice singing a popular song in a strong Northern accent. When Susanne got near enough to see, she stood and watched the live duo performing. The girl was wearing a scarlet dress covered all over with sequins which glittered under the pub lights. The smile she wore while she was singing never left her face, and yet her eyes were bored and contemptuous. The pianist's hands flew over the keys as if they knew all the moves, and his head was tipped back slightly in a parody of enjoyment. But he also seemed dull and mechanical, as if he were a doll who had been wound up just before the show. Susanne stood and regarded the couple in fascination for a few minutes, while she sipped her coke and tried to pretend that she was only waiting for someone. A few heads turned to look at her and, standing there alone, she was the target of some enquiry.

Susanne decided she would have to move somewhere, and either find a place to sit or give up and leave the pub entirely. So she put her half-full glass on a table and started once more to push her way through recalcitrant bodies. She wasn't even looking for Jeff—was concentrating mainly on escape—when she saw the familiar golden head bobbing up and down behind the arm of a man in front. She attempted to follow his head with her eyes and caught another glimpse of him walking away from the bar. In a moment of pugnacity, Susanne thrust her slender body between the chattering pair in front, who were obscuring her view of Jeff's retreating head. She repeated the maneuver twice more, to find herself in a clearing facing the corner of the room, where benches covered in burgundy velvet lined the walls.

Jeff was there as she had guessed, sitting on a stool with his back to her. And with him sat a girl. She had short orange hair, gelled into a stiff coif above her pale face and wore a matching blouse cut embarrassingly low, beneath which her braless breasts wobbled as she talked. Susanne watched in mounting agitation as the girl leant over the table, grasped one of Jeff's large hands and smoothed it over her right breast. Jeff's initial reaction was hidden from view, but the girl must have spotted Susanne observing them, for he suddenly whirled round and looked full at her.

She bolted for the door, wishing desperately that he hadn't seen her and trying to forget the look on his face. Now, she just wanted to get away from there as fast as she could. The narrow streets were quiet and the full moon shone down and lit her way, seeming to mock her with its brightness. Her head was throbbing and her feet hurt in their tight shoes. She tried to pretend to herself that it was all a dream, that she was just in a nightmare that would end soon. But the hollow sound of her footsteps hitting the cobbled pavements as she ran home was evidence that she was still awake.

It wasn't until she was in her bed at Coral Cottage that her heart stopped palpitating. She took a few deep breaths and tried to relax. Although it was a warm summer night, she was shivering with cold and she wrapped the duvet tightly round her. She squeezed her eyes tightly shut, but the image of Jeff and the girl was still there behind her eyelids.

Ten minutes later the sound of Jeff's key in the front door below warned her of his return. She waited in apprehension for his measured footsteps on the stairs, and when the bedroom door opened she had turned to face the wall and closed her eyes, the duvet pulled up over her head. She heard Jeff crossing the floor and felt his hand lift the covers away from her face. Now unable to resist opening her eyes, she saw with pleasure that he looked anxious.

"What's the matter with you?" His voice was gentler than his words. Susanne was silent but—he could see from her expression—not uncompliant. He pulled back the covers to expose the top half of her body, lifted her up by the shoulders and perched on the edge of the bed, holding her. She felt as limp as a rag doll in his arms, and it was easy to force himself on top of her.

It was the first time in two weeks that they had made love. As usual, Susanne's pleasure or pain was soundless, her body showing neither acceptance nor rejection, her face betraying an absence of emotion. In three minutes it was finished, and Jeff rolled over and fell into a heavy sleep.

Chapter Two

The stench of vomit made her nauseous and the dry retching began again. Exhausted, she couldn't stop her empty stomach heaving and heaving.

Presently, she splashed her face with the cool water that gushed from both taps and felt safe enough to lift her head, catching her reflection in the bathroom mirror-tiles. Her skin was chalky white and there were dark circles under her eyes. Strings of damp hair clung to her forehead.

She reached into the airing cupboard and mopped her face with a clean towel, inhaling its lavender perfume. Then she flung the casement open wide and leaned out, looking on to The Promenade and beyond that, to the sea. The air was stifling and oppressive, the ocean still as a sheet of glass, the sky washed with a film of dingy gray. A couple strolled by arm in arm and behind them an elderly woman struggled with a shopping bag. A burst of screaming rent the noiseless air, as a flock of seagulls swooped down for their prey. Then, as if in reply, the leaden chimes of St. Bartholemews tolled a quarter to three.

There was time for a good long walk before dinner. Her mother always prescribed fresh air for any ailment.

Susanne wondered what her father's opinion might have been, had she known him. But he wasn't even as familiar to her as a character in a novel. Since his desertion, her mother mentioned him rarely.

The sea being unenticing and the town too crowded at this time of year, Susanne chose to visit the Abbey. Her body, though, felt so unnaturally heavy, as if someone had filled it with sand, that the hundred and ninety-nine steps leading to those gaunt ruined walls seemed almost insurmountable. Among the silent stones, Susanne stood gazing at the drops of bleached light that fell through the traceries, but the place seemed to have had some of its magic worn away by the trampling of strangers' feet.

Until recently, she had felt it to be a mystical place: haunted, perhaps, but by ghosts that were benign. Several times she had brought her small box of watercolors and artist's pad, given to her as a leaving present by the hospital, and tried to express her feelings of awe and mystery on the white paper. But when she looked at the finished painting all she could see were lines and blobs of color, which didn't resemble the image in her mind's eye. After a while she had grown tired of Jeff's taunts that a painting was never as good as a photograph anyway, and had put away the pad and the watercolors in a forgotten corner of her wardrobe.

She tried to escape from a cluster of American students carrying backpacks, and in turning a corner of the Abbey wall, literally bumped into a middle-aged man walking his dog. More precisely, the dog was walking its master—pulling the little man along on his leash—and on encountering Susanne, it stopped and sniffed interestedly at her heels. The wet touch of muzzle on her ankles distressed her and she gave a small cry of disgust before making off across the grass.

"Sorry miss," the man called after her, "he doesn't mean you any harm."

But she was already on her way home.

*   *   *

It was Sunday afternoon. Susanne had left Jeff in the kitchen reading the *Express* and had come upstairs to change the linen in the master bedroom, recently vacated by the Flynn family. She enjoyed the Sunday ritual of bed-stripping. As a child, it had been the one chore she had always volunteered to help with. She remembered her nurse's training, folding the sheet and blanket into a neat triangle at each corner and tucking it under the mattress. All Susanne could hear of the music from below was the steady beat of the bass guitar. She recognized the song, though, and hummed along, in a voice that was mostly breath, practically a whisper. Years of training to be quiet had made it impossible for her to sing out loud.

It was her mother who had enjoined her to be quiet. Being brought up in a bed and breakfast meant that, even as a small child, Susanne had been aware of the needs of other people, had known that the guests must never be disturbed and that her place was to merge into the background of the hotel like some friendly ghost, a little girl who would be seen but not heard. And the seizures she had been prone to had only made matters worse, and heightened her mother's desire to hide her away like a secret that she was ashamed of. Susanne was afraid of her fits and afraid of that other part of herself that rose up like a monster from the deep sea of her subconscious.

Even at school, she had felt isolated and different from the other children. Continually taunted for not knowing where her father was, she started to claim that he was dead, and then began to believe her own lie. It made things easier, to think that he'd been taken away by Fate and hadn't deserted them of his own accord. She was unpopular with the other children who were frightened of her fits, and the teachers found her periods of vacancy difficult to deal with. When Susanne reached adulthood she grew out of her fits, but they had left a mark on her that went deeper than mere memory.

Susanne was enjoying making the beds and felt perfectly happy. She had no inkling of what was about to occur. But it was as she was straightening up to throw the bedspread over the second bed, that she had an eerie sensation of being lifted up and thrown into a whirling current. The roaring sound of the waves which enveloped her drowned out the radio and she was washed into a dark and sonorous cavern.

When she awoke, an hour or so later, she realized what it must be. Jeff said it was just one of her dizzy spells, but she knew this was different. She had been surreptitiously to the chemist the day before to get a *Predictor* test. The results were positive.

"You can't believe them things, Su" said Jeff, without lifting his head from the paper. The couple were having afternoon tea in the living room, and Susanne had just confronted her husband with her knowledge. She hovered over the table, too tense to sit down.

"That's how Denise found out she was pregnant. She didn't believe it either, but then the doctor—"

"Oh all right. Well, what are you going to do about it?"

"Do?" Somewhere in the back of her mind, she had hoped that Jeff, presented with a fait-accomplis, would simply accept. A lock of golden hair was entwined about her index finger and she twisted it till her head ached.

"I thought you was taking precautions." Jeff flung his paper down and gave her a suspicious look.

"I am taking precautions. It must be an accident."

"You'll just have to get rid of it."

"Oh Jeff!" She dropped into a chair, her eyes big with tears. "I can't, you know I can't."

"I don't wanna talk about it." The newspaper was still on his lap, and he was staring at it sullenly. There was a silence, as both of them wondered how to respond.

"You never said you didn't want children" Susanne stammered, glancing tentatively at her husband.

"It's not that I don't want them, Su. It's just…not now."

"Why not now?"

Jeff sighed and moved to the window. He pressed his nose against the glass and looked out over the garden, like a caged animal who longs to escape.

A hot tear welled up in Susanne's left eye and rolled conspicuously down her cheek. Another one joined it and another and she made no attempt to wipe them away. Jeff turned and looked at her.

"Oh, don't cry!" he complained in exasperation, "For God's sake…"

"Please don't make me get rid of it," she sobbed, "I couldn't go through with all that. Please let me keep it."

Unable to stand the sight of her tears, Jeff moved behind her chair and patted her shoulder roughly. "All right, all right. I didn't know it was so important. But stop crying now, will you."

Susanne removed a cotton handkerchief from her pocket. "It's just...you don't know how it feels..." She stuttered between sniffs, "when Denise rang me last Friday...I thought...I want to have a baby...and I'd be a good mother, I know I would..."

"All right then" Jeff capitulated, "if that's what you really want. But it'll make things more difficult for the pair of us. Just remember it was your decision."

A week later, a maid came to live at Coral Cottage. Jeff was easier to persuade than Susanne had imagined, perhaps because of the Trust Fund her mother had set up in the event of any grandchildren. Mrs. Hardcastle was well known to Susanne, having helped out during her mother's attack of hepatitis when Susanne was six. Then, she had been maid, nurse and godsend to Mrs. Gray and her small daughter.

She had bright restless eyes, a small pointed nose and those thin down curving lips that you often see in women of the North East coast, as if they've spent their lives battling against a harsh, blowing wind. She had a strong body, a strong voice and a strong character. It was she who ordered Susanne to put her feet up when she felt faint and let her husband wash up or hoover the guest rooms. She never mentioned a family of her own, and yet she was an inexhaustible fund of knowledge on every subject relating to babies. Babies were the topic discussed at every possible occasion: what times of day babies should be fed, how many hours sleep a day a baby should have, when babies start to teethe, when babies start to bawl and when her baby would start to walk. Jeff would come home to find Susanne and Mrs. Hardcastle both knitting a tiny cardigan, pair of trousers or little booties. He would turn the radio on in the kitchen to hear the soccer results, only for Mrs. Hardcastle to enter and smartly lower the volume, saying that too much noise would be bad for the baby.

Susanne basked in the attention.

One day in late September, she went shopping for maternity clothes. She hardly showed any bulge but Mrs. Hardcastle had persuaded her that this was a good opportunity to splash out on a new dress.

"You go out and enjoy yourself for a change, dear" she said, giving Susanne an affectionate pat on the arm, "and when you come home, I'll have some tea ready."

Susanne was heading for Marks and Spencers with a voucher her mother had given her for her birthday, but she couldn't resist calling in at *Second Hand Rose*. A print dress in crepe de chine was on display and it caught her attention. It appeared to be patterned with blotches, but when you looked closely you could see that each blotch was a pair of faces looking at each other fondly, like something from a film poster of the thirties. The loose-fitting curves were certainly flattering to her figure, however big it might become. Susanne bought the dress and then went to *Mandy's* for her hair appointment. Coming home, she was pleased to elicit some wolf whistles from three men on a building site.

She got back to Coral Cottage in the late afternoon and found Jeff with his feet up watching soccer on the television. When she entered the front room, he turned round with what seemed to be a guilty look.

"Hello love" he said, with more enthusiasm than he had shown for weeks, "Your hair looks nice. Have you had it done?"

Susanne nodded and showed him the dress she had bought. He pretended to like it but it was obviously not to his taste. His attention was half focused on the soccer but he dragged himself away from the screen with an effort and offered to make tea.

"Oh it's all right" Susanne replied, "Mrs. H. said she'd do it. By the way, where is she? Is she in the garden?" She couldn't understand why Jeff hovered by the swing doors, looking as if he had bad news to tell.

"Mrs. Hardcastle had to leave" he said.

"Oh" responded Susanne, "when's she going to be back then?"

"No, I mean, she had to leave forever, completely." The waving of his hands tried to convey his message, but Susanne still looked perplexed.

"She had a phone call from her sister in Jersey. Her little niece has been taken sick. She had to go and help out. Sorry love" He smiled apologetically.

"She never told me she had a niece" said Susanne, in a weak voice.

"Yeah I know, secretive old…" Jeff gave a little nervous laugh and looked at Susanne's crestfallen face. "Don't worry, love. We can always get another maid. I'll make you a cup of tea."

He disappeared into the kitchen and Susanne sagged on to the sofa. She still held the dress, crumpled in her hands. The pairs of faces were glaring at each other now, ready to start an argument. It was a silly design anyway, tasteless and old fashioned and the colors were dull. She twisted a strand of hair round and round on her finger.

Chapter Three

▼

A massive oak tree, from whose russet branches the leaves had been thrown down like a tawny carpet, dominated the surrounding field. On one leaf perched a small bird, pecking at the hard green ground in its search for grubs.

> *Now summer's gone, the falling leaves*
> *Will usher in the cold.*
> *But take heed of the little bird,*
> *Whose song will ne'er grow old.*

reminded the calendar in archaic script beneath the October scene.

Susanne's October scene, as seen through the bay window of her front room, was altogether different. Here, all was gray and covered in that fine English mist that presages rain. Cars made a swishing sound in the street as they passed. It had rained unremittingly for days, shrouding the coastline in an envelope of gray.

Thursday October 23rd—the date Susanne was looking at with jaded interest—was circled in red ink, with a message beside it saying 'Dr. Freund 12.30.' She glanced at her watch and saw that the time was 11.30 am. A vacuum cleaner was grinding along the carpeted floor of one of the bedrooms above, and as Susanne became aware of the din, it began to irritate her.

She flitted noiselessly up the stairs to the small guest room on the first floor where Mr. Finch, the Canadian travel writer, was staying for the week. The bedroom door was ajar and Susanne glimpsed Tracey skillfully maneuvering herself round the furniture with the long-necked hoover. Six weeks before, Jeff had brought the girl to Coral Cottage, pronouncing her to be Mrs. Hardcastle's successor. Susanne's first irrational thought was that she was far too attractive to be a maid, with her luxuriant dark tresses, expressive brown eyes and full lips that seemed to retain their pinkness without lipstick, yet there was nothing in her work that could be complained of. There was nothing overtly disrespectful in her manner either, but something about her quiet self-possession—so unusual for a teenage girl fresh from school—made Susanne feel that their roles had been subtly reversed.

The noise of the hoover died down. "Tracey…" Susanne's voice seemed unnecessarily loud in the sudden silence.

The girl turned, surprised. "Oh, hello Mrs. Martin. I didn't hear you come up."

"I've got to go to the hospital now. I don't think I'll be long. Can you look after things?"

"Yes, of course."

"And if the phone rings, take a message."

"Yes, I will."

She felt embarrassed again, as if the girl were secretly mocking her, as if as soon as her back was turned, a peal of delighted laughter would be intended for her. She walked stiffly down the stairs.

*   *   *

The waiting room was emptier than usual today. Susanne fidgeted and tried to get more comfortable on her plastic chair. Idly, her eyes were drawn to the heap of grubby plastic toys in their cardboard box in the corner and the posters on the wall demonstrating how to brush your teeth correctly and how to use the Green Cross Code. Then she noticed the woman sitting opposite. The bulk of her immense body with its huge flabby arms and stumpy hands gripping the worn copy of *Reader's Digest* were strangely fascinating. It wasn't until the woman lifted her head and looked at Susanne, that she realized she'd been staring.

"What are you in here for, love? Not a mother-to-be too, are you?" Her voice was wheezy and high-pitched, not at all what Susanne had expected from that enormous frame. She seemed determined to be friendly, though, and when Susanne simply nodded in answer to her question, she made an effort to crease the fleshy folds of her face into a smile.

"Don't look it, does she?" the woman said to her companion in the next seat, who was abnormally thin with scrawny shoulders and a neck that seemed to consist entirely of lines. Susanne wondered why these two were sitting next to each other, when the waiting room was full of empty chairs. They were so dissimilar, it seemed impossible that they could be friends.

"No, she doesn't" said thin woman to fat woman, "but on some people it doesn't show for months. I was like that myself when I had my first," sadly patting the bulge under her skirt.

They both dissected the object of their conversation. Susanne could feel her cheeks glowing. She wondered if she would ever—after five children, say—resemble this scraggy woman, whose distended stomach seemed not to belong to her.

"It's the tummy muscles" said the fat woman, "you've gotta exercise them right after the birth. Then they won't get too relaxed."

Susanne was trying to imagine the woman exercising her stomach muscles when a voice interrupted her reverie, calling her name. It was the nurse standing outside the surgery door and beckoning her in.

Dr. Freund smiled hugely and shook Susanne's hand as if he had known her all his life. Of course, he had known her all her life, having been present at her birth, but he couldn't be expected to remember that. He asked her all the usual questions: *how was she feeling? any more morning sickness? sleeping all right? how was her mother?* Stiffening her body, Susanne submitted to the blood pressure test, which she always hated. While he was reading the results from the black dial, she glanced at his notes, which were upside down on the desk, and could just make out one lengthy word scrawled under her name. The doctor noticed her curiosity.

"Hypoglycemia, Mrs. Martin. Sounds rather a long word, doesn't it, but all it means is that your blood sugar level is a tiny bit down, as we found out from the results of your blood and urine samples last week. Now, your blood pressure's rather low, have you been feeling at all faint recently, dizziness when you first get up, anything like that?"

"Yes, sometimes."

"I thought so. Well, no need to worry, we can give you something for that. And for the insomnia, I'll just prescribe a mild tranquilizer to help you sleep. You'll just have to stop worrying, won't you?" He gave her one of his huge smiles and winked. "Believe me, there's nothing to worry about, you'll be as right as rain. It's perfectly normal, though, most women find it a stressful experience, giving birth. What we call prenatal tension. You can tell that one to your husband if you like, when you want him to do the washing up, just say, Sorry love I can't do it, I've got prenatal tension." The doctor smiled and winked again.

She got the bus into the center of Hazelmere this time, so she could collect her prescription from the village chemist, then she walked the mile or so to Fairbanks. A delicate drizzle had progressed to heavy plops of rain and she sloshed along the pavement in her white plastic sandals. She felt sluggish and dispirited and would have postponed the visit, but for fear of her mother's reaction.

The nurse at the door remembered her this time, even acting as if she were expected: "Miss Gray isn't it?" she said with a smile.

Susanne didn't correct her but dutifully followed her starched white skirt as it swished down the narrow corridor.

"Your daughter is here to see you" announced the nurse when they reached room 204, as if to allay any misunderstandings once and for all.

Susanne, meanwhile, slunk into the room and was surprised to see her mother lying prone in bed. A few wisps of gray hair, followed by a pair of startled eyes—still violently blue, though old now and fuddled with sleep—appeared above the edge of the coverlet.

The nurse said again, but louder "Your daughter's here Mrs. Gray. She's come from Whitby to see you" at the same time propping her up behind two pillows like an old china doll.

Mrs. Gray gawked at Susanne and waited until the nurse was out of the room and far enough down the hall for her swishing skirts to be inaudible, before remarking, "You look peaky".

"I have been a bit tired" replied Susanne as she seated herself in the armchair by the window and began to stroke the rubbery leaves of a begonia.

"I don't know why *you* would get tired" remarked Mrs. Gray. "What do you have to do with yourself all day?"

Susanne—used to these kind of comments—took little notice: "I have to run the hotel, mum. And I'm pregnant."

"Pregnant?" queried her mother, her lips puckering with shock.

"You know I am. I told you before, several times. You never seem to remember."

"When are you going to have this…baby?" She said the word *baby* as if it was something she couldn't imagine her daughter having.

"It's due next April."

"You—having a baby? But…you're only a baby yourself" asserted Susanne's mother.

Susanne sighed and scratched a bit of dirt off the sleeve of her jacket. "I'm not a baby. I'm twenty three."

"No you're not" replied her mother with conviction, as if she'd been dying for this chance to argue. "You're sixteen next birthday."

Susanne didn't bother to contradict her. She got up and stood by the window, looking out. She noticed dully that the grass on the communal lawn had become overgrown and needed cutting. The gray sky seemed to blur at the horizon, as in a bad watercolor where the paints seep into one another.

"I'm so tired" announced Mrs. Gray, seeking attention. Susanne turned dutifully. "Are you, mum?"

"Oh dear, oh dear" her mother murmured, smoothing the sheets on her bed as if they were worry beads. "I get tired too, so tired and unwell I can't even drag myself out of bed." She gave a long sigh to prove her point. "But I suppose you'll be wanting me to come and look after you."

Susanne didn't answer that. "I brought you some jellies, mum" she said, laying the box in its brown paper bag on the table.

Her mother seemed not to hear. "I've had three or four people to see me this week. Doctors and specialists, examining me. I'm not well you know, Sannie." Her mouth was quivering. "These people here aren't very bright. They think they know what's good for me but they've no idea." She pursed her lips in triumph, like a schoolgirl who's discovered her teacher fibbing. "Yesterday a young man came to see me. He said he wants to do tests."

"What sort of tests?" asked Susanne, sparked into interest by this last revelation, and sitting again in a chair by her mother's bedside.

"A brain scan, he said. He wants to have a look inside my head. They'd turf me out of bed, in my condition, and take me to some horrible hospital. I tried to tell them I don't want to go but they'll do it anyway, they don't care about my feelings." She leaned forward as best she could, her head wobbling pathetically in an attempt to be conspiratorial. "Can't I come home, Sannie? I don't like it here."

"But mum, I can't—" began Susanne.

"Ah, I know, it's that boy isn't it, turning you against me" she said with sudden venom. "I knew the moment I saw him he was after your money. He waited till I was safely out of the way, then he moved in and started to turn you against me. But what am I to do? I've got no home to go to!"

Susanne rose and stood nervously by the bed, trying desperately to placate her. "Don't get upset, mum. It's not that…what you think…you don't understand…"

"He's always hated me, hasn't he? That boy. He's never liked me. But I'm your mother. Your only mother!"

"He doesn't hate you. Of course he doesn't. It's just…he doesn't have time to…" Susanne couldn't think of any more excuses for her husband. She knew that what her mother said was true. She didn't want to admit that not only did he not love his mother-in-law, he probably didn't love his wife either. It was like the pain of an illness that gnawed away at her all the time, that she kept suppressed deep in her belly.

Mrs. Gray's hands were alternately smoothing the coverlet and gripping it like talons. "I suppose you think it's fun being cooped up here all day with no one to talk to, none of my own things around me."

Her mother's voice was rising in incipient hysteria, and Susanne was frightened: "No, no, mum. Don't get upset. Please don't be cross."

But the old lady continued: "Nobody's nice to me here, not even polite, they just push me and bully me and tell me what to do morning noon and night. Just treat me like

a…oh…oh…Sannie, where are you, I can't see you…"
She began to choke and fight for breath; her jaw dropped
and locked into a silent O; her eyes bulged unblinkingly
from their sockets; her hands clawed the coverlet,
beneath which her limbs seemed to be engaged in a battle for freedom.

Susanne quickly pushed the button marked with a bell
beside the bed and tried to hold down the thrashing body.
She was terrified. She didn't recognize her mother any
more. She was just an old lady, the victim of an attack and
Susanne felt like an observer.

To Susanne's relief, within seconds the nurse arrived.
Taking in the situation instantly, she seemed to know
what to do and she asked Susanne to step aside for a
moment. Susanne didn't look while the nurse injected
Mrs. Gray with some substance that had an instantaneous
calming effect.

"It's all right, you needn't stay" said the nurse to
Susanne, "She'll sleep like a baby now. The phenobarbi-
tone always does the trick."

*   *   *

In the heavy quiet of night, the kitchen was filled with
the solitary sound of a wall clock, ticking away each second with precision. Susanne blew on the mug of hot
chocolate till it was cool enough to sip, testing the temperature with the inside of her lip. She studied the label on
the bottle she had been prescribed, *One or two to be taken
at night as required,* unscrewed the childproof cap and
placed two of the orange pills on her tongue, swilling
them down with a gulp of liquid. She was halfway through

the romance story in *Woman* and as she continued reading, the words appeared to blur a little.

The kitchen door opened without warning and Susanne turned to see Jeff squinting in the sudden light. "I thought you were up" he said. "What are you doing down here?"

"I couldn't sleep."

"Again?" He shambled to the stove. "You woke me up an' all this time. What are those?" pointing to the bottle of pills on the table.

"The doctor gave me them. To help me sleep."

"You shouldn't need pills to sleep."

"Well I do. I can't help it."

Jeff turned from the kettle and raised his eyebrows.

"I get tired…because of the baby…tired in the day and then at night I keep awake. It's not my fault, is it?"

Jeff had lost interest now, and was preparing his mug with a tea bag. "No, well, that's why we've got Tracey in to help, isn't it" he said with his back to her.

Susanne held herself in silence for a moment, rehearsing a dozen different responses. Finally she said, her cheeks on fire, "I don't think Tracey's much help."

"Of course she's a help, she does the work doesn't she?" he said lightly, pouring water into his mug.

"Yes but…when I came home today after visiting mum, Tracey had gone out. I told her to wait in and take messages."

"Well, that's nothing to make a fuss about." Jeff seemed to be laughing at her, his lips very slightly curled in amusement.

"And she'd left the back door open" she continued, indicating it with her finger, as if that would strengthen her argument. "Anybody could've got in."

"We all make mistakes—"

"Anyway, we don't need her anymore. I don't need her. I'm all right without a maid."

"Don't be daft, Su." Jeff was taking her seriously now. "Look at you. You just said you're tired all the time. You're not well, are you? You can't go round hoovering and lifting beds."

"Couldn't you help me a bit?"

"Look, I'm not doing all the bloody work! We can afford a maid, can't we, so we might as well have one. I'm not the bloody skivvy. And right now, all I want to do is get some bloody kip." He stormed out of the kitchen, leaving a trail of tea drips along the floor.

She wanted to follow him and say something that would make amends, but her body suddenly felt so incredibly weary, as if an iron weight had been attached to her shoulders and was pressing her into the chair. She wanted to stand up and make her way back to bed, but somehow it was easier just to relax forward, rest her head on her arms and fall into a dark and dream-filled sleep.

*   *   *

On Sunday, Tracey took a day off and Susanne spring cleaned as much of the house as she was able, starting with the front bedroom where she and Jeff slept.

She flicked the dust from a porcelain milkmaid then reset it on the bedside table, doing the same with a glass earring tree, a lamp with a tasseled shade and a tortoiseshell hairbrush. The white dressing table with its oval mirror was rid of every speck of dust by her searching cloth. On the flowered bedspread she had dropped a roll of waxed lining paper, which she would use to replace the newspaper Jeff had put in the bottom of the drawers.

Starting with the top drawer, she gathered a clump of Jeff's underpants, vests and socks and threw them on to the bed, changed the paper and replaced them in more orderly fashion. The second drawer contained an assortment of bras, knickers and tights in nylon or cotton, kept sweet-smelling with a sachet of dried rosemary.

The bottom drawer was one she rarely had cause to look in. She knew Jeff kept things in there that he considered none of her business, like back copies of *Survival*, his fishing tackle and a spare set of darts. But she set about withdrawing all these objects, fighting her fatigue, determined to prove herself a better housekeeper than Tracey.

The last thing she took out was tucked into the back right hand corner. It was an unfamiliar white and red cardboard box with a silhouette design.

She cleared a space for herself on the bed and sat down with the box, bracing herself for sounds of anyone approaching on the stairs. There was nothing.

Cautiously, she opened the box and slid the contents out into her palm: a small gun, jet black, which reminded her of the starting pistol they fired to begin the relay race on sports days. It lay flat and seemingly harmless in her hand, like a sleeping cat. She had used a gun—several times at Hull Fair when she was in her teens—and had been the proud winner of a coconut and a plastic bag of goldfish. Picking up the big rifles at the firing range and hitting a moving target had been easy, easier for her than for her cousin Neil, two years her senior. In fact, he was so envious of her superior marksmanship that he told his parents he had won the prizes and had given them to Susanne out of pity.

A piece of vellum paper had also been stuffed into the box. Underneath the logo of crossed rifles and a heading in large red letters, proclaiming 'Scarborough and North Yorkshire Shooting Club' the letter thanked Jeff for renewing his membership and advised him that his firearms license had almost finished its three year term and would be up for review in December.

Just then, she heard the soft thump of feet coming up the stairs. She shoved both letter and gun back in the box, flinging it into the drawer, together with the other things she had taken out.

When Jeff entered a couple of minutes later, she was sitting on the bed carefully folding her underclothes into neat piles. She looked up at him with an expressionless face.

Chapter Four

The road was pitted and uneven. Through the window the desert yawned and sent up clouds of parched yellow dust at every jolt. She sat sweltering in the back of the jeep, aware of the steady drone of the motor and clutching a saucepan, her talisman. Tracey took both hands from the steering wheel, turned to her, gestured to a barefoot figure standing alone, his arms held up, pleading. It was Jeff.

They came to a large stone gray fortress. She followed Jeff through thick iron doors into a long dining hall, bare except for faded tapestries, the echoes of forgotten splendor. Water trickled from the ceiling, each drip emphasizing the silence. She grasped the handle of her saucepan, safe in her pocket, knowing it was really a gun.

Jeff faced her now, a large black beast who snarled softly, then drew back his lips to expose pointed canines. She drew the gun from her pocket and shot swiftly and certainly. The bullets tore the air with a whine but none of them touched the dog. He advanced, jaws open and drooling in delight, till his eyes were level with hers and she could smell his rank, fetid breath on her face. She pressed the trigger again and again but the shots backfired and hit her in the stomach, splitting it apart, drenching her body in pain…

Susanne woke up.

She opened her eyes wide and stared into the darkness. Her heart thumped wildly against her chest. All was black.

After a few seconds, she distinguished a thin sliver of pale morning light penetrating the curtains. She scanned the gloom for familiar objects and made out the whitish amorphous shape of her dressing gown hanging on the back of the door. Little by little her tensed body relaxed.

She knew she was awake but the dreamed pain was still there. Maybe it had prompted the dream. She had an appalling cramp in the pit of her stomach, as if someone had taken her innards and wrung them out like a dish-cloth. The pain made her nauseous. She gently eased back the covers and slipped out of bed, heading across the hall.

In the bathroom she could hardly stand and she sank on to the toilet seat in a semi-swoon, capable of nothing for a few minutes but cradling herself in a fetal position. When she could, she fetched the Kaolin and Morphine from the wall cabinet and the chalky mixture soothed her enough to return to bed and doze for a couple of hours, though she was too afraid of dreaming again to fall properly asleep.

At 7 o'clock the alarm began its shrill serenade. Susanne rolled over and was surprised to find the other half of the bed empty. She got up and dressed hurriedly, feeling debilitated after the rigors of the previous night. At least the stomach pains had gone.

She opened the door for December 9th on her advent calendar and revealed a gold-frosted Christmas tree, then drew back the curtains to look out on the real world. A coating of frost fringed the outside of the windows, looking almost deliberate in its symmetry. The sky was a dark bluey-gray.

Downstairs the kitchen was empty but the overhead light and softly babbling radio indicated that it had only recently been vacated. Susanne filled the kettle and put it on the stove to heat. Deliberating over how many teacups to put out on the table, she finally decided on a pair, feeling sure that Jeff would return soon.

She picked up the teapot in her right hand, ready to move it to the table, but her fingers suddenly felt powerless and numb. She lost her grip on the heavy pot and watched it slide from her hand and fall with a crash to the floor. Leaping back from the scalding water, she let out an involuntary cry and stood over the mess for a few seconds, too shocked to move.

While she recovered from her temporary paralysis, Jeff entered having heard the scream. "What the hell is going on?" he demanded.

Susanne could feel irrational tears begin to creep into the corners of her eyes but she struggled to keep calm. "It's all right. I just dropped the teapot…that's all."

Jeff eyed the china debris and sodden patch of linoleum then looked at her curiously. "What's the matter with you?"

"I don't know" she whimpered, foundering to her knees. "It just happened."

Jeff reached into the cupboard and took out the dustpan and brush. Handing it to her, he said more kindly "Is it something to do with being pregnant?"

"Yes" she nodded, scraping the bits from the damp lino with weary strokes, "I think so. I woke up in the night with cramp—"

"Yes I know. I heard you get up."

"It's gone now. But I couldn't sleep after that. I feel…funny." She finished sweeping up and tossed the contents of the pan into the pedal bin, then sat down, the brush still dangling listlessly from her hand.

Jeff meanwhile, realizing that he would have to fend for himself this morning, was making instant coffee. "I thought those pills were supposed to help."

"They usually do."

"You're still not sleeping though."

Susanne was silent and impassive.

Jeff looked at her a moment, then took the chair opposite hers, stroked his chin for a few seconds and breathed in carefully before speaking. "Su?"

She looked up at him questioningly.

"I've been thinking. While you're like this, not able to sleep and that, why don't I move into one of the guest rooms? Just for a while, like. I mean you're keeping me awake too, you know. It would be better. For you too. What do you think?" He studied her face for a reaction, but saw none.

"It's not that I don't want to sleep with you anymore. It's just that…well, you know…practically every night I hear you getting up, going to the kitchen. I mean, what do you do down here anyway? Sometimes you're up for hours."

Her face was ashen. She didn't move a muscle.

"Well look, Su, it's no good for me. I haven't had a good night's sleep for weeks. If you can't sleep, why don't you do something about it? 'Stead of taking all those pills?"

"What am I supposed to do?"

"Well I don't know, do I. I'm not a doctor."

"Dr. Freund said I needed rest. He said I was overdoing things."

"Yeah, well, you are overdoing things. I said you should let Tracey do the work. That's what she's here for. But you have to do everything yourself."

"I told you before, I don't like Tracey. I don't want her here. But you forced me—"

"I never forced nothing."

"Yes you did. I never wanted her to come here in the first place. But you didn't bother asking me how I felt. You don't care how I feel."

"That's not true" he said defensively.

"If you cared about me you'd help me with the work yourself, instead of getting some stupid maid I never wanted anyway. But you don't want to help. You're never even here. I don't know why you bothered marrying me and taking on this hotel." Her voice was rising in incipient hysteria.

Jeff left the table and started abstractedly rinsing his coffee mug. "That was your idea" he countered.

"What do you mean?"

"I only live here to satisfy you. I could have done other things."

"Other things! What other things?"

"I've had jobs, you know."

"What, you mean that one on the building site where they sacked you after two weeks for fighting? And I bet Mr. Ormerod didn't think much of you when he caught you with your hand in the till."

Jeff glowered. He was furious with her for remembering these things and using them against him. "I don't have to answer to you for nothing. You may be my wife but you can't tell me what to do!"

"I just wish you'd help, that's all—"

"Look, this place is nothing to do with me. If it comes to that, you never asked me if I wanted to run a guest house, because I bloody well don't."

"Well I don't either. I want to be a nurse."

"That's your problem. You should have stuck up to your mam."

"You don't care at all, do you. You don't give a toss. Just so long as everything's all right for you!"

"Oh shut up!" he shouted.

She burst into noisy tears, alternately sobbing and sniffing and hiding her face in her hands.

The sight of her uncontrollable weeping infuriated him further. "I've told you before, I can't stand that bloody crying. Stop it, will you. Shut up! I told you to shut your friggin' face!"

The sobbing continued unabated. Incapable of containing his rage, Jeff shook her violently by the shoulders, shouting at her through clenched teeth. Her body weight was so light that, almost without realizing it, without intending to, he pushed her and the chair over backwards on to the floor. Her head knocked with an audible crack against the sharp edge of the cupboard door and she crumpled to the ground, where she lay still and white, her lips slightly parted as if sleeping.

Jeff rang the surgery in a panic and Dr. Freund made an uncommon house call, diagnosing mild concussion, which warmth and rest would soon cure. To Jeff's relief, he completely accepted the story that Susanne had slipped on the wet kitchen floor and fallen over by accident. Susanne lay in bed unconscious for two days.

On the third day, when she awakened still dazed but well enough to sup chicken soup, she had a telephone call from Miss Johnson at Fairbanks. Her mother apparently had had another stroke, this time much more serious, sending her into a coma from which it was feared she might never return to consciousness.

Chapter Five

Even Jeff had expressed surprise at how little Susanne reacted to her mother's death. Maybe because it happened so suddenly or because it had been impending for so long, she had felt nothing. Even when her mother's eyes had flickered in what could almost have been recognition, just before the end when she had seemed to be straining to speak or to hold on to life with one last frantic gasp, Susanne had felt no grief or loss or any of the emotions normally associated with death. At the cremation she had been calm and efficient, dispensing grave hellos to the few relatives who managed to turn up for the funeral. They knew, of course, that it wasn't like her to fuss. But they gossiped later about the absence of her husband and the unhealthy pallor of her skin.

All, that is, but Auntie Mabel. She was a surprise visitor, who had come all the way from London to attend the funeral. She seemed genuinely moved by the event: several times during the ceremony Susanne caught her dabbing her eyes with the corner of her scarf. Perhaps she felt guilty, that she had waited for her sister to die before coming back to Whitby. Or perhaps the sight of Susanne's swollen belly made her wish she had had some children of her own. At any rate, before stepping into her red Fiesta for the long drive home, she pressed four £10 notes into her niece's hand, plus a slip of paper on which she had written her London address in large black letters, assuring her that she was always welcome to visit.

It being close to Christmas, Tracey had gone home to her parents for the weekend. There were no guests at Coral Cottage but Jeff insisted that Tracey should return on Sunday night and stay for the remaining week until the holiday. After that he swore he would give her notice.

Susanne believed him. And yet, here she was in his room, the guest room he had adopted as his own since her accident. Here she was, with an unquenchable urge to spy on him, knowing that he would be out all day and there was no one else in the house.

She had read her horoscope that morning in the new issue of *Woman* and had been amazed at its accuracy: *'Unexpected disruptions in your home life (always an area of concern for you) could test your goodwill this Christmas. Don't allow those closest to you to ignore your needs. Now is the time to put any long term plans into action. You are especially fortunate this month in money matters.'* She had disregarded the last sentence, but most of the prediction had seemed to speak directly to her.

Jeff had been unusually solicitous towards her in the last few days. That morning he had asked her whether she would like him to fetch her anything from Scarborough, but she had replied in the negative, feeling a twinge of regret that he hadn't made similar overtures to her before, before it was too late.

Now she stood on the threshold of his room, looking in at the chaos. Sleeping apart from Susanne had increased his potential for untidiness. The bed was unmade, the curtains drawn, a pair of jeans lay in a discarded heap on the floor, a half-empty tumbler of stale beer perched unsteadily on its beer mat on the bedside table. There was a strong, unpleasant smell in the room which Susanne couldn't identify.

Both pillows were still crumpled from the previous night's sleep. It was a double bed, this being the largest bedroom in the house and the one reserved for couples and families. Coverlet, blanket and sheets had been hastily pulled back, revealing the creased under sheet. The sight of untidiness was upsetting to Susanne and she moved to the side of the bed and plumped the pillows.

On one pillow lay something that made Susanne's heart stop. Deliberately, and with a ghastly mixture of excitement and fear, she picked it up between thumb and forefinger and held it up to the light for closer inspection. What she saw made sense of her bad dreams, the times she had woken early in inexplicable agitation and her unaccountable desire to see inside this room.

It was a long black hair. Treacherously long and curling at exactly the same angle that Tracey's curled when it hung loose over her shoulders.

Susanne stared at the hair for a long time. There was a knot in her stomach that wasn't exactly a pain, more a feeling of constriction as if she couldn't breathe. She tried to discipline her mind into ordered thoughts, but in vain. Unwanted emotions, like rebellious children, clamored at her mind's door. She could feel nothing but the knot her guts had twisted themselves into.

She slipped the hair furtively into her pocket. Standing there in her flowered pastel housecoat, she suddenly felt dowdy, old and alone.

Her fingers had dug so fiercely into her left palm that the nails had left a deep impression. She left the room and shut the door firmly behind her, closing the lid on that Pandora's Box. In the top cupboard of her kitchen she found the pills. She had been hiding them there recently and telling Jeff she was managing without. She read the label: *Do not exceed the stated dose without consulting a physician,* but she chose to pretend she hadn't seen it. At any rate, she had completely forgotten whether she had taken some pills that morning or had more than her usual quota last night. And anyway, it didn't matter.

She waited for the lovely numbness to overcome her. *My mother is dead,* she thought. *Jeff doesn't care whether I live or die and neither do I.*

*   *   *

Jeff returned from the club at 5.15 on Sunday evening, feeling invigorated by his day out at the shooting range. The weather had been perfect: crisp clean sunshine with a breeze that stung your cheeks, not too cold and not too warm. Plus, he'd impressed the lads with his shooting prowess. They couldn't help admiring the way he'd hit those five bullseyes, one after the other. He never bothered to tell the wife, though, as he didn't fancy enduring her awkward questions.

Tramping into the house while humming the only tune he could ever remember—'When the Saints Go Marching In'—he removed his fur-lined leather jacket and hung it on the hat stand, pausing on his way to the kitchen to give his hair a quick preen in the mirror.

The gun was in a yellow plastic bag which he took through into the kitchen and laid on the work top, intending to give it a good cleaning and take out the ammunition later on. Although not generally a tidy person, he was very meticulous in some things, like the cleaning of guns, which he considered important. Dicky always said *you should treat a gun like a woman, take care of her and she won't turn out dangerous.* Being the club's manager, Dicky knew all there was to know about guns. But Jeff considered himself more of an authority on women.

It was unnaturally quiet. The stillness lay like a blanket and the house seemed to be holding its breath waiting for something to happen. Jeff turned the radio on for company and started to make himself a cup of tea. When he turned back to the table, he was startled to see Susanne standing in the doorway and his body gave a twitch of shock.

"I didn't hear you come in" he said.

She was dressed in her nightgown and slippers, her face was white and her small frame so gaunt, apart from the slight bulge below the midriff, that it was almost spectral.

"Well don't just stand there, love. Sit down. I'll make you some tea." He tried to disguise the slight edge of embarrassment in his voice. It discomfited him to see her so pale and silent with her big eyes staring. She had quite shaken him out of his jovial mood.

She wafted to a chair and sat down. "Where have you been then?" she breathed.

Jeff didn't feel like telling her the truth. "I was out with some mates, you know, Bill and Paul. We did a bit of angling down the pier, didn't catch nowt, then popped in at the Falcon for a quick one. You know their lunchtime closing hours, we didn't get out of there while five o'clock!" His short chuckle didn't inspire any reaction from her.

He put a cup of tea on the table and she reached for it with a shaking hand. "Were you at home Friday night?" she ventured.

Jeff puzzled a moment over the question, then replied "At home? Course. Where else would I be?"

"Did you sleep in your room?"

"Well where d'you think? What are you on about, Su?"

"Nothing. Just wondered."

Jeff wanted to think of some remark that would stop her stupid questions but there was nothing to say. So he sat opposite her and threw her furtive glances over the top of his cup. She had only had two sips of the liquid before sagging back in her chair with eyes half closed. Jeff decided to take action.

"Are you feeling all right, Su?"

She opened her eyes dazedly and looked at him as if she wasn't sure who he was.

"You're tired aren't you. You better go to bed. Come on." He lifted her limp body from the chair and practically carried her up the stairs. She had about as much life in her as a rag doll. He left her in bed and went into the front room to watch television. He tried to relax with a couple of cans of beer, but she'd put him in a bad mood and the programs bored him.

*   *   *

There was music in her ears—a low throbbing like the beating of a heart and a high-pitched wailing like a single violin. A cacophony of sounds rushed through her head.

She opened her eyes. She was alone and in her room. She didn't know what time of night it was or how long she'd been lying there. The clock said five past eight but its ticking had stopped. She struggled to sit up, felt sweat trickling between her breasts and touched it with her fingers. A clump of damp hair was matted to her forehead. She drew back the covers and put one foot on the floor, following it slowly with the other foot, then stood up shakily, clutching the bedpost for support. The room was dark and she had forgotten where the light switch was.

She halted there for a few moments, shivering in her nakedness and rocking to and fro on her heels. Only the cold told her she wasn't dreaming.

She put on her dressing gown and progressed by small shuffling steps out into the hallway, which was also dark. She negotiated the stairs carefully one at a time, clinging to the bannister, till she had safely reached the kitchen.

She saw a yellow plastic bag lying on the work top. It was unfamiliar and yet it seemed to call her to it, willing her to peek inside. In the bag was a white and red box with a black symbol. She recognized the symbol. Casually she slipped the gun out of the box and into her hand. It seemed to fit her palm. She felt a queer sensation come over her, holding the gun. A feeling of power, of invincibility.

There was a creak above her, a rattling at the door, strange voices. She whirled round to face an adversary but there was none. Maybe it had been the wind.

The wind was buffeting the walls of the house and soughing through its crevices. She went to the kitchen door and looked out into the dim hallway. There were shapes in the shadows, lying in the corners, waiting to spring. She clutched the gun more tightly.

And there were definitely voices. Rustling, whispery voices and muffled laughter coming from upstairs. Susanne floated up to the first floor, feeling her way in the gloom.

The house was silent. Susanne stopped. She was a fool. She had imagined the voices. It was all in her head. She was only dreaming.

But then she heard it again, more clearly this time. A stifled giggle. She carried on up the stairs to the second floor. She was as stealthy as a cat in her bare, slipperless feet. She was as pale as a ghost in her white dressing gown, the black gun clutched in her hand.

The bedroom door stood ajar and light gushed into the hall. Susanne lurked in the shadows, hearing the well-known voices.

"Come here, you."

"Where do you want me, sir?" Giggles.

"You know what I want, don't you. You're gorgeous, you are."

"Don't talk so loud. She'll hear you."

"Fat chance. She's sleeping like a baby. I sent her off to sleep with some nice pills."

"Are you sure?"

"Don't be so nervous. Come here and let me feel you."

More giggles. Snap, rustle, smack. Flesh on flesh, lips on lips. Susanne walked into the glare. But like a wraith, nobody saw her. Jeff had his back to her and his naked body gleamed in the light. The muscles on his back rippled as he stroked her smooth legs with his strong arms. He bent down, his mouth seeking her breast, and her mass of black curly hair appeared over the top of his head. Her arms were entwined about his waist, caressing his buttocks. Their coupled bodies gyrated in the light, cavorted in mutual pleasure.

Susanne felt a black cloud of hate suffuse her until she was permeated with rage. She had turned into a small hard steely ball of hate. She was a bullet, searing into their soft pulpy flesh, tearing their bodies apart, sundering their limbs forever.

She raised the gun, leveled it at Jeff's head and squeezed the trigger. "You never lifted a finger" she screamed, "You never lifted a finger!"

An animal-like roar of pain filled the room, then he lurched back with the force of the blow and sprawled on to the bed. Tracey stood paralyzed with terror, stiff as a mannequin, her hands held up. Susanne squeezed again. She closed her eyes but saw behind her lids the mass of red, heard the splintered bone and scattered flesh, smelt the mingled odor of sulfur and death.

Like a reed in the wind, she shuddered from head to foot.

Chapter Six

Rain spattered on to the carriage window, making dozens of tiny rivulets. Each drop smashed itself against the glass and descended, slowly at first, then joined with other drops to aggravate its weight and hurtled to destruction. Susanne mused on the short and uncomplicated life of a raindrop, lulled as she was by the train's rhythmic pattern. Through a haze of image-distorting rain, gaunt trees sped by, their branches naked and shivering; thorny hedgerows; fields that had once been green and slant-roofed country houses. Each person in each house was trapped in a human life, just as she was trapped in hers.

Susanne trembled with the cold. Never having traveled a long distance by train before, she had expected to be too warm and had packed her jumper. She stood up and reached for her suitcase in the overhead luggage rack, but immediately the man in the dog collar who sat opposite her leapt to his feet and offered assistance. Up until then he had worn a perpetual grin, but now he took the opportunity to smile properly, showing an unruly mass of teeth which looked as though they wanted to escape from his mouth.

"It is quite cold, isn't it" he said as he watched Susanne remove a maroon chunky-knit jumper from the case and pull it over her head. His voice was smooth and refined with no trace of an accent.

Susanne, unable to think of a suitably noncommittal reply but not wishing to ignore him, murmured in agreement and nodded her head, looking away.

He continued to stare interestedly at her. "Are you traveling far?" he inquired cordially.

"To London."

"For the first time?"

Again she simply nodded, desperate to retreat from the conversation before it became too intimate. She stared fixedly out of the window until the priest gave up his attempts at chit chat and retired once more behind his copy of *The Name of the Rose*.

Her white handbag lay on the seat beside her. Covertly, she undid the zipper of the purse compartment and checked to see that her wad of twenty pound notes was still intact. The young man in the main Post Office at York had seemed to look at her strangely when she asked to withdraw all the money in her account, but it wasn't his job to ask questions.

She looked in her wallet to see if she still had the address of her Auntie Mabel in London. Yes, it was still there. *13b Tooley Street, Westbourne Grove.*

Mabel. The name on Coral Gray's lips as she lay dying: "Mabel, put your scarf on, you'll catch cold". Her younger sister, and the one she had loved the best. What had happened between them to cause such a rift that they hadn't spoken for nearly twenty years? Susanne had never found out.

Mabel had come up to Whitby once to visit, when Susanne was seven. Susanne only remembered two things about her aunt, she was improbably rich and she knew Harold Gray. She was the only person who dared mention Harry in his daughter's presence and her words had stayed locked in a chink of Susanne's memory: "Harry's not all bad you know, Corrie, he left you the house didn't he, and he never lifted a finger against you. He always seemed such a gentle man to me."

"Oh no, he never lifted a finger" he mother replied "but he hurt me right enough, leaving me all on my own with a child to support."

Susanne wondered how Auntie Mabel would react to see that she had accepted her invitation so quickly. And would she be willing to prolong the "visit", while Susanne had the baby? She didn't know, but she had no one else to turn to.

*   *   *

Susanne was walking up a street called Queensway. On her way out of Bayswater tube station she had asked the ticket collector for directions, showing him the map that the woman in the tourist information office at King's Cross had drawn her. He was a black man who spoke in a blend of Jamaican and cockney that was unintelligible to her ears, and though she pretended to understand him, the only part that made sense was "turn left on to Queensway".

It didn't look remotely like a Queens Way. She had imagined a wide avenue flanked by elegant white houses. Here was a busy shopping center, which would have resembled the center of Scarborough, but for the diversity of nationalities. Susanne had never seen such a motley conglomeration of people of all colors and nationalities, some extravagantly dressed, some drab, some from the pages of fashion magazines. The confusion she had felt all day deepened almost to panic as she was swept along on this tide of strangers in a strange city.

Flashing fairy lights hung from the street lamps; Christmas greetings were sprayed in white on shop windows; from each boutique and delicatessen blared a different selection of carols; outside the butcher's stood Santa Claus, looking bored and handing out leaflets about a prize draw. And everywhere the shoppers scurried, desperate to get the last gift, the last card, the last mince pie.

Susanne felt that she must be the only person in the world not participating in this great event. Her suitcase felt heavier and heavier and banged against her legs, the sharp edge of a book jabbing her calves.

At the top of Queensway she turned left into Westbourne Grove, from which she found the side street leading to Tooley Street. Here were the houses she had expected to see, not elegant but white and with an air of past grandeur, now faded. Passing by one house, she saw a pair of trousers hanging out to dry in the garden. Cold and frost had stiffened them, so that at first sight they resembled animate legs, footless and torsoless, twitching on the line.

With a stab of pain, she remembered her dream. She had tried to push it out of her memory, but it was so appallingly vivid that it kept surfacing to her conscious-ness. She had shot Jeff and Tracey in the bedroom.

But it was only a dream. A horrible dream. It felt like reality, but then dreams often did.

She knew none of that had really happened. Tracey was staying with her parents for Christmas. Jeff was in Scotland with the shooting club and Susanne was visiting her aunt in London, to ask for help with the baby.

Here it was. Tooley Street. She walked down the street until she came to number 13. She couldn't see a 13b, but maybe that was one of the flats. It was a large gabled house, white like all the others and with its name proudly displayed above the door: *Arundel Villas.*

Underneath was a sign saying 'Bed and Breakfast: Vacancies'. No mention of *a* or *b*. Susanne stood and stared in bemusement.

The front door opened and a woman appeared. She was short and stocky in a knitted woolen dress and thick stockings. Her hair was brown with gray at the temples and she wore a lot of rings and jangling bracelets. She had a wide face and her swarthy skin was wrinkled like an old leather bag.

"I seen you from the window. You want a room miss?" she queried in a gravelly voice.

"I'm looking for Miss Hazlett, Mabel Hazlett, does she live here?"

"This is a bed and breakfast" she said, jabbing impatiently at the sign with one beringed finger. "Nobody lives here, except me. You want a room?"

Susanne considered her hot, sticky feet and her aching body and decided that she could afford one night in a hotel. She would look for Auntie Mabel tomorrow. "Yes" she replied.

The woman led her into the house and into a dark room stuffed with heavy wooden furniture, where an upright piano lurked in the corner, covered with framed photographs.

A large leather-bound book was thrust into her hands. "Sign the guest's book, please miss."

Susanne picked up the pen attached to the book by a piece of string and wrote slowly, 'Tracey Nightingale'.

STORY THREE

Chapter One

<hr>

FRIDAY MARCH 13th, 1992

Driving home bleary-eyed, Graham cursed the weather, the Camden Road traffic which was heavy even at that hour, the freezing temperature inside his vehicle since the failure of the car heater, and chiefly his job and everything that went with it. A profession that dragged him out late at night to investigate a completely motiveless killing with no clues, then sent him home—he consulted his watch— three hours later, tired, disillusioned and hungry, having achieved absolutely nothing. He'd be better off with steady employment as a road-sweeper.

His bad mood was exacerbated by discovering that someone had parked outside his house in St. John's Wood, and he was forced to waste a further ten minutes driving round the block before finding a space.

"Typical" he muttered crossly to himself as he trudged through the blinding rain, stubbornly refusing to run, even though he could feel water seeping inexorably through his coat, shirt and vest. As the day had started out fine that morning, he had neglected to carry an umbrella.

Once indoors, Graham couldn't resist snatching a peek at Serena from under the silk cloth draped over her cage. Her head was nestling snugly under one wing. He removed that day's copy of *The Hampstead and Highgate Express* from his briefcase and flung it on the pile in the living room. As usual, he hadn't had a chance to read through it properly yet.

Taking off his sodden overcoat, he shook himself dry like a dog and toweled his hair, using the downstairs bathroom so as not to disturb Pat. After helping himself to some cold ham and egg pie from the refrigerator, he tiptoed up the stairs but forgot about the top step, whose loud creak punctured the silence. Graham eased open the bedroom door, listened for Pat's stertorous breathing and slipped out of his clothes and into his pajamas, feeling his way in the gloom.

"You were out a long time" mumbled a drowsy voice, as he lodged himself between the sheets.

Graham answered with a curt monosyllable, not wishing to start a conversation that might delay his rest.

"Where did you go?" Pat asked, rolling over to face him and drawing a knuckle across her eyes.

Graham sighed but decided it was simpler just to answer. "A discotheque in Camden Town."

"Oh…"

He could feel her willing him to elaborate and it irritated him. "Do I really have to tell you all the details now?" he complained, making his voice sound as exhausted as possible.

"I'm just interested, dear. You *are* about four hours later than I expected."

"Yes I know, I'm sorry" he said unrepentantly. "There was a murder and I was called out to investigate. A boy was knifed to death in a ladies toilet."

Pat gave a small groan of dismay. "How horrible!"

"Do you want to hear all the sordid details or can I get to sleep now?"

"There's no need to get cross, dear—"

"Look, I'm sorry but I've had rather a rough night and I'm not exactly on top of the world at the moment."

"I just thought it might be nice for us to talk, since you've been out all evening. But if it bothers you that I take an interest in your work, never mind, you just come home in the middle of the night, fall into bed without speaking to me and I'll ignore you—"

"Oh, for heaven's sake!"

"I *did* want to talk to you about Gemma actually, as she *is* your daughter as well as mine, but maybe it had better wait till tomorrow morning when you're less crabby."

"No, all right Pat, I'm thoroughly awake now, so let's talk" said Graham resignedly, sitting up and turning on the bedside lamp.

"Are you sure you're interested?" she insisted.

"Yes!"

Pat sat up too and took a sip of water from the tumbler by the bed. "I had a long chat with Gemma on the phone this evening."

"What did you ring her for tonight? Couldn't you wait till Sunday?"

"I didn't ring her, she rang me. Or rather *us*, but since you weren't home…"

"All right, all right, what did she say?"

"Apparently, she's not happy at University—"

"Not happy. Why on earth—?"

"Please stop interrupting, Graham, and you'll find out." She paused briefly, registering his compliance, then continued. "She hasn't mentioned this before because she didn't want to worry us and she thought she could manage, but now the situation's getting a little out of control. She had been seeing a boy called Julian, another student, for about three months. But a couple of weeks ago she decided to break it off with him. I don't exactly know why, I suppose she must have had her own reasons. Anyway, he must be completely besotted with her. She doesn't want to be unkind but he's interrupting her studying, just at the time she needs all her concentration if she's to get through her exams. But he won't stop pestering her, he rings her up every day, comes round to her room in halls, tries to meet her in the students bar, and generally makes her life a misery. Anyway, the upshot of all this is, she wants to come home."

"What? But she's about to finish the course."

"She says she's near enough to finals and has put in enough work at the beginning of the year for the University to let her study at home. She could maybe commute one day a week to Sheffield for tutorials—"

"She can't come home. It's absolutely out of the question." Graham had a fleeting, vivid image of the young girl's corpse on Hampstead Heath, the life battered out of her before it had hardly begun, her innocent, once lovely face. The killing was random; it could have been anyone, it could have been Gemma.

"Don't be unreasonable, Graham. Why not give it some thought? It must be pretty important to have prompted her to say anything. She's never made a fuss easily—"

"I *have* given it some thought and my answer is no. She's over-reacting." Graham lay down and turned his back to his wife, indicating that the conversation was at an end.

"Well, I think it's a shame, you're so uncaring about your own daughter you'd reject her just when she needs you." Pat waited a few moments for Graham's response, then realizing he wouldn't be drawn, gave up, turned out the light and went to sleep.

Graham lay awake for what seemed like hours, his mind in turmoil. He had surprised himself by the violence of his reaction to Pat, brought on by the sudden connection in his mind of his own daughter with the girl who'd been murdered. Although he didn't like admitting it, there were similarities between the murders in Hampstead and Camden Town. In both cases, the murder weapon was the first available object to hand, seemingly grabbed on the spur of the moment with no premeditation. There was no apparent motive for either attack. And both murders had been botched and amateurish, with no attempt to conceal evidence. It looked like the work of a psychopath with a low mental age. Someone like Charlie Hackett.

*   *   *

A few days later, Pat was in the living room knitting a jumper for Gemma and half-listening to the television, when she heard her husband's name. By the time she had turned up the volume, however, the attractive dark-haired girl with the melodious voice had changed to another topic:

"…so if anybody was in the vicinity of North London College in Camden Road at about ten o'clock last Friday night March 13th and saw anything suspicious, please could they contact the Incident Room at Temple Green police station, or alternatively give us a ring here at *Watch Out for Crime*. The lines are open 24 hours a day…"

Pat switched off the television. She didn't want to hear any more. It had jolted her to hear Graham's name. It made her feel as if he was public property and no longer belonged to her.

She returned to the knitting but found it difficult to concentrate. Her thoughts kept straying to Graham. His attitude towards Gemma really was intolerable, not to even listen to the poor girl or try to do something to help. It was as if he didn't care. He'd always worked hard, but now he'd become so completely wrapped up in his work that it was impossible to communicate with him on any-thing but a superficial level.

These days, they only ever talked about the day to day things that linked them like bills and house repairs. There was never the opportunity to discuss anything deeper, like why their marriage was falling apart like a pack of badly-stacked cards. Graham was always so distant, avoiding her with his gaze or looking through her as if she were invisible. She wanted to cry out to him that she needed attention, that she was a person with feelings not just a house-keeping machine. Sometimes she thought of confiding in a friend, but her attempts to open the subject always died on her lips and she heard herself repeating the same stale old lies: "Graham's fine, everything's fine."

The sound of the post being delivered broke her reflec-tion, and she rushed to the front door, ever eager to hear from Gemma, but it was just a garishly-colored circular inviting her to play a competition, which she threw straight into the bin. When she returned to the living room, her optimism surfaced. She told herself that things must change for the better soon. She had only to wait.

*　　　　　*　　　　　*

It was remarkable how the mere sight of one man could put Graham on edge, even to the extent of making him physically ill. Graham hoped nobody else could hear the churning of his stomach, as he faced Charlie Hackett. He fingered some indigestion tablets in his pocket, but he didn't care to display his sickness by eating one in front of his suspect.

Charlie had brought his solicitor with him—a squat woman with cropped black hair and a broad, sallow face—and she sat opposite Graham with a grim expression, as if expecting trouble.

"These friends you say you were with on Friday the 13th" Graham recommenced, "Can you give us their phone numbers so that we can confirm you were at the pub with them?"

"Marty don't have no phone" Charlie sputtered. "He works at the pub. You can find him there."

"That's the *Mean Fiddler*, is it?"

"S'right."

"The same pub you were at on the 25th February?"

"Yeah. I told you. Fridays, I goes there" asserted Charlie, with a look towards his solicitor.

Graham wrote a name down in his notebook. "And Dominic?"

"Dunno where he lives. But he works on the buses. Number 31. Stops at Camden Town."

"I see. He shouldn't be too hard to locate, then." Graham paused for a moment to weigh things up in his mind, scratching one earlobe distractedly with his finger. "It seems very convenient that you were at the same pub, with the same friends, on both Friday nights when the murders took place."

Charlie grinned, showing yellow tar-stained teeth. "Inspector Brunswick," piped up his solicitor in a shrill voice, "My client has been completely co-operative and has given you the names of two people prepared to give him an alibi that he was nowhere near the crime location on either of the evenings in question. I really think that should satisfy you."

"Yes," Graham replied, "We'll speak to them again, of course. Meanwhile, I'd be grateful if you could make sure your client remains contactable until we finish our enquiries into this case…these cases."

"I'm sure Mr. Hackett is quite happy to comply with that" responded the woman, with a look to her client for confirmation.

Charlie grinned again, like a satisfied schoolboy: "I got nowhere else to go" he said.

The solicitor glanced at her watch, picked up her briefcase from the floor and rose, pulling down the edge of her suit jacket with one hand. "I *do* have somewhere else to go, I'm afraid. I have another appointment in twenty minutes, so…if that's all, Inspector?" she inquired unsmilingly.

"Yes, I don't think I'll need to detain you any longer" Graham replied with as much politeness as he could muster.

The solicitor turned to her client and gave him a pat on the arm which was unexpectedly tender: "Sorry to rush off, Charlie. I'd stay for a chat, but with having to squeeze you in at short notice I'm already delayed. You don't need me any more, do you?"

Charlie looked down and shook his head.

"Anyway, you know where I am." She left the room without another word to the police officer.

Graham stood up and hovered by the door. "You might as well go too, Hackett."

Charlie's grin spread all over his face. "I'm afraid I must be going" he said in an exaggeratedly posh voice, mimicking his solicitor. "I have another appointment." Then back to his normal tone: "In the pub!" His shoulders shook up and down and he wheezed with laughter.

"Get your coat" Graham ordered tersely. "And get out of here. This place smells." He waited till Charlie had thrown an old jacket over his scrawny shoulders and was by the door, before holding him back by the scruff of his collar and whispering fiercely: "What the hell did you say to me when you first came in here?"

Charlie wore his most innocent expression. "What d'you mean?"

"*I know about your woman* you said. Who were you referring to?"

"No one."

Graham pulled him back roughly till Charlie's back hit the wall with a thud. "Ow! Didn't mean no harm." His face level with Graham's shoulders and his eyes fixated on Graham's chest, he creased his brow into a frown.

"What woman?" Graham insisted, pressing his face close into Charlie's.

"You should know" Charlie replied in a small voice, letting his eyes travel slowly up to Graham's, a smile hovering about his lips, "Her name's Ruth."

Graham took a quick intake of breath and released his weight from the little man for a second. Shocked at how much Charlie already knew, he braced himself for the worst. "You said you knew about her. What exactly do you *know*?"

Charlie replied casually, as if unaware of the significance of his statement. "Know where she lives, don't I."

"What the hell—?" began Graham, almost suffocating Charlie with resumed pressure against the wall.

"I ain't done nothing wrong" squealed Charlie. "No law against it. Seen her in the street is all. Seen her with you."

"Were you following us?"

"No" Charlie denied, wide-eyed.

"Just leave her alone, you hear? Leave her out of this" warned Graham.

"No law to say I can't call, is there?" said Charlie, jutting out his chin defiantly. "It's a free country."

"Not for buggers like you, it isn't. Not when I catch you" Graham replied in a cold voice, his gaze on Charlie intense.

"Don't threaten me" whined Charlie. "I'll tell my solicitor."

"I know your little game" Graham growled. "But you'll play it one too many times." He shook Charlie roughly away from him. "Now get out of here!"

Charlie recovered himself and shambled away down the corridor, leaving his stench behind him like a memento. Graham burned Hackett's retreating back with his eyes, unable to relax until he'd seen him leave the building. Charlie had almost reached the end of the corridor when, with a sudden thought, he turned back to the policeman and hissed, waggling a dirty finger: "She's a pretty girl. But she might not stay pretty. Just you leave me alone."

Graham's face darkened with rage. But before he could retaliate, Charlie was gone.

Chapter Two

Pat was putting on some face powder in the tiny cubicle laughingly referred to as the "Ladies" at the back of the kitchens, prior to leaving for home. It had been a long hard shift tonight and she hadn't been able to concentrate on the job or take her usual pleasure in recognizing familiar faces and dispensing food and warmth to the needy. She had been too preoccupied by thoughts about her husband.

She regarded herself sternly in the stained wall mirror. She had been pretty once, very pretty in a wholesome sort of way. But now she just looked like any other middle-aged woman who did the best with her appearance. *What is wrong with my marriage?* she pondered. *Am I somehow, inadvertently, driving Graham away?* She always tried to do the right things. Life was so unfair.

"Self-pity won't get you anywhere, Patricia" she said aloud to her reflection. "Go home and put your feet up." She often spoke to herself in this manner, when no one else was around to hear. It was quite a good way of combating loneliness.

She let herself out of the cubicle and made her way to the front entrance, checking to make sure that all unnecessary lights had been switched off before saying good night and exiting through the glass door. Sarah had gone home and the hostel residents had mostly retired to the bedrooms, a few insomniac stragglers remaining in the dining room huddled around the television. Suddenly, Pat became aware that somebody had crept up behind her. She turned to see a young girl she knew standing on the pavement, looking characteristically lost and disorientated.

"Oh…hello…" the girl stuttered. She was dressed as usual in faded jeans and a thick red jumper, with no coat. Pat wondered if she might be cold.

"Hello my dear. You're too late I'm afraid. The dinner's over, and I was just leaving."

"Oh." The girl was obviously disappointed, and she continued to stand in the street as if unsure what to do next.

Pat felt a rush of sympathy for the girl. She inwardly chastised herself for being so concerned with her own troubles, which were meager compared to those of other people. This girl, for instance, had no money, no job, no husband, probably nowhere to live. "Do you have somewhere else to go?" inquired Pat.

"Oh…yeah…" Despite this assertion, the girl hesitated and stood gazing at the locked door as if it might provide an answer to her problems.

"I'm afraid all the beds in the hostel are taken tonight. It gets full so quickly."

"It's all right…I'm O.K.…."

Pat didn't believe her. The girl was obviously too embarrassed to admit that she was homeless. Pat thought of the empty room in her house that had been Gemma's, and of the fact that Gemma probably wouldn't be coming home now until the holidays. She thought of her own feelings of isolation and of the comfort of having another person in the house when Graham was out, indeed of the pleasure she got from giving to others. She thought of all the people, like this girl, who were down on their luck, probably through no fault of their own, and whom society neglected and ignored. She thought of how lucky she had always been, to have a nice home and a family, and she wondered how she would manage if she were in this girl's shoes.

She knew that none of the other helpers at the hostel took strangers into their homes, in fact they had been discouraged from doing so by Eric Tideman. She remembered the warning he had given her when she first volunteered for the job: *Don't get carried away by your good intentions. These people bite the hand that feeds them. They'd not worry about robbing you if they got the chance.*

Pat found Tideman unnecessarily cynical. She preferred to believe that if you expected good from people, good was what you got. There had been other down-and-outs at the hostel she'd been drawn to, but not in the same way as this girl. She had an air of lost gentility about her, as if she'd been plucked from a safe middle class existence and tossed into the alien world of the streets, a world where she didn't belong. Pat didn't believe this girl could rob anybody, even if she wanted to.

"There's a spare room in my house," she declared impulsively "If you need somewhere."

The girl stared at her in apparent bewilderment, the offer clearly having taken her by surprise. "Your house?" she echoed.

"You're welcome to come and stay with us for a while" Pat restated. "Of course, it couldn't be for ever because our daughter Gemma comes home from university in the holidays, and she'd need the room then. But she only visited us recently, so she won't be back down to London for some time. I don't imagine Graham would be too keen, but after all he's hardly ever there and it's my house as well." Pat's words tumbled out of her mouth in a rush of good feeling. She felt a little rebellious thrill at going behind Graham's back and deciding to do something without his sayso.

The girl thanked her politely. She looked both grateful and unsure whether to accept.

"Well anyway" continued Pat, "you don't have to come, but it's there if you need it."

"Yes. Thank you."

"I'd better write down the address for you, hadn't I? And the telephone number. So you can just give me a call and we can take it from there." Pat tore a slip of paper from the address book in her handbag and wrote down the details on it, then handed it to the girl.

"It's very kind of you…I might come…I'm all right at the moment…bye bye."

The girl walked off, clutching her slip of paper, and Pat looked after her. She felt much happier all of a sudden, and pervaded by a mood of unexpected optimism. Graham and she were just going through a difficult patch; they'd been through them before and the marriage always survived. In any case, she had a life outside her marriage with people who she mattered to and people who needed her.

CHAPTER THREE

Graham scanned the selection of limp salads on display under the glass, hesitating for so long that the person behind pressed hastily past him. Ignoring the seductive aroma of chili con carne, he opted at last for prawn and egg mayonnaise salad.

Nicky, the checkout girl, handed him the change from his five pound note with a smile designed to be winsome. She was so plain that he always felt constrained to be extra polite to her, and she unfortunately had taken this as encouragement.

"Ooh, aren't you being good today, Inspector!" she enthused, giving him a grotesquely flirtatious wink.

He smiled wanly and took his tray to the only unoccupied table in the noisy canteen, erecting his newspaper as a shield from interference. As he chewed desultorily on his second mouthful of salad, a tray was plonked down opposite him. He raised his head, ready to tell the intruder that the seat was taken, and saw Tom regarding him with a smirk.

"Absorbed are we, mate? Reading the story?" asked Tom, seating himself at the table.

"What story?"

Snatching Graham's copy of *The Hampstead and Highgate Express*, Tom flipped through the paper and located an article on page 4, which he held up for Graham to see. "Here. *Grisly murder on Hampstead Heath.* You've got a mensh."

"Oh God" groaned Graham, "Where did they get that photo?"

"Ah well, Curnow does a nice little business with the Ham and High on the side. You don't expect him to live on a copper's wages, do you?"

There were times when Graham wished Tom weren't always quite so jovial. And now was one of them.

"Don't you want to read what it says about you?" demanded Tom, slurping his coffee between bites of a large Danish pastry.

"No I don't."

"Ah, publicity shy, eh? You vant to be a-loon…right?"

Despite his mood, Graham was forced to laugh. "That must be the worst German accent I've ever heard. Thank God you didn't go into show business."

"Too right. It was a Swedish accent. Glad you can still crack a smile anyway, old son. I can see you're eating a salad but what's eating you?"

"Oh…nothing much." Graham carried on eating.

"You're brooding again" stated Tom.

"Maybe" replied Graham enigmatically, chewing his salad.

"I never could understand why you didn't jack in the job nine months ago, like you said you would." Tom's bluntness was not always unintentional: he gave Graham a quizzical glance over the top of his coffee cup.

"Thanks a lot" replied Graham sardonically.

"You know what I mean. All that spiel about not believing in yourself any more, about the Force not being what it's cracked up to be, do you still think that?"

"Nothing's happened to change my mind" said Graham, a little sadly.

"I thought so."

Graham felt the urge to open up a little and get a few things off his chest. "The truth is, I sometimes feel I'm losing my touch. And if I don't believe in *myself*, what chance have I got of convincing anybody else?"

"Anything in particular set this off?" Tom had an inkling that he knew the cause of Graham's current crisis of confidence, but he wanted his friend to volunteer the information.

"I pulled in Charlie Hackett yesterday. Gave him a thorough grilling."

"I'll bet you did."

Graham objected to Tom's sarcastic tone on that remark, but he decided to ignore it: "Hackett's got alibis for the Heath murder and the knifing in Camden Town. Two names he gave me, both of whom corroborate his story."

"I didn't know he had that many friends" Tom said sardonically.

"Surprised me too. But they're sticking to their guns. If they're telling the truth, Hackett was nowhere near either of the crime locations at the right time."

"Hang on" Tom interrupted, "Wasn't that pub he claimed to be at in Camden Town as well? That's a bit bloody coincidental. He could have popped out for a few minutes in the middle of his drinking—would anyone really have noticed?"

"I thought of that. They were playing one of those trivial questions pub games—you know, the ones where they give you the scores at the end with the players' names and the time the game ended? Fields went over there this morning to check and it's there in black and white on the machine—CHAS, which is his code name, and the score and the time completed as six minutes past ten. The game lasts a good half hour and Dominic swears Charlie was playing the whole time with him and Marty. The murder happened about ten o'clock, so there's no way he could have got back to the pub in time, even if he did pop out for a quick knifing."

"Any way he could have nobbled his witnesses again?" suggested Tom.

"Anything's possible" Graham said with a sigh. "But if they won't tell us, there's sod all we can do about it."

Tom picked up some crumbs of pastry off his plate with his fingers. "So we're back to square one, then?"

"It's so confusing. You see, it has to be somebody short, because of the angle at which the knife went into Mark Winstanley's chest—"

"I remember reading the description. He was quite a tall lad, wasn't he?" Tom threw back the last drops of his coffee and leaned in towards his colleague.

"That's right, five foot or eleven or thereabouts. But the person who knifed him must have been a good deal shorter, because they were stabbing from underneath, upwards." Graham ran a hand through his thick thatch of gray hair. It was a trait of Graham's when trying to unravel the finer points of a case.

"Like the Heath murder" Tom pondered.

"That's right—Sturgeon said he thought the log was swung upwards. And we've got the blonde hairs on Mark's t-shirt like the blonde hairs on the log—forensics confirmed they're 90% certain to be from the same person."

"So, what have we got—a short arse with blonde hair who kills for no reason and who isn't Charlie Hackett. Has he got a twin, by any chance?"

Graham didn't laugh at Tom's comment but replied gloomily: "I wish he did. Hackett was the best suspect we had."

"Had?"

"I couldn't detain him when his alibis checked out. His solicitor was getting stroppy."

"The mad bitch of Carmarthen" said Tom with a smirk.

Graham took a slurp of tea. "I don't know why she has to treat it as some kind of racial thing. I haven't got it in for all her countrymen."

"Just for Charlie Hackett" mused Tom. "Any other leads?"

Graham shook his head and pursed his lips. "I keep going through the statements from the students at the disco to see if anything leaps out at me."

"Not even got one of your famous hunches?"

Graham stroked his chin in thought: "Those kids were all so ordinary. I can't believe they were a specific target. Remember what Hackett said when we asked him why he did it?"

"Because they were there."

"Because they were there. They were there—he was there. Bingo! That's how his mind works. I don't know. If it's not Hackett, it's somebody like him. With the same madness."

"Look mate, I'm not being funny but…I think you're leaping to conclusions. With only two murders, it's a bit early to say we've got a new serial killer on our hands."

"That's just it, though. It's *not* early, it's not early at all. Two weeks after Hampstead and we're still floundering, no nearer a result." Graham wiped his mouth with his paper napkin and glowered at his companion, daring him to reply.

There was a pause while Tom ruminated. He seemed to study the profile of a pretty WPC sitting at a table across the room for a few moments, then he began again. "I thought you *were* going to leave, you know, nine months ago."

"After my job, were you?" quipped Graham.

Tom ignored this comment: "You said it was Charlie Hackett that set you off, but I wondered at the time if it went deeper than that." Graham looked at him speculatively, but said nothing. Tom continued: "I mean, a cop's only human. He makes mistakes sometimes, like everybody." He shrugged. "Some of us can handle that, other's can't. Know what I mean?"

Graham stared at the remains of his salad. He wanted to be honest with himself. "I suppose it was the Hackett case that triggered my…I don't know…my discontent." He put down his fork and leant back in his chair. "Up to then, you see, I'd always felt…I knew it wasn't a perfect system and there has to be room for human error, but I felt it worked overall."

Tom nodded. "Yeah" he said. He knew what Graham was driving at.

"But with Hackett, the system *didn't* work, the system broke down."

"It wasn't the system—"

"Yes it was! We are here…our whole function is to make sure that justice is done, that the criminals are caught, that they're put behind bars where they can't be a danger to society. How can it be that we know someone is guilty of murder, beyond a shadow of doubt, we arrest him, we take him to Court, we have the evidence—"

"Not enough evidence—"

"We *knew* he was the one!" Graham smashed his hands down on the table in rage and frustration.

"There have to be laws, Graham. To protect the innocent."

"Yeah, and to protect evil psychopaths like Hackett, so that he can walk the streets terrorizing other people. And meanwhile, we sit here on our arses and wait for him to do it again."

"We'll get him. It's only a matter of time."

Graham's anger was spent now. He picked up his knife with a sigh and buttered a bread roll. "I hate feeling so helpless. I should be able to do something."

"You're still here, aren't you. Why *did* you stay on?"

Graham stalled, marshaling his thoughts, and chewing on a mouthful of bread. He had pondered the question many times in his own mind and was still unsure of the answer, so he gave a flippant reply: "I've got to redeem myself, haven't I? I couldn't quit on a downer like that."

There was more to explain, but DC Smart distracted him by appearing at his right shoulder. "Sorry to disturb you at lunch, sir. Message from Superintendent McGivern, sir."

"Got us bugged has he?" muttered Tom.

"What does he want?" asked Graham.

"He'd like to see you first thing after lunch, if you don't mind sir."

"I don't mind. Thank you, Smart."

As soon as the constable left, Tom grinned at his friend and asked "Your chance to redeem yourself?"

"Huh" Graham barked sardonically, "I hardly think this case'll win me promotion. With no suspects? I'm sure I'll be teacher's pet."

"Just a word of advice, mate, but if I were you I wouldn't let McGivern in on your hunches. You know what he's like."

"I've no intention of telling McGivern anything."

*   *   *

Being a typical West End pub, it was usually crowded and noisy in the King's Arms on a weekday lunchtime, and today was no exception. Ruth pushed her way through a group of jabbering men in business suits, clutching her pineapple juice and Ploughman's lunch, to reach the others at her table. It was company policy not to buy rounds of drinks, an idea that appealed to Ruth, who always drank far less than her colleagues.

Ruth squeezed in between Tony and Maggie, who had left a place for her marked by her briefcase. "Here she comes, the Women's Champion" quipped Tony, as he moved aside for her. It was a long-standing joke and nobody laughed. On her left, John and Tony were in the middle of an argument about who was responsible for the hiss on the microphone in the last shot. On her right, Maggie and Tanya had their heads bent over the production schedule. Maggie was drinking strong coffee and

Tanya was stuffing herself with tortilla chips washed down with Perrier.

Ewan sat opposite Ruth. He winked at her over his glass of bitter, as Ruth tucked into her French bread and cheese. He was not a talkative man, but he had a warm smile and an easygoing manner, and he was Ruth's favorite among the technicians. She reflected that perhaps she liked him because he was a little older than the others, in his forties perhaps, about the same age as Graham.

Ruth hadn't meant to think about Graham, but he'd been on her mind since their telephone conversation the week before. She was known for her courage and honesty, and often teased for it by her work mates. But in this she'd been a coward. Nine months she'd spent letting the situation ride, waiting to see what would happen, not daring to face Graham with the question: *Who would you choose?* But she knew it wouldn't be long before she did ask. And whatever his answer, she would just have to bear the consequences.

A muted bleep began to sound from somewhere near her. At first, Ruth was too lost in her thoughts to notice. But then Tony nudged her and demanded: "Is that yours?"

"Oh—yes, maybe." Ruth had put her briefcase on the floor between her legs, and she heaved it on to her lap and fumbled with the lock, flinging back loose strands of hair that fell in her eyes and obscured her vision.

"I don't know why she brings that thing in here with her" commented John, leaning across Tony to Ruth and aiming the remark at her.

"She's a very important person" replied Tony. "You never know who might need to get in touch."

"You know jealousy's a sin" remarked Ewan, character-istically dry, from across the table.

Ruth ignored them all, picked up her mobile phone and held it to her ear: "Hello."

The voice on the other line was muffled and unclear, but she could tell it was a man. At first, she had a wild speculation that it might be Graham, but soon dismissed the idea. The voice was one she'd never heard before. "Is that Ruth?"

"Yes. Who is it, please? Sorry—I'm in the pub, you'll have to speak up."

"I'm glad I've managed to get hold of you" the voice crackled. "I rang you at work but they said you weren't there. Gave me this number." To Ruth's amazement, the person laughed after saying this.

A bit disconcerted, she didn't know how to react, but decided to remain polite for the time being. "Was it some-thing important? Who is it, please?"

"You don't know me…" After that, the voice distorted so much that Ruth couldn't hear what he said next.

"Sorry—I can hardly hear you. I'm going to have to move. Just a minute." She grappled her way past the oth-ers, pushing unwilling knees aside as nicely as she could, and made for the pub's entrance, where the reception was clearer. "There—that's better. What were you saying?"

"You don't know me, see. But I know you."

"Who *is* this?" Ruth was becoming impatient now. The mystery caller had put her to a lot of bother already, and if he was just going to talk in riddles she didn't think she'd waste much more of her time with him. But she was too curious to hang up just yet.

"I seen you on the telly."

"Yes—so have a lot of people. What is it exactly that you want?"

"You get on with policemen, do you? With a policeman?" The voice laughed again, an unexpectedly childlike giggle. Ruth could detect an accent, but she wasn't sure where from. She was trying desperately to place the voice and put a face to it. Perhaps it was a hoax call—she did occasionally get them, although they didn't usually manage to get through Tanya's vetting and on to her mobile number. Or perhaps it was somebody with important information about one of the cases she was covering. She couldn't be sure. It was difficult to tell whether the man was old or young, as his voice was light and high pitched and with a slightly breathy quality.

"What are you driving at?" Ruth asked uncertainly.

"I know him, your fancy man. I seen him only the other day." The voice was getting fainter now.

"Who are you talking about?" Ruth knew, but she wanted him to say the name.

"You know. Treats you good, does he? Tells you he's going to leave his wife? He won't. He's all talk, that one."

Ruth felt a shiver go up her spine, and she was suddenly cold. "Get to the point, whoever you are" she hissed. He had touched on a raw nerve and she hated him for it, whoever he was.

"No offense, miss" the voice appeased, unconvincingly. "Just thought you might want some help is all."

"What sort of help?" snapped Ruth. She almost turned the phone off at that point, but was glad she'd hung on when she heard the next sentence.

"You don't know who done it, do you? You haven't got no clues. Neither of you. But I got information."

Ruth suddenly had an inkling who the caller might be. She remembered Tanya telling her about the unknown caller who'd rung into the program they'd done the week before and hadn't left his number. "What are you referring to?"

"Those murders on your program. The boy in the disco. And the people in the park. Isn't that what us public do? We rings you with information."

"Well, people usually go through my assistant, yes, but—"

"It's you I likes to speak to. Straight to the top, that's me."

Ruth guessed that he was hedging. She wondered if he really did have any useful information, or if this was just an excuse to harass her over Graham. And it was worrying that he knew about Graham. Did that mean he'd been deliberately following her? Why? "What is this information?"

"Can't tell you now. It's private, see." The voice was even quieter. She wondered if he were moving away from the phone, if he were going to hang up again before saying anything worth hearing.

"So what *do* you mean? Do you want to meet me? Is that what you're saying?"

The voice didn't reply, so Ruth continued: "I don't just go around meeting strangers who call me up, you know. Do you think I'm a complete fool? What assurance have I got that you're not just playing with me..." Ruth realized that there was absolute silence on the other line. She shook the phone impatiently and held it to her ear again: "Hello? Hello? Are you still there?"

But nobody responded. The phone had gone dead. The *recharge battery* sign was flashing red, and Ruth realized that her caller had gone. She placed the phone pensively in her jacket pocket and stood for a moment in the pub doorway collecting her thoughts before she rejoined her companions in the pub.

*   *   *

The balding head of Superintendent McGivern was bent over a typewritten paper, as Graham entered his office. "Take a seat, Brunswick" he barked, without looking up.

Graham perched on a black leather armchair and watched the Scotsman's index finger as it underscored each line. The loaded silence of this room was in marked contrast to the rest of the station and to Graham's office in particular. It was five minutes before the superintendent finished his reading. Then, he tipped back his reclining armchair and joined his hands in front of his chest, as if in prayer, fixing on Graham the basilisk stare which had earned him the nickname 'Old Stone Eyes'.

"This report on Booker Mulholland" McGivern began, "The drug squad sent it over to me. I understand he's a suspect of yours, for the Hampstead Heath murder."

"Not a suspect exactly, sir."

"Not a suspect? He was seen on the night." He glanced at the report. "February 25th—8 pm—Mrs. R. Cavendish, 19 East Field Lane."

McGivern's voice had an edge to it like crackling paper, dry and sharp. It always irritated Graham. Today, though, he did his damnedest to keep cool. "Forensic evidence doesn't match up with Mulholland, sir" he said.

"But was he involved? Waiting to give a tip off?"

"It's unlikely, sir. We've questioned him thoroughly and he has a firm alibi from ten thirty onwards. The murder can't have happened before midnight, taking into account the couple's movements after they left the cinema. Booker's girlfriend made a statement that he was with her all the rest of the evening at her flat in Tufnell Park."

McGivern gave a derisive snort. "How reliable is this girl? Drug squad found marijuana at her flat. They're both drug-users, apparently. Mulholland's been charged with drug offenses before, among other things. He's got a list of previous as long as my arm. "

"With all due respect sir, the boy's a petty criminal, not a murderer. His previous convictions are all minor offenses: breaking and entering, T.D.A., shoplifting, drug possession. No record of violence."

McGivern shook his head slowly and narrowed his granite eyes. "I take your point. But you've no other suspects, have you? Or have you?"

"Well..." Graham was disinclined to tell McGivern about his interview with Charlie Hackett. But the superintendent got there before him anyway.

"I heard you had Hackett in here again the other day. Got any evidence against him?"

"There are certain facts—"

"Any *firm* evidence? That might stand up in Court. We don't want to go getting his solicitor rattled again, do we? She made quite a stink for us last time."

Graham ignored these barbed comments and carried on: "The forensic evidence suggests that the killer was short. And there were blonde hairs at the scene of the crime, of both the crimes."

"There's a lot of short people out there, Brunswick. And the hairs could have got there from some other source."

"Also the random nature—" Graham began.

McGivern leaned over to him with a confidential air, piercing him with his cold blue eyes: "Not wanting to get in your way at all" he said sarcastically. "But I've been consulting the files. And I'm not too happy with what I see. Give it a rest with Hackett, we won't beat a confession out of him this time either. I suspect you're pursuing him for your own reasons."

"With respect, sir, I've told you my reasons."

"Not good enough, I'm afraid" snapped the superintendent. "We can't afford to make any more mistakes."

Graham was silent.

McGivern stroked his chin thoughtfully. "I'm inclined to pull in Mulholland on sus."

Graham could feel the skin under his collar beginning to prickle with the effort of remaining polite: "If you'll excuse me sir, we've already questioned him."

"Maybe you weren't thorough enough."

"There's nothing to link Mulholland—"

"He was seen at the location at about the right time. He may know more about this than we realize."

Graham knew that Booker was an easy target, and just a sop to make the police feel they were accomplishing something. It was just this sort of shortsightedness that had made him want to leave the Force. And just at the moment, he wished he had acted on his first impulses. "We're wasting our time with Mulholland. The boy's no murderer, not even an accomplice."

"So you'd know that, would you? Is that a fact or an intuition?" sneered Graham's superior. "Have you got any better leads?"

Graham just shook his head.

"Bring in the lad, Brunswick. Have a little chat—just for my sake. You know something? You're too sensitive." The superintendent rose and walked over to a chart on the wall. "You've got one of these. Looked at it recently?"

Without regarding the Monthly Analysis of Crime Patterns, Graham knew exactly what McGivern was driving at—the red lines indicating crime levels which rose steeply for February and March. Graham wanted to shout with frustration. How did McGivern always manage to corner him with his petty bureaucratic mind?

"I might write that on your Annual Qualification Report, Brunswick. You're too sensitive. Aren't you?"

When Graham returned to his office, he saw the Forensics Report from the disco murder lying on his desk. According to the report, the fingerprints on the knife which had stabbed Mark Winstanley did not match any on Police Records. So it was looking increasingly unlikely that Hackett had anything to do with the disco murder. Maybe Tom was right, they were unconnected and the similarities were sheer coincidence. Graham was beginning to doubt his judgment on everything.

Chapter Four

Ruth had been brought up to appreciate nature and the countryside, and she enjoyed these visits to her father and her childhood home, not just for the pleasure of seeing him, but also for the delight of recapturing the peace and tranquility of a rural setting. She loved the hectic pace of London, but every now and then she needed to refresh herself away from the city.

What she loved most was the opportunity to forget about work for a while. She didn't have to be back at the television station till the following Wednesday, and she had made the decision to leave her briefcase at home and do her research on Tuesday. Thus, she intended to enjoy a few days with nothing to occupy her apart from her favorite form of relaxation, which was browsing through the local papers and enjoying their banal and often bizarre mix of gossip and inconsequential news items.

It was a glorious Spring morning and Rodolfo Ramon sat in the big carved wooden armchair by his desk, his head tilted back in relaxed contemplation, listening to the strains of Verdi's *Faustus* coming from the hi-fi which dominated one corner of the room. He was a tall, solidly-built man, still handsome despite his seventy years, with dark hair only just beginning to change color, a swathe of white on the top of his head making a dramatic contrast to the rest. His fingers were long and elegant, and danced in the air to the music, as if conducting some imaginary orchestra—a habit which his daughter often teased him about.

The room—his study—was small but carefully furnished with dark wooden shelves on which stood innumerable books, well-thumbed but kept in pristine condition. The place was dark but not somber, and French windows led out to an extensive garden full of brightly colored flowers and plants which were in profusion at most times of the year, but had reached their zenith on this unseasonably warm day in late March.

Outside in the hallway, Ruth was having a serious conversation on the telephone.

"It was just so weird" she was saying, "It made me feel really peculiar, to think that he knows about us. How on earth has he found out? D'you think someone could have told him? No, that's paranoid. And anyway, I've told no one at work. But otherwise, he must have actually seen us together."

"I can let you have police protection if you're really worried about him" the voice on the other line replied.

"Oh no—no…"

"Are you sure? I don't want you to be in any danger on my account."

"I don't really think he's dangerous—"

"Oh, come on! Not dangerous? If it really was Hackett who called you, he's dangerous all right. You can take it from me."

"Whether he is or not, I can look after myself. He just gave me the creeps, that's all." Ruth paused, twisting the telephone cord round her finger thoughtfully. "Do you think it *was* Hackett, then?"

"From what you've told me about the voice, I'd be almost definite that it was. When did you say he rang you?"

"Last Wednesday, it would have been, because we'd just broadcast the new program and we were in the pub for our lunch break."

"That doesn't surprise me" Graham said with an air of certainty.

"Oh—why?"

"Well—I'd pulled Charlie in for questioning on Monday. Couldn't pin anything on him and had to release him pretty quickly, but it obviously got his goat. Also—I didn't want to tell you this, but…"

"Tell me."

"I suppose I shouldn't be surprised that he rang you, because he threatened you when I interviewed him on Monday."

"What did he say?" Ruth's voice had a tremble in it.

"Oh, nothing much. I think he was just trying to frighten me. I'd still be happier if one of our lads was watching your house, just in case."

"Good heavens, no" Ruth expostulated. "There's no need. That's obviously what he wants, to put the wind up you and make you afraid for my safety. Don't pander to him. Anyway, I'm always careful. I can look after myself."

"Well just remember that if you need anyone you only have to ask."

"I will."

"I think you're right, though. It's me he's trying to get at. I used to worry that he might go after Gemma. But I think he's too clever to actually do anything to harm either of you. If that was his intention, he wouldn't have bothered to alert us. He's just sussed out my Achilles heel and it amuses him to play with my feelings. I imagine he gets some sort of sick kick out of it."

Ruth pondered for a moment. "Do you think he did have something to do with those murders?"

"I still can't make up my mind. Did he actually give you any information in the end?"

"No. He was cut off—my phone went dead—before he could say anything useful." Ruth could hear the faint strains of her father's music wafting through from the study, and she wondered if he was eavesdropping on her conversation.

Graham continued. "Perhaps he's got nothing useful to say. Anyway, let's stop talking about that psychopath. I can think of better subjects. How are you enjoying seeing your father?"

Ruth smiled. Graham had read her mind. "Oh—same as ever. It's nice to be the little girl again, and be looked after for a change."

"I'm looking forward to seeing you tomorrow."

"I'm looking forward to it, too. Listen, Graham, I'd better go. Pa'll be cross with me for spending so long on the phone." She gave him a perfunctory kiss. "Till tomorrow."

"Till tomorrow. Goodbye."

Back in the study, Rodolfo heard a telephone receiver being banged down. His door opened with a creak, and Ruth appeared, wearing some old black jeans and a t-shirt with an embroidered leopard. "Morning, pa" she announced.

"Up at last?" her father responded, sitting up in his chair. "It's ten o'clock already."

"Already, already" Ruth teased, "You're showing your Jewish ancestry, pa" and perched on the corner of his desk, her legs dangling over the side like a child.

Rodolfo patted her knee. "Want some coffee, my dear?"

"Hmm, sure do" Ruth replied, stretching her arms over her head, and glancing through the windows. "What a fantastic day."

"Who were you telephoning?" Rodolfo asked, as he made his way into the kitchen, with Ruth at his heels. The kitchen was all in dark paneled wood and immaculately tidy.

"Graham."

"Who's Graham?"

He put a large bowl of fresh coffee—French style, without handles—in front of her on the kitchen table, and poured himself one.

"I've told you about him."

"Not that…that police officer?"

"Yes. He's working on a murder case that we're covering for the program. I had some information to give him."

"I'm sure that wasn't the only reason you called him."

"Maybe not" Ruth admitted, sipping her coffee.

"But didn't you say he was married?"

"Yes" she replied simply, knowing that whatever she said would only increase her father's displeasure.

"Oh, Dios!" Rodolfo swore, hitting his forehead with his palm, "Why do you waste your time with him?"

Ruth sighed. "I enjoy his company, and he enjoys mine."

"But there's no future for you—"

"Of course there's a future. People get divorced" she asserted, meaningfully.

"People do, yes, but he's not going to."

"How do you know?"

"I just know" her father blustered, "I can feel this is not a good thing for you. There's no future for you with him. What you need is a good man to marry" he insisted.

There was silence for a moment, as they both sipped their coffee and considered what to say next. It was an old battle between them, and they were like two weary gladiators recovering themselves for the next bout.

Ruth spoke first: "I know you want to protect me, pa. But really, I've got to make my own decisions."

Rodolfo sighed. "Well, I can't stop you."

"No, you can't", she replied with a childish grin.

*   *   *

Ruth could smell Spring on the air—a fresh, clean smell, as if everything had been washed new, a mingling of flowers and newly mown grass and past rainfall that clung in dewdrops on the rapidly burgeoning leaves. It was warm enough to wear just a light jacket and skirt. Ruth walked beside her father, enjoying the playful breeze that blew her hair back from her face like a caressing lover.

She and Rodolfo ambled through the trees of the wood near his home, not speaking much now but just enjoying each other's company. Rodolfo's golden Labrador—Boxer—ran on ahead and every now and again turned to look at his human companions, panting excitedly and wagging his tail as if to egg them on faster. The sun trickled through the trees, making patches of light on the ground. When Ruth stumbled upon a large, weird-looking mushroom in the woods, they stopped to discuss it and debated whether or not to pick it and take it home. Rodolfo said it was perfect as it was and should be left in its natural environment. Ruth had a secret urge to pluck it and even try cooking the thing, but on this occasion—as on many others—she let her father get his way.

Later on that afternoon Ruth put her feet up in the sitting room and took up the local paper that she'd bought the day before at Hull Paragon station on her way to her father's. It was a copy of the *Hull Daily Mail*. She made a habit of keeping up with the national papers as part of her work, so a local paper by contrast was light entertainment. Her father was in the kitchen making dinner: his Spanish heritage meant that he had no illusions about the kitchen being a woman's domain. Ruth, therefore, was enjoying the luxury of unhurried reading.

It was during this relaxed perusal that she came across an article on page 4 under the headline: Body Found in Humber:

The body of a young woman was dredged out of the Humber river at Spurn Point earlier today by a local fisherman John Coxhouse. The corpse was badly decomposed and post mortem experts believe it had been lying in the water for several weeks before a freak tide washed it ashore. The body has now been placed in cold preservation at Hull Public Mortuary pending identification.

North Humberside police believe the body may be that of Mrs. Susanne Martin, 23, of Whitby, North Yorkshire. Mrs. Martin disappeared from her home last December in suspicious circumstances. The bodies of Jeffrey Steven Martin, her husband, and Tracey Nightingale, a young girl who was working for the Martin's, were found on Boxing Day last year, in the Martins' bedroom. Both had been shot at close range with a .22 caliber automatic pistol licensed in Mr. Martin's name. Police have so far described the case as homicide by person or persons unknown, and were trying to locate Mrs. Martin to help them with their enquiries.

North Humberside police are still trying to trace any relatives or acquaintances of Susanne Martin, who may be able to make a positive identification of the body.

Ruth's father came into the living room clutching two glasses of sherry. He had on the plastic chef's apron that Ruth had given him for Christmas, and his face was slightly red from the heat of the kitchen.

"Here you are" he said, placing one of the glasses on the occasional table at Ruth's side.

"How awful" Ruth muttered, without looking up.

"What—the sherry?" Rodolfo quipped.

"No, this." Ruth pointed at the paper. "An article I'm reading."

"You shouldn't read papers. Full of horror stories, doom and gloom." He turned over the record that had just finished. "Life should be for beautiful things, as much as possible."

"You're a hedonist, pa" mused Ruth, swallowing her sherry. "But isn't it a normal human urge to read horror stories, because we're glad it's not happening to us?"

"I must not be normal, then. I would never have such an urge."

Ruth smiled at him. "Well, we can't all be like you. Most people would be fascinated by this story, I mean, it's really gripping stuff. I'll bet you it gets made into a movie one day."

Intrigued despite his skepticism, Rodolfo glanced at the article, skimming through it quickly. "So there are some bodies in a bedroom. What's so interesting about it?"

"She killed them, didn't she."

"Who?"

"The woman. The one they're looking for."

"Susanne Martin?"

"Yes, it's obvious."

"She's dead apparently, anyway."

"Well, maybe she committed suicide because she couldn't live with the guilt. Yes, she probably did."

"How do you know she killed them?"

"In the bedroom of her house, there's her husband and a young girl. What do you think? Her husband was having an affair, of course, and she discovered them and bam!"

"You're making a lot of assumptions."

"The obvious ones. I think it's a shame, though."

"Why a shame?"

"Look at that picture. She was just a young thing, and really pretty too. What a waste of her life."

"If she killed someone, I don't feel sorry for her."

"She might have had good reason."

"There's never a good reason for killing. Except in war."

"There you are, you've thought of a 'good' reason. How come men are encouraged to kill, honored for killing in a war, but a woman who's been wronged by a man—"

"You don't know she was 'wronged'—"

"No, nobody knows or bothers to try and find out, but I bet she was wronged, I bet he messed around with other women all the time and she just couldn't take any more. But because she killed in a moment of passion she could no longer restrain, she's branded a murderess and put away in jail for life!"

"What does it matter, she's dead anyway?"

"It's the principle though, pa."

"Oh, you and your principles." Rodolfo always tired of arguing before his daughter did, and he rose now to attend to the dinner. At the door, though, he gave a parting shot: "What about you, now? If your precious…Graham's wife found out about you and decided to shoot you, would *she* be in the right?"

"That's…different…"

"Why is it different?"

Ruth was flustered. "It's not just an affair we're having, it's a meaningful relationship, and it's not something Graham does all the time. And he's not cruel to his wife…"

"You're just making excuses. It's the same thing. Marriage is marriage. And murder is murder. Now let's stop all this talking and eat. I'm hungry."

Chapter Five

▼

A small heap of soot blew through the cracked window and landed on the inside sill, the smell almost dispersing the strong stench of urine in the room. Charlie pulled his overcoat more tightly around his shoulders and kept his head bent over his work. He was enjoying himself too much to feel the cold. He stamped his almost numbed feet a little on the bare floorboards, to get the circulation going in them again. His stubby yellow-stained fingers wobbled so much as he held the scissors that he frequently slipped up over a letter and had to re-cut it. But he was patience itself, the corners of his mouth working in concentration and his ears deaf to the sounds around him—traffic in the street, the wail of an ambulance siren in the distance, a baby yelling next door.

He'd picked up the newspapers from empty seats in the tube, while riding round and round the Circle Line that morning. They were grubby and dog-eared but perfectly good for his purposes. The main problem was eking out the small amount of tape he possessed so that he could stick down all the letters on to the paper. He was proud of the scissors, new and sharp-sided, which he'd shoplifted from Smith's while the counter girl wasn't looking.

He paused for a moment and studied his handiwork, then put the scissors down and clapped his hands together a few times to warm them up. This set him off on a coughing fit which lasted several seconds and shook his whole body. He would have given anything for a ciga-rette. Or a whiskey.

The page was shaping up nicely. On one side, *To Graham Brunswick* in letters of varying sizes, and on the other he'd already completed the first two words of his sentence: *Her face*

He smiled. Despite the cold and the emptiness in his stomach, he was happy.

*   *   *

Graham had to wait a while after pressing the door bell and, hearing raised voices, he glanced across the street. A mini cab driver appeared to be arguing with a garage attendant, claiming that he'd been given leaded petrol by mistake. Graham felt glad that he wasn't on duty.

Two or three locks were pulled back before the hefty door opened to reveal Ruth in a pink silk shirt and match-ing trousers. Her ebony hair was piled into a chignon, leaving several artfully casual tendrils to frame her face. At the sight of Graham she smiled, kissing him firmly on both cheeks, then invited him to follow her up the stairs.

He visited Ruth at home often, and every time he was enchanted afresh by her well-structured chaos. Each wall was crammed with pictures vying for attention: 'art' posters from exhibitions she had seen; photographs of

Marilyn Monroe and Dustin Hoffman; postcards from abroad; her degree certificate in a clear glass frame. It would take days to look at everything, with at least one day devoted to the newspaper cuttings and cartoons covering the walls of her tiny bathroom.

A melting pot of sounds fell upon Graham's ears, a combination of soothing Chopin on the compact disc player in the living room, loud-voiced newscasting from the radio in the kitchen and a children's serial from the television in the bedroom.

"Drink?" offered Ruth, taking Graham's overcoat and throwing it over an armchair.

"I'd love a scotch, thanks. I brought you some wine, by the way."

Ruth motioned him to sit on the rolled up futon and carried his bottle into the kitchen, an annex of the living room separated only by a half-partition. Graham took a look through the magazines and newspapers which littered the mosaic top of her coffee table. Several back issues of *Cosmopolitan*, last Sunday's *Observer* color supplement and a *Hull Daily Mail* from the previous day, dated Saturday March 21st.

"That's a rag" said Ruth as she handed Graham his drink, seeing that he'd picked up the newspaper. "But there's an interesting story on page 4", indicating the one she meant to Graham, who glanced at the headline. "Although that's another story in itself. Pa and I had a bit of a barney about it—you wouldn't credit it, would you, arguing about a story in a newspaper? But that's us. Both trying to set the world to rights. Both as stubborn as mules." She wandered back into the kitchen.

Graham started reading the article, while he shouted to Ruth over the drone of music. "Is he still wanting you to give up your job?"

"Oh yes, of course" she shouted back, as she took the dinner out of the oven. "I've told him it's not the money. But he doesn't understand. If he had his way, I'd be on the first train back up North and married to some nice rich accountant…Damn, I forgot to put the mats out."

"Can I help?" Graham volunteered, hoping she'd refuse.

"No, no, won't be a minute." She came back into the living room and started taking some ethnic-looking raffia table mats out of a drawer in the sideboard.

"What was it you argued about?" Graham asked. He wanted to know what would be important enough to Ruth to make her lose her cool.

"What? Oh—that story. Well, this woman that they're looking for—what's her name? Sylvia Martin or something?"

"Susanne Martin" replied Graham, looking up the appropriate section.

"Yes, well it seems pretty obvious that she killed her husband and the girl with him…"

"Tracey Nightingale. Hmm" mused Graham, "I wonder if she sings."

"Yes, so I said to Pa that she might have had good reason to kill him."

"Good reason?" responded Graham, horrified.

There was a brief pause in the conversation while Ruth brought through the steaming hot casserole dish and placed it on the table. "It's this whole double standard thing between men and women."

"What's that got to do with it?" said Graham, coming to the table and pulling up a chair.

"We had this case on the program where a man had killed his wife for nagging him—just nagging him, mind, no physical abuse—and he got off with a two year suspended sentence, because he'd acted on the spur of the moment, so the murder wasn't premeditated. Are you hungry?" She hovered over his plate with the serving spoon.

"Hmm, certainly am. It smells good" Graham replied with false gusto. It was the usual brown mess that passed for vegetarian casserole, but Graham was hungry.

Ruth continued talking as she heaped his plate. "Now, imagine if that had been a woman convicted of murdering her husband."

"I imagine it would have been exactly the same."

"No it wouldn't" Ruth countered, as she heaped her own plate, and Graham tucked in to his food. "Because women don't act on the spur of the moment. They might put up with years of abuse, including physical violence, threats to their children, before they can gather the courage to strike back. Women's anger is slow-acting and deep, men's is quick and impulsive. But they're both just as valid as reasons for homicide. There shouldn't be any discrimination."

"Murder is murder in my book. You take another life, you should be punished for it."

Ruth suddenly smiled at him. "You're just like my pa, you know. Maybe that's why I like you." She turned her face away, a little embarrassed. "Anyway, why am I arguing with a policeman?" Graham smiled and there was silence for a few moments, as they both concentrated on eating.

Graham felt pleasantly mellow. The scotch was going to his head. Relaxing him at last. He certainly needed relaxing. These days he was always so tense. He liked Ruth's company, even if he did always feel that he had to do mental press-ups before visiting her. She was like a man—he didn't have to hide things from her or talk about "feminine" things, like he did with Pat.

"Are there any times when you think murder isn't acceptable?"

"Of course!" She looked up at him, then realized he was ribbing her. "Of course there are, you idiot!" she said lightly. "Like the murders you're working on at the moment, they're not acceptable—"

"Even if they were done by a woman?" teased Graham.

"Who ever did them. There weren't any reasons. Not as far as I know, anyway. By the way, have you got any leads on that?"

Graham was suddenly serious. "To be quite honest, I'm very confused by this case. I thought at first there were connections between the two murders. But now I'm not so sure. I've already told you about Hackett's threats, of course. They may mean something, and they may not—the man's a joker, he likes playing with people and winding them up. And he knows very well how to wind *me* up."

"Plus he'd have every reason to want to, since you were the one who almost put him away."

"Exactly" agreed Graham.

"I think there *are* some connections, though" Ruth asserted.

Graham looked up, surprised. "You do?"

"They were both couples. And the girls looked the same."

"The second girl wasn't attacked—"

"Only because she was locked in the toilet, the killer probably heard someone coming and ran away before he could get to her."

"That's a very tenuous link, Ruth."

She persisted. "I was looking at the photographs of Jenny Hunt and Annette Payne, and I was struck by how similar they were. Same hair color, same age, roughly the same build and height. That might not be a coincidence."

Graham chuckled. "You're in the wrong job."

"You could be right", she said meaningfully. Ruth started to clear away the plates. "Finished? Did you like it?"

"Delicious" asserted Graham, smacking his lips.

"Really? I made it myself, from a packet." She laughed, an incongruously girlish giggle. "No, actually, there's a brilliant health food shop just around the corner and they do these packet sauces with no preservatives or additives, so I keep a stock of them in the house for special occasions."

"And why not?" He wished he hadn't said that. He knew Ruth would object to his patronizing tone.

She answered somewhat defensively. "I literally do not have one minute to prepare meals from scratch. I mean, it's OK if you're not working and housework is your main function in life—" She broke off, and took the plates back into the kitchen, adding them to the pile in the sink. "Where does Pat think you are tonight?" she asked, as she came back with the bowls of ice-cream.

Graham had hoped to avoid this topic. He attempted to treat her question lightly. "Oh, at the police station, I expect. She's used to my working late."

"It's a wonder she believes all those lies you tell her. You must be awfully convincing." Ruth's tone was sad rather than angry. She remembered what her father had said: *If he lies to her, he can lie to you. People get divorced, but he's not going to.* Perhaps there was some truth in what he said. Parents often have an uncanny instinct about what's good or bad for their children.

Graham started to feel uncomfortable. He looked at his ice-cream, but didn't feel like eating it. He hadn't come here to thrash out his relationship with his wife. What was the point of having the same argument again and again? He looked at Ruth trying to ascertain her mood, but her eyes were averted. "Look, Pat and I get along fine. She doesn't know everything about me but I don't know everything about her either. That's often the way marriage works."

"So it *does* work, does it?" Ruth hated the little whine her voice got in it when she started to feel emotional. She looked steadily at Graham, determined to maintain her composure.

But Graham hesitated too long before replying.

"I thought you told me that things weren't working between you. It was a slight variation on the 'my wife doesn't understand me' theme." She was glaring at him. The words had come out of her mouth before she could stop them. Well, she was on a roller coaster ride and she had to just go where it took her. She had to know how Graham really felt.

"Things aren't perfect between us, of course. Like I said, we married young, we're not particularly compatible, we don't have much in common—"

"Except Gemma" interrupted Ruth.

Graham wondered if he could detect envy in her voice. But why? She always said she didn't want children. "Yes, all right, I suppose we've stayed together for Gemma, not that it's ever been spoken about, but…Gemma's very important to me, and I've always thought divorce is damaging for children. I mean, for God's sake, look at your parents, you told me that their divorce was the most traumatic thing—"

"I was eleven at the time. So it was slightly different. Also, I got over it, and emerged, I think, relatively unscathed."

Her voice was so cold that Graham knew he would have to placate her, in order to salvage the rest of their pleasant evening. "You're absolutely right. But then, you're a very strong person, Ruth."

She said nothing but he could tell by her silence that his remark had flattered her. He continued. "Pat's not as strong as you are. She might fall apart if I left her now."

"She's probably stronger than you think" countered Ruth, thinking of how she would feel, "She'd probably be grateful if you were honest with her."

"It's not that easy. She's stuck by me through thick and thin for twenty odd years, I can't just walk out. We may not have the romance of the century but I've no right to hurt the woman, have I?"

"But you *are* hurting her, Graham. And you're hurting me as well." Ruth didn't want to be selfish. She felt pity for the woman she'd never met, not rivalry. But it wasn't fair to be fobbed off with these sort of excuses. Graham had to choose between them, for both their sakes. She put down her spoon, leaving her ice-cream untouched, and moved over to the futon.

"Oh come on, I'm not hurting you. You knew what you were getting into." Graham rose and joined her, putting an arm round her tense shoulders. "You're very important to me, Ruthy, you know that. I wish I could do something to make us all happy. But it's not as simple as that. I don't know what to do for the best. Now's the worst time I could choose to leave Pat. She hasn't recovered from Gemma leaving home and she needs to find other interests. Maybe in a few months…"

"So you're saying that if and when she's strong enough to bear it, you will consider divorce?"

Graham searched his mind desperately, trying to come up with a non-committal answer. "Possibly" he replied at last.

"No!" Ruth declared, breaking free of him and standing up. "Possibly isn't good enough, Graham. Why should I hang around waiting for you to 'possibly' divorce your wife? You've been seeing me for nine months. You ought to know your own mind by now."

"I *do* know my own mind" Graham said, moving close to Ruth and drawing her gently to him, "I've told you how I feel." As he kissed her, he could feel her desire for him vying with her anger, and he thought he knew which would win eventually. "All right. I will tell her. When I think she's strong enough. You're right. She deserves to know the truth."

Ruth didn't believe him, but she gave in to him, seduced by his strong arms and warm male body. She knew she would hate herself in the cold light of day, for succumbing to his charms. But just now, she couldn't resist.

*   *   *

She took the knife in her hand. She thrust the blade into his chest. It sank easily into the soft flesh, as if slicing a peach, but the juice of this fruit was vermilion red. She opened her hand, releasing the knife, and stepped back to watch the weapon continue its work. *Slash said the knife as it struck for joy, slash I'll take the life of the boy.* Scarlet paint oozed from the waxy figure and dripped down his chest, covering his white shirt. His mouth gaped and she waited for a shrill scream, but instead he did something far more horrible. He was not screaming but laughing, laughing at her, blood red tears falling from his eyes in amusement and rolling down his puffy cheeks. His legs writhed in a paroxysm of hilarity, he was not dying but rising, two more jerks and he would be upon her. She turned and ran.

But as she looked down at her running feet, she saw a cold stone floor peppered with spots of blood and strands of hair, tufts of black hair.

She ran back into the noise. The floor pulsated with the beat of drums thumping the ground. She was surrounded by people, whirling like dervishes, surrendering to the ground's heart beat, every one screaming. They knew. She had killed Jeff. First she shot him with a pistol, then she stabbed him in the heart with a kitchen knife.

She ran again.

She came to white ground beneath bare trees on a moonless night. When she panted, her breath formed a frozen cloud that hovered in the air. The sound of her steps was muffled by the softly fallen snow. Ahead in the darkness, she could see two figures preceding her and she followed like a stalking shadow. As they passed beneath a street lamp, their hair was lit up and she knew then who they were. Jeff and Tracey walking arm in arm.

She could hear their low patter of laughter. She knew why they laughed.

Through the tattered trees they wove a tortuous path, trying to throw her off the trail. But she, secreting herself in hollows, a few paces behind, was cleverer than they thought. Before a giant arching tree they stopped and held each other in a long embrace and she seized the fallen branch in her icy fingers.

Crunch said the branch as it whirled through the air and smashed his head like an eggshell cracked into a bowl. *Crack* it said, resounding against the bone of Tracey's skull. Now they were done for…

Susanne woke up.

She was shivering again, though fully clothed, and sitting upright in bed with the covers flung aside. Another bad dream. The cold gave her nightmares.

She retrieved her hot-water bottle from the bottom of the bed and took it across the hall to the bathroom to refill it with steaming tap water. While there, she heard the floorboards creak outside and a soft rap. Could it be her door?

She peered out into the hall. A girl was standing with her back to Susanne, knocking at the door of the room next to hers. She had black curling hair. Susanne knew at once who it was. She pulled her head back into the bathroom like a tortoise retreating under its shell. Her heart had begun to thump.

So Tracey had followed her here after all. How had she managed to find her? Jeff had obviously taken the room next door to Susanne's and they were arranging a lover's tryst, to taunt her. She heard low voices and a stifled laugh.

She knew that laugh all right. She heard the door open and shut with a click.

She took the hot-water bottle and crossed the hall to her room, noticing a light under their door. The light in the hall, on a timer switch, snapped off just as she entered her room.

A paraffin lamp stood on her mantelpiece with a large ornamental globe. Mrs. Kurowski had put it there in January during the threatened miner's strike, in case the electricity ran out, but it had never been used. Susanne unscrewed the brass top which held the wicks and tipped the paraffin out into a plastic beaker. It was pale pink and smelt musky like an exotic perfume. Mrs. Kurowski had left a box of Swan matches by the lamp and Susanne slipped them into the pocket of her skirt. She extinguished the light in her room and waited in the darkness.

She sat inert and listened to the sounds of Jeff and Tracey in the next room. Muted voices—a low male rumble and a light female refrain—the squeak of bedsprings, a hint of laughter. She spoke to her fear, begging it to leave her. She needed all her strength now.

Taking the beaker, she padded into the hall. There was no light under their door and as she opened it silently and crept inside, all she could distinguish in the gloom was a heaving shape on the bed. Her heart constricted as she heard a groan of pain, a moan of pleasure. She had to work quickly and without thinking.

The coverlet twitched as if alive, and she sprinkled paraffin on to the edge and dropped the beaker on to the carpet with trembling fingers. She drew the matches from her pocket and struck one, watching the tiny yellow flame lick the soaked coverlet and steadily grow.

She ran from the room, locking the door behind her with the key that sat ready in its hole. She heard startled cries become wails for help, then sounds of coughing, spluttering and rattling of the door handle. She couldn't bear to listen any longer. Throwing on her green duffel coat, she grabbed her handbag and raced down the dark stairs.

Susanne fled down the deserted street. Glancing back at the house for an instant, she saw the top right hand window lit up like an orange beacon and she thought how beautiful the flames looked, reaching from the building, like fingers of fire, into the night air. She ran, just as she had always run in her dreams, only this time, she thought, the nightmare would never end.

Chapter Six

Pat was contentedly snoring, when the urgent sound of a telephone bell yanked her into wakefulness. She fumbled for the bedside extension, her heart jumping, hoping it would be Graham. "Hello. 2938".

"Oh hello Pat, Tom here. Sorry to call so late. Didn't wake you up, did I?"

"Oh…no, not really."

"Could I have a word with Graham, love? I'm afraid he's going to lose his beauty sleep tonight."

"Graham? But…he's not here. I thought he was with you. Isn't he at the police station?"

"Er…well, not at the moment. What time did he leave home?"

"About seven o'clock. He said he had something important to do at the station. Haven't you seen him?"

"No, I only just got here myself, as a matter of fact. Look, don't worry, I imagine there's been some breakdown of communication our end, he probably set off before I got here or something. Maybe he's already on his way to the job. I just got called out about quarter of an hour ago, you see. There's been an attempted homicide over in Westbourne Grove—"

"Oh dear, do you think Graham—?"

"No, no, look, not to worry, love. There's obviously been a cock-up—excuse my French—but we've got this new lad on night duty and he's not too sure of the ropes yet. Shall I get Graham to ring you as soon as he's free?"

"Yes, yes, if you would, I'd be grateful."

"Certainly, can do. Meanwhile, you get back to bed now and I'll speak to you soon, O.K.?"

She heard the dialing tone as Tom hung up, and replaced the receiver slowly. For the first time in her marriage, she felt betrayed.

*   *   *

"Hello mate."

"Tom—how did you know I was here?"

"Process of elimination, I'm afraid. I rang your home first."

"You what? Oh Christ…"

"Well, if you will go sneaking off—"

"Yes, yes, all right. What are you ringing about?"

"We've got a call out to Westbourne Grove. There's been a fire in a bed and breakfast and it looks deliberate."

"Right. Any casualties?"

"A couple of people were taken to St. Mary's Paddington with carbon monoxide poisoning. Nobody else hurt, fortunately."

"Is the fire out? Did it spread at all?"

"No, it was very easily contained, in fact only one room in the house was damaged, as far as I can gather."

"Anderson's lot must have been quick off the mark."

"Well yes, I think the fire brigade were pretty efficient, but the main thing is, the fire started in one of the top rooms and then somebody locked the door from the outside and took away the key."

"What, with people in there?"

"Looks like it."

"Hmm, that does sound pretty deliberate. I'll grab my things and get down there now. Where is it?"

"Arundel Villas, Tooley Street. I'll meet you there."

"Fine. Oh, and Tom?"

"Yeah?"

"You didn't mention anything to Pat did you, about where I was?"

"Listen mate, if you want to make a prat of yourself, it's none of my business. But I don't like covering for you. Next time, let me know will you?"

*   *   *

She walked quickly, weightlessly, her body seeming to hover above her feet as they skated over the ground. She had heard somewhere recently—maybe the snatch of a radio program—about a man who had died and come back to life. It was like going through a long, dark tunnel, he said, then suddenly experiencing a dazzlingly bright light. Susanne expected at any moment to be hurled into that tunnel, almost hoped, in fact, for some strong irresistible force to take charge of her actions as if she were a puppet.

But instead she was walking, still walking. Her feet wouldn't stop. There was nothing else she could do. An urgent need impelled her forward. Some time ago, she had wanted to speak to someone about something. She hoped to remember why later on. Meanwhile, her blistered feet walked, half-ran, dragging her body with them like an unwilling accomplice.

All the time, her head was aswirl with images, crowding in on one another. Herself in a white night dress clutching a gun—a room in a blaze of light—two bodies, naked—long black hair curling on a pillow. A couple arm in arm walking in the snow—laughing, jeering at her, holding a gloved hand to their mouths to stifle a snigger. A baby, the body of the child that was hers, born faceless, nameless, dead. The pair of them dancing, holding each other close, dancing in a room, dancing on the bed, always laughing, as if they knew, as if they'd planned it, indestructible…

      *   *   *

The room had been burnt to a skeleton, leaving only a pile of black mattress springs and the remains of a paraffin heater in the corner. Graham tried to open the small window which overlooked the communal gardens and found that it had been locked with a key. No wonder the fire had worked so quickly. Noticing a misshapen lump of plastic on the floor, he picked it up and studied it but couldn't tell what it had been.

Noxious fumes still clung to the air making him want to retch, and he left as soon as he could. In the passage, he nodded to Tyson, who was fingerprinting the door handle. "How are you getting on?"

"Not much luck, I'm afraid. Too many prints on the damn thing and most of them are smudged."

Downstairs in the dining room, four hotel guests were supping tea in gloomy silence and refusing to look at each other. Tom stood warming his back by the gas fire, smoking a cigarette. "Do you know where that Kurowski woman's got to?" Graham asked him.

"The landlady? She could be in the kitchen making tea. Then again, Tyson might have got so sick of her nattering that he's gagged her and stuck her in the broom closet."

One of the guests tittered. Graham left the room. Tom could be irritating in his sarcastic moods.

Mrs. Kurowski looked up as Graham entered the kitchen, then continued pouring hot water into a huge aluminum tea pot, which she covered with a knitted cozy. "You wanna cuppa tea or something, Officer? It's just fresh and made" she said, beaming.

"No, not at the moment thanks. Would you mind if I asked you a few questions?"

"Yeah, sure, you go right ahead. I got nothing to hide. Why don't you take a seat."

Graham perched on the edge of the large central table and took his notebook from his pocket. "First of all, do you think anyone could have come into the hotel this evening without your knowledge?"

"No, no way. See, I let everybody in myself. Don't believe in front door keys, too dangerous. This area, somebody might get robbed, their keys stolen. Then what do I do? I have to change the lock four times a week! No, forget it. I'm always here or someone of my family. We let in the guests when they ring the doorbell."

"So how many people do you have staying here at the moment?"

"Well, first there's Mr. Dowdeswell in Room 6, he comes here from time to time on business, he travels about a lot, you know—"

"That was the man who was taken to hospital?"

"Yes, and that girl with him, Polly Rendek, she doesn't stay here, but sometimes she comes by to visit. I don't usually let guests have visitors in their rooms, but Mr. Dowdeswell, I known him a while, he's a special case." She leaned over the table to Graham for this last sentence and he got a strong whiff of garlic. Then she rose and started to pour herself a cup of tea. "Anyway, I seen this girl a few times before, I know she works at the Foxes and Hounds around the corner. But you know, I hope they don't say nothing about all this in the papers. Mr. Dowdeswell, he's got a wife in Manchester, I don't want him to get into no trouble."

"I'm sure it'll be all right. Does Mr. Dowdeswell have any other…acquaintances here in London?"

"Oh no, not that I know of anyway."

"Business partners? Drinking companions? Anyone at the hotel?"

Mrs. Kurowski shook her head and smiled eagerly. Graham had a feeling she reveled in the drama. "Right then. What about the people in the dining room?"

"So, there's Mr. and Mrs. Al-Awadhi, they're over here for a month to visit their daughter who just married an English boy. Very nice couple but they don't speak very well English. Then there's Mr. Higton, he's been here six months or so waiting for the council to rehouse him, he got made redundant about a year ago, used to work for London Transport. And a Chinese girl, I think she studies

English, can't never pronounce her name, she's been here since last Tuesday."

"You certainly find out a lot about your guests" Graham said smiling. "So that's the lot, is it?"

"No, but I forgot one" she exclaimed, tapping her forehead with her right hand. "Tracey Nightingale, the little girl in Room 7. I forgot all about her, 'cos she gone out."

Graham jotted down the name. Something indefinable was bothering him, but he pushed it to the back of his mind and continued with the questioning. "So what time did Miss Nightingale leave?"

"I don't know, this evening sometime…oh yes, I remember, I was having a little nap in the front room and I heard her running down the stairs, it woke me up. So then I look out the window and I seen her leaving the house. And that was just before I first notice the fire, because I went into the kitchen to make tea and then it was I heard the noise upstairs, the screaming and shouting. "

"I see. And which room does Miss Nightingale occupy?"

"Room number 7, it's at the top of the house, next door to number 6 that got burned."

*   *   *

It was always the same. When Ruth couldn't sleep, there was nothing for it but to get up and do something. She'd tried listlessly flicking through the pages of *Cosmopolitan*, but she couldn't concentrate on reading. Her mind kept coming back to the scene that night with Graham, and his abrupt departure at around midnight. It was two hours later and she was still wide awake, with a raging headache that didn't respond to any amount of patient massage and soothing music from her "Peaceful Islands" tape.

She took a pen and began to doodle on the back of a circular letter, in an effort to shape her thoughts. The droning notes surged upwards towards their crescendo, as the faces she had drawn glared back at her.

All of a sudden, the idea sprang into her mind, perfectly formed, as if it had been there all along. The time for action had come. She had waited long enough for Graham to make a decision. It was up to her now.

She still had two days of her leave left. She'd told Maggie she was visiting her father until Tuesday, but she'd come home early in order to spend the evening with Graham. Tomorrow was Monday. So she had plenty of time to go and see Pat. She would get up early, clear up the mess from last night and have a wash, make a list of what she wanted to say and prepare herself mentally. Then, sometime in the afternoon perhaps, she would drive to St. John's Wood—to the address on the back of a little card she'd never been able to throw away, that had come with some flowers from Graham after their first date—and meet his wife.

*   *   *

The door of Room 7 was unlocked. Graham glanced over a single bed with a faded pink cover, a dull brown wardrobe with a cracked full-length mirror, a chest of drawers covered with chipped white paint and an armchair with ragged upholstery. The floorboards were barely covered by a square strip of worn carpet. Striped brown and olive curtains hung at the window. A white linen runner lay on top of the chest of drawers, on which was placed an unused glass ashtray, a bottle of baby shampoo, two 10p coins, a near empty bottle of pills with no label and a tortoiseshell comb. In the top drawer—which was open—lay a few female underclothes and what looked like hand-knitted baby clothes. The other two drawers were empty. A beige toweling dressing gown hung on the door hook, underneath which lay a pair of fluffy pink women's slippers. In the wardrobe hung a blue flowered dress, a tartan skirt and a white cotton shirt, plus a folded blue raincoat and a large red jumper which had been thrust into the back corner. The room had the unlived-in quality of a passing visitor, yet Mrs. Kurowski said the girl had been staying there since Christmas.

"What do you know about Miss Nightingale?"

Mrs. Kurowski frowned and paused for the first time that evening. "Difficult to talk to her. There's always something strange about that one."

"What do you mean exactly?"

"Well, for a start, why does she come here at Christmas time when most folks is with their family? That I think is strange. But I'm not one to pry, you know. But I likes to have a little chat with the people here sometimes, specially if they're here for a while…but that one, a dark horse, couldn't get nothing out of her. No idea where she's from, though I know it ain't round here. Dunno what she does for a living, what she does all the day. Seems to me like she just walks the streets or something. And then she's so quiet, so timid like a little mouse, and looks so pale and…" She searched for the word but gave up in confusion with a wave of her hand. "I couldn't help myself to worry about her. Not specially after the baby and all…"

"Baby?" Graham, in spite of himself, was finding the subject of the woman's monologue more and more intriguing.

The woman suddenly seemed hesitant. Her hand flew up to her mouth, as if she'd revealed something unwillingly.

"Baby?" repeated Graham. "Perhaps you could tell me more about that, please."

Mrs. Kurowski breathed in and crossed her arms in front of her chest. "When she comes here she's pregnant. I can see that. She not showing much, but I know this here not just the stomach, you know what I mean?" She indicated a protruding belly with her hands. "I'm used to these things you know, I got five grandchildren myself. Anyway, I ask her if she wants to see my doctor—he's a good man, has his surgery just up the road here. But she say, no, she don't like doctors. So I thinks, well, it's none of my business, I just the landlady, I keep my nose out of her affairs. You know, I try to help, but if she no want my help what can I do?" She shrugged and opened her hands, holding them palms upwards. "I try to get her to go to the hospital but she wasn't having none of that, too scared she says, scared of doctors, hospitals, all that."

"Did she have the baby, then?" asked Graham.

Mrs. Kurowski sighed and looked down. "Tracey was in pain, like labor pains. And I ask my cousin Irena to come, who is midwife. But it was too soon—the baby born dead—how do you say…?"

"A miscarriage?" suggested Graham, who knew little about such things.

"Ya, that's the word Irena said. She said Tracey not pregnant for long enough, only twenty weeks or something, and so impossible to save the baby. And once it has gone, there is nothing we can do. I felt sorry for the girl, but she never talks about it. Acts like she forgot the whole thing right away. But every day she looks more and more pale, like a little fragile flower or bird or something that's just gonna fade away. Walks around like on tiptoe."

The woman paused for breath. Graham stared at his note pad for a moment, deep in thought. "Do you know where Miss Nightingale was going this evening, when she left the hotel?"

"Oh no, no, she keeps herself for herself always, I don't know." Mrs. Kurowski shook her head sadly.

"Wasn't it rather unusual for her to go out so late?"

"Well, yes…maybe…I guess so."

"What would you say her manner was, as she was leaving?"

"What do you mean, manner?"

"Well, did she seem happy, depressed, excited—?"

"Excited, yes I would say she was a little excited, she seemed in a hurry over something."

Graham sighed slightly. "Did you not think to ask her where she was going, in a hurry, late at night, when it was unusual for her to be leaving the hotel?"

"Now one minute, I had other things to think about at that time. So maybe I wondered for a little where Tracey was going, then I heard these screams and noises from upstairs and I ran up there and found the door locked and saw smoke puffing out from the room and I think my hotel is going to burn to the ground! Then comes the fire brigade and I have to wake up the other guests, I had things to think about!" Her face had flushed dark red with indignation.

"There's no need to take offense, Mrs. Kurowski" Graham said quietly, "I'm just trying to find out what happened."

"Yes, O.K., O.K. I'm a little upset over all this business. It's a difficult thing running the house on my own, and now this. I don't need these problems."

"Yes of course, I can understand that. Could I just ask one last thing? We'll need to have a physical description of the girl. It may help us to locate her, if she decides not to return to the hotel."

"But she left all her things—"

"Nevertheless."

"Well, she's about my height, that is quite short you know, I don't know how much to say in inches. But then she's much skinnier than me, she don't eat so much! Also she has long yellow hair, light eyes, very pale—I told you that. What else should I say?"

"Thank you, that'll do. You've been a great help, Mrs. Kurowski."

CHAPTER SEVEN

She was trudging down a street, somewhere in London, her hands in the pockets of her duffel coat, her head down, watching her feet in the muddied sneakers. Some joker had got inside her mind and rearranged all her memories into pieces of a jigsaw puzzle that wouldn't fit together again. Now he was laughing at her, as she struggled to remember how she'd come to be in this place.

But there's one memory you can't hide from me—she said to him defiantly, lifting her head into the piercing wind— *I still know who I am. I'm Susanne Gray, aren't I?*

Why did you call yourself Tracey Nightingale then?—he asked with a smirk.

Because I didn't want to be me any more—she replied— *I'd had enough of me.*

She stepped on a loose paving stone and splattered her ankle with cold rainwater. The pavements here were so filthy, litter lay everywhere. The people that walked by her—their faces gray and sullen—looked at her as if she were more litter on the ground.

She saw a girl on a corner. The girl sold red tomatoes which matched her florid face with its fierce little eyes.

Her ruddy hands in the fingerless gloves grubbed about in a cardboard box, snatched handfuls of the pulpy fruit and piled them into brown paper bags which tore with the weight.

"Want anything, love?"

The question startled Susanne, and she shook her head, wide-eyed.

An old woman spoke behind her, straining for the tomatoes on the stall, her hand already outstretched. "Pound of the salads, please. Could you give me ripe ones, I want to eat them today."

At the next stall a man sold bananas. He held up a yellow pistol and pointed it at Susanne, intoning "Two pounds for sixty pence bananas, fresh today, come on now."

Further along the street, a blind man played the harmonium. He had a white stick slung over his shoulder and he seemed to stare at Susanne through his sightless eyes, squeezing the instrument in and out, suffocating it with his strong fingers. An arm reached out to her and offered her a silver metallic balloon. She pushed the arm away and stumbled on.

*   *   *

A ray of late afternoon sun pierced the net curtains and fell on to a heavy wooden table in the center of the kitchen, around which two middle-aged women sat. One of the women poured treacly black coffee in a thick stream from an espresso machine into a little cup. "You want Grappa?"

"Oh Elisabetta, you're too good to me, you know that?" Marte Kurowski laughed gleefully and shook her hands so that her bracelets jangled on her swarthy arms.

"The sun in your eyes?" Elisabetta pulled one of the heavy woolen curtains halfway across the window, then sat down heavily in a chair opposite her companion. "So tell me more, Marte. When I seen you last, at New Year's, the girl was pregnant, no? How come she run out of the house like that? What happen to the baby? She want to kill the child?"

"There's no baby. Didn't I not tell you? Oh—that was the time you and Leon were in Israel. So much has happened since we last talked. Jesus, that girl, what a story!"

Marte took a melodramatic pause while she sipped her coffee, and her friend gazed at her across the table with mounting curiosity. "So, what happen?" Elisabetta prompted at length.

"Sometime after New Year's, about two months ago, I don't know, I try to get her to go to the hospital. I says I know they'll treat you good in there, but she says no, no, don't want no hospital, no doctor, nothing. I says what you gonna do, just have it here on the bed? Yes she says. On my bed!"

Elisabetta shook her head and tutted in conciliatory disapproval. Taking the stopper from a bottle on the table, she poured some of the clear liquid into a tiny glass and placed it next to Marte's cup.

"So one day, about the end of January it was, I hear her crying in her room, and I go up to see what the matter is with her. And she moaning and groaning and say—oh, these pains like knives in my belly, like the curse only worse, much worse. And I know what's happening. I seen this thing before—back home when I was a kid and one of the farmer's daughters, just fifteen she was, got pregnant and tried not to tell no one about it—her time came too quick. So, I thinks fast I need some help with this, so I calls up my cousin Irena, she's a mid-wife, you know? So she luckily was at home, so I says come quick and help me. Meanwhile the girl is screaming and Lord knows what the other guests are thinking, they think I murder her or something!"

Elisabetta hid a giggle behind her hands, filled her own glass with Grappa and waited for more.

"Well, and you know how I feel about blood, and this little girl she is bleeding all over the sheet—I have to take it and the mattress off the bed and burn them both later. She bleeding and bleeding and I think she gonna die, and we have to wait nearly one hour for Irena to get here from Turnham Green. But anyway, so, Irena comes finally and she delivers the baby—I didn't stay in the room with her—and when it's all over I asks her, well, is the little girl all right? and she say, yes the mother O.K. but the baby too small, hardly a baby at all."

"Sometimes they can save them, even the little tiny ones, the premature babies. They put them in an incubator. I've seen it on the television" said Elisabetta with enthusiasm, her blue eyes wide over the rim of her coffee cup.

"Yes, but this one too small and too soon it come. I seen it later when Irena showed me, and it not like a baby at all, like a very tiny little skinny doll with skin all shiny. We don't know what to do with it and the girl unconscious, so we wrap it up in newspaper and bury it in the back garden. See, the girl was only five months pregnant or thereabouts, says Irena. They've saved babies six months but not before then. Anyway, she tells me it was born dead—a proper little body and all but no face, just skin."

"She must have been upset. The girl, I mean" Elisabetta prompted.

"I dunno if she was upset. She stay in her bed for three days."

"So you didn't tell no one about it?"

"Why for should I tell anyone?" demanded Marte. "What harm she do? Irena tells me, even if the girl go to hospital they don't save the baby there. She tells me many women lose their babies like this, although not many so late as this girl. So—maybe I should have told a doctor or something, but why? What can he do for her now? She gone anyway. And I told you, the girl said she don't want no doctor. After all, it none of my business if she don't like doctors. She's not relation, just a lodger in my house. I not supposed to take care of her."

"What about the legal? In this country are there so many rules. You maybe should have told someone, I don't know." Elisabetta shook her head warily.

"Irena tells me, we don't need to tell no one—the baby born dead, the pregnancy only five months, it's O.K. And my cousin she work in a health clinic, she knows about this. If the girl was six months, then we must tell because the pregnancy—what was the word she use? a word I not heard before—*viable*, something like that."

"So did you tell all this to the police when they come round?"

"I had to say something. The man was asking so many questions, and looking at me funny, you know? I was nervous he was gonna tell me I done something wrong, send *me* to jail! But he just stood there and ask the questions—he want to know all about this baby thing, and his eyes big like he thinks it's important—and then they left."

"And what happen to the girl?" asked Elisabetta.

"How should I know? She gone somewhere and left all her stuff. And she owes me lots of money, she didn't pay the rent for a month but I have no heart to throw her out. Now look at where my good nature has got me! But you know, the queerest thing, if I said to her something about the baby she looked at me as if I gone mad."

"Maybe she just wanted to forget about it."

"Yeah. Or maybe she already had forgotten about it. Just like it never happened. So peculiar. I never seen anyone like her before."

Elisabetta took a thoughtful sip of her Grappa and reset her glass on the lacy white tablecloth. "Your coffee's getting cold, Marte" she said.

*   *   *

Graham hated hospitals. Even this one that he'd visited many times before in the course of his work. The smell of disinfectant and the jumble of noisy confusion in the Casualty wing always disquieted him. Here was human suffering he could do nothing about, it was another situation out of his control: he couldn't help this couple and he couldn't stop mindless killers terrorizing innocent people. He sat glumly in the hallway waiting to be called to the ward, too tired to read.

"Inspector, you can see them now. Sorry to keep you waiting." The short dark-haired nurse gave him a brief harassed smile, as he got up and followed her down the corridor. He was led into a small room with a single bed, where the curtains were drawn against the morning sunshine.

"Is she on her own?"

"The man was more seriously burnt. We're keeping him in intensive care. Please don't be too long, Inspector, she's still very weak."

"Of course."

The nurse hurried away and Graham saw the girl's eyes flicker wanly open and look at him in surprise. She was obviously pretty, despite her pallid complexion and the assortment of bandages covering her thin arms. Her small white face seemed lost in a sea of black hair which lay in a swathe on the pillow.

"Hello Polly", Graham ventured. "I'm Detective Inspector Brunswick, and I wanted to ask you a few questions about what happened last night."

"What do you want to know?" she croaked.

"When did you first notice the fire in your room?" began Graham as gently as he could.

"It was when…Ken and I were in bed, had gone to bed. And I noticed a smell."

"A burning smell?"

She nodded with an effort. "Like on Guy Fawkes night." She tried to laugh and it turned into a short, breathy cough. "When I looked down at the coverlet I saw these flames. So we jumped out of bed and I started screaming for help and Ken ran to the door but it was locked."

"From the outside" Graham confirmed, writing in his note pad.

"Yes. I ran to the window and rattled it but of course that was locked too, as a security measure I suppose, and we didn't have a key."

"Do you have any idea who might have locked you in?"

The girl shook her head and her mane of black hair rustled on the pillows. "I had some crazy idea it was Mrs. Kurowski. But no—why should she? She's always been friendly to us."

"Is there anyone else who might have a key?"

"Oh—anyone could have taken it. It was in the lock."

Graham looked at her in surprise, raising his eyebrows.

"Ken always left it there for some reason. I told him he was too trusting. But you don't expect this sort of thing, do you?" She blinked her eyes slowly, as if it was hard to keep them open.

"Just one more thing" Graham solicited. "Is there any way this could have been an accident—a burning match fallen from an ashtray or something like that? Do either of you smoke?"

"Oh no" the girl replied. "That smell I noticed, it wasn't just burning, it was paraffin. Like from one of those paraffin lamps or a heater."

"There was a paraffin heater in your room—in Mr. Dowdeswell's room" recalled Graham.

"Yes" the girl admitted, "But it wasn't lit, neither of us like those heaters, I can't stand the smell. Plus, there was nothing to set it off. Ken never has any matches. And the door couldn't have locked itself by accident, could it?"

*   *   *

She felt so tired that she leaned against a wall and tried to rest her head on the cold stone, but the wind only made her shiver. She saw a telephone box ahead and went in, hoping for shelter from the wind, but when she pulled the heavy door closed behind her, she noticed that one of the panes of glass was missing and the cold air rushed in. The box smelt of stale fish and chips, old beer and urine.

A finger tapped on the glass and Susanne turned to see a woman in a head scarf. She didn't want to give up her box, even if it was cold.

She picked up the receiver and listened to the dialing tone, then saw a flashing sign, which read: 'Insert money—minimum 10p'. In the purse section of her handbag she found a 10p coin and inserted it. In her left hand pocket was a crumpled slip of paper with a telephone number scribbled on it. She couldn't remember whose it was, but it was a number and she had to ring someone.

"Hello. 2938" said the voice.

Susanne froze.

"Hello. Hello. This is Pat Brunswick speaking. Is anybody there?"

"Yes" croaked Susanne.

The joker had been kind. He had released one of his memories and let her take a look. She saw a warm, motherly face, a middle-aged woman saying she could call her any time, if ever she was in trouble.

"I…it's…Tracey Nightingale…you gave me your phone number…you said—"

"Oh yes, of course, I remember. How are you, Tracey? Are you all right?"

"I…"

"What's the matter? Is anything wrong?"

"No…it's just…I need somewhere…to sit down…somewhere to rest up…"

"Where are you calling from?"

"I don't know" she said pathetically. Mrs. Headscarf was tapping on the window again. Maybe she could over-hear their conversation.

"Can you make it to St. John's Wood?"

"St. John's Wood."

"Try and make it to St. John's Wood tube station" Pat said urgently. "I'll meet you there."

"When should I—?"

"Just get there when you can and I'll be waiting for you. All right? Is that all right, Tracey?"

"Yes, that's all right." Susanne hung up and leaned breathlessly against the glass.

Once outside the box, Susanne steeled herself and asked the nearest passerby how to get to St. John's Wood. The words came at her in a blur but she remembered some of them later as she trudged up what seemed an inter-minably long road: "…about a twenty minute walk…" "…straight on in that direction…"

She felt she must have been walking for at least an hour when she noticed a street sign on her left, saying *St. John's Wood Road*, and she sighed with relief that she was almost there. Her head pounded, her throat felt dry and there was a bad taste in her mouth. Her fingers closed around a small plastic bottle and she drew it out of her pocket and saw that it was empty. As if by magic, a chemist's shop appeared on the other side of the street. She crossed the road and went in.

"Can I help you please, miss?" inquired the Indian man at the counter. His voice was gentle and high-pitched and he put his head slightly to once side when he spoke.

Susanne approached the counter and held out the empty bottle to him.

"Ah, Triazolam, is it? You want some more of these?"

She nodded, her face serious.

"Yes, we have that. But I can only let you have 20 tablets without a repeat prescription from your doctor. Is that all right?"

She nodded again.

"Wait a moment then, please, and I will get them for you."

When she walked out of the shop, the wind slapped her in the face. She wanted to go back into the warmth, but she had no more money to buy anything.

*   *   *

At about the same time, Graham was driving back to Temple Green through heavy traffic. He had tried to put last night's scene with Pat out of his mind, but it kept popping back again. All right, so he was in the wrong over Ruth—he'd admitted it, hadn't he?—but he still felt a wave of justified anger over Pat's sulky and uncommunicative mood this morning. Why had he spent two hours of his time last night—precious time when he should have been sleeping—trying to explain? Useless now to aver that he would have told her anyway or that Ruth was just a passing infatuation: Pat wouldn't have believed anything he told her. And how could he make any promises, when he didn't even know himself what his feelings were? Women always had to pin you down, force you to make your mind up, make a commitment, when sometimes, all you needed was time.

He'd slept dreadfully. The living room sofa with a blanket draped over him was not his idea of comfort, but he and Pat could hardly have shared a bed after the words that had passed between them. He tumbled and tossed from one position into another, his brain full of jumbled emotions and memories that itched his consciousness and made his head feel like a pressure cooker about to explode.

Graham thought of Dowdeswell and his barmaid mistress, the pretty girl he'd just visited in hospital: what if it had been himself and Ruth trapped by a fire, how would Pat have reacted when she read in *The Standard* 'Police Inspector trapped in love nest by burning blaze!' Despite his preoccupations, Graham couldn't resist a smile at the idea.

Something else was tugging at his memory demanding to be heard, as if he were trying to recall a dream that wouldn't quite surface to consciousness. It was the thought of a newspaper article that had sparked it off. Something to do with newspapers. Something he had read recently...

Graham had a capacity for storing names in his mind and recalling them later—a natural talent, honed during his years on the force. It was a name that he had heard somewhere before...a woman's name...the name of a bird?

Graham slammed on his brakes and just missed a pedestrian who had suddenly appeared on a zebra crossing. The old gentleman waggled a finger at Graham as he doddered across the street. Graham didn't even notice. His heart was racing and his hands trembled slightly on the steering wheel.

Tracey Nightingale—the name of the girl in Room 7— had struck a chord when he heard it last night, but he wasn't sure why. Now he knew where he had heard it before. Of course, there may be no connection, but it wasn't exactly a common name. He had to find out more, and as soon as possible.

*   *   *

The arms of her chair were so large and soft, Susanne felt pleasantly enveloped, as if she were lying in a cradle. She didn't want to raise her eyes, and anyway the lids were too heavy. So she sat and stared at her hands, which shook slightly, making the thin china teacup rattle against its saucer. The left half of her face and her left thigh burned with the heat of the magicoal fire. She shifted her position in the chair, keeping her eyes lowered, and listened to a sympathetic voice which floated over to her from the other side of the room.

"Are you feeling better?"

Susanne gave a faint nod and took another sip of tea. She didn't want to speak. She was afraid her voice would tremble or crack or something worse. She liked the woman and was grateful to her, but she longed for the questions to cease.

"I really was quite worried about you when you called. You sounded so upset. Is there anything wrong, Tracey, anything I can help you with?"

The voice came closer, soft and comforting. It sat in the chair opposite. The woman crossed her legs in their thick nylon stockings. Susanne made a tiny movement of her head up and down.

"There is? Is it the room? I said you could have Gemma's room, didn't I...well, I don't see why Graham should object, after all, he..."

Susanne dared to look at the woman. She seemed to be thinking of something else, she was fidgeting and looking around, as if there was something else she wanted to say.

"I've nowhere to live." Susanne hadn't meant to say that, but the words had fallen out of her mouth. Her voice wasn't her own: it sounded high and pleading, as if it belonged to a stranger.

"Of course you can stay in Gemma's room, of course you can" the woman said emphatically. "For as long as you like. Graham will just have to put up with it. I did mean to ask you, Tracey" she hesitated, "Do you not have any friends in London, or any relatives? Someone who could help you get back on your feet?"

"I've got an auntie."

"An auntie?" The woman sounded surprised.

"She said I could stay with her. I tried to find her, but...when I first came..." Susanne stumbled, confused, trying to piece together the fragments of memory.

"Didn't you have her address?"

"Oh yes...I went there, but..." Susanne still had the bit of paper, with Auntie Mabel's address, crumpled up in her handbag. She had kept it as a sort of talisman: she believed that if she threw it away, she would lose all hope of ever finding her aunt. Now, she pulled it out of her purse, uncreased it slowly and handed it to the woman.

"136 Tooley Street" read Pat, looking at the paper.

"No...13b"

"What?"

"13b Tooley Street" repeated Susanne. That was something she knew for sure, Auntie Mabel's address. She'd spent long enough looking for it, looking again and again at the scrap of paper and wondering why Auntie Mabel had written it down wrong. Maybe she had done that on purpose, never wanting Susanne to visit her at all.

"I think you've made a mistake, my dear. It looks like a b but it's a 6, I'm fairly sure of that." The woman suddenly smiled. "Maybe that's where you went wrong! Don't worry, Tracey, we'll find your auntie after all. I'll come with you myself, and make sure to find her."

The woman sounded so pleased. Susanne didn't say anything: she was too stupefied by this new information. Surely it couldn't be possible that Auntie Mabel had been in the same street all along, but at a different number?

"You didn't say much about yourself when you came to the hostel. Only that your husband had left you, and you'd lost your baby."

There was a question in the woman's voice. She paused, waiting for a response, and then continued. "I was very sorry to hear about your baby, Tracey. I know how awful it must be—well, it hasn't happened to me, but I know what a comfort a child can be when…other things go wrong."

Susanne relaxed her body a little. All her muscles ached, all her bones seemed to be crying.

"Did you want a baby very much, Tracey?"

Susanne didn't answer. There were too many questions, and her mind felt fuddled. She decided not to say any more. Maybe the woman would give up eventually and leave her alone.

"Children can be such a blessing. Our Gemma will be eighteen in May. She's in Sheffield at the moment, at University, studying psychology, maybe I told you that before? She always was a clever girl. We've been very lucky with Gemma, she was never any trouble. Graham used to call her his little sunshine when she was a child, we couldn't have wished for…"

The voice tailed off. Susanne was confused. Why had the woman stopped talking? Was she staring at her now noticing something strange?

Susanne lifted her head and saw to her amazement that the woman was weeping silently. Her face was serene and composed, but the pale eyes brimmed with tears which fell along her downy cheeks.

"What is it?" Susanne said, forgetting her decision not to speak.

The woman smiled at her and wiped her face with a white linen handkerchief. At first slowly and falteringly, then with increasing confidence, she told Susanne the story of Graham's liaison with Ruth.

*   *   *

Ruth was in the bath when the telephone rang. She cursed herself for not having remembered to leave the ansaphone on, but she struggled out of the water and draped herself with a towel, before hurrying dripping into the bedroom to pick up the extension. Graham's voice was the last one she had expected to hear.

"Didn't wake you up did I?"

"I don't sleep that late. I was in the bath, actually." She tried to keep her tone light, but it had an unfriendly edge. "Are you calling from work?"

"Yes. Listen, could you do something for me?"

"What?" Time was she would have agreed to any favor, without asking what it was.

"You know that paper you brought from your father's?"

"Which? The Hull Daily Mail?"

"Yes, the one I read last night at your place. D'you think you could get it over to me?"

"What, now?" What on earth could be so urgent in some local rag that he would need it right away? Perhaps this was some excuse and Graham really wanted to see her.

"Yes, it's rather important. Perhaps you could get it biked."

No—it was obviously the paper he wanted to see, not her. "What do you need it for, Graham?"

"Or maybe you could just fax me the one page, it's on page 4 about halfway down, but just fax me the whole page, you've got a fax at home haven't you—"

"Graham, why do you want it?" Ruth insisted.

Graham sighed. He felt it was a waste of time to tell her about his hunch over the common name, but he gave in and explained. Ruth didn't seem as surprised as he had felt when he made the connection. At his request, she found the relevant article and read it over the phone to him.

"Can I ask you something?" she inquired, "You say you went to visit the couple who got burned in the hospital this morning—"

"Well, just the girl, the man wasn't allowed visitors—"

"What was her hair like?"

"What?"

"Her hair. What was it like?"

"I don't know what that's got to do with anything…erm…there was lots of it…"

"Dark?"

"Yes, black I suppose."

"Right" Ruth replied, with an air of conviction. "I'll bring the paper over myself right now."

"Won't it take you too long?"

"Of course not. I can be there in half an hour. And Graham, I suggest you find out everything you can about the woman who disappeared."

"Susanne Martin. Yes, I was going to do just that."

*   *   *

"I'm sorry, I really didn't mean to burden you with my troubles, I'm sure you have enough of your own. I'm not normally like this." Pat rose and fetched a tin of biscuits from the Welsh dresser which she offered to Susanne. "I'm afraid you've been rather unlucky. You've come at a bad time." Still smiling grimly, she reseated herself and pulled her skirt down over her thighs, as if wishing it were longer. Susanne didn't know why she should have been chosen as the recipient of the woman's confidences, but she was interested and keen to know more.

"Anyway…maybe because I've no one else to tell…I suppose I might tell Gemma if…no, I don't think I'd want Gemma to know. But I want to tell someone. Is that all right?"

"Yes" said Susanne.

"I had no idea, you see, that all this was going on. I was under the impression that our marriage was…that Graham was happy, with me…well, actually, I knew something was wrong, I've known it for months, I tried to talk to him about it but he wouldn't…I thought it was something to do with his work, you see. I never imagined it would be anything like this. I found out, about Ruth, by accident." She stumbled over the name. "But now, what am I to do? He tells me he doesn't love her. But he's been seeing her for nine months, he must feel some-thing…I don't know whether to believe him or not, I don't know anything any more. It's ridiculous—I feel like my life's fallen—oh, I don't know, I wish I could just accept it, find a way to accept it. But I can't. Do you understand?" Her eyes were so pleading, so trusting, so bemused. Susanne nodded.

Pat sighed deeply and revived herself. She got up again. "Well, there's nothing to be done at the moment. Best just to forget it for the time being, wouldn't you say? Anyway, you must be starving, dear. I'm afraid there's very little to eat in the house. If I'd known you were coming—but never mind. It's early closing today, if I hurry I can catch the shops before one and get us something for lunch. Will you be all right here on your own? Or would you rather come with me?"

"No, I'll stay here."

"All right then. I won't be long. If you get bored, there's plenty to read, mainly newspapers. Graham never gets round to throwing them out."

Susanne waited till Pat had left the room before she reached down for her handbag and took out the bottle of pills, fingering them gratefully. She'd tried to do without but she couldn't cope with her panic attacks and the thoughts that constantly threatened to surface, thoughts she wanted to forget. She much preferred the comforting fog of a mind becalmed, she didn't care how.

The rest of her tea had gone cold and was covered with a brown film, but she gulped it down with two of the pills and lay back in the chair, feeling the aches start to go and the numbness take over.

To her surprise, after a few moments, she was bored. What had the woman said? There was enough to read. It was a long time since she had read anything.

Underneath the coffee table lay a stack of newspapers. They all seemed to be different issues of the same paper, *The Hampstead and Highgate Express.* Susanne read the most recent one, which was on top.

There was a headline on the front page, about a murder on Hampstead Heath. Susanne's mind began to reel and her body to shake. The joker laughed.

Chapter Eight

▼

"I've got the print-outs for you."

Graham disregarded the voice, which was smothered by the general office cacophony, until he felt Tom's bony hand slapping him gently on the cheek.

"Wakey wakey! Show a bit of enthusiasm. You were ready to kill for these an hour ago."

Graham gave a snort of laughter that was also a gasp of surprise and seized the white sheets. "Thanks Tom, thanks a million." He smiled.

"That's more like it. What are these for anyway? What's the sudden interest in North Yorkshire?" Tom pulled a black plastic chair from Sergeant Corby's desk to Graham's.

"Hang on, er, Tom my old chum, as you're standing…"

Tom sighed with mock fatigue. "Coffee, white, two sugars" he recited on his way out.

"*No* sugar" corrected Graham.

He took the phone off the hook and studied the faint type on the flimsy papers, sifting through the wodge of information to find the relevant bits, which he plucked out like gems and transferred to his notes.

Tom returned with two plastic cups of frothy brown liquid which he put down before seating himself, splaying out his long legs under Graham's desk and lighting a cigarette.

Graham spoke softly and rapidly. "Don't spread this about, but I believe there's a connection between the homicide attempt last night and a shooting that happened in North Yorkshire on Christmas Eve last year."

"What's the connection?"

"A name. Tracey Nightingale, one of the guests at the hotel, the one who left the house just before the fire was noticed, has the same name as the girl who was shot last year. It could be coincidence, but I doubt it."

Tom sat up and rested his elbows on the desk. "How did you find out about this?"

"Pure luck, really. I happened to read about it in the paper. The name rang a bell. And the description of the girl, Mrs. Kurowski said she wasn't local." Graham was leaning over his desk, gripping the papers.

"You lucky bugger!" exclaimed Tom, raising his hands to heaven "Why don't things like that happen to me?"

Ignoring the rhetorical question, Graham pushed on. "Right, now, I've made a note of the salient points from all this bumph here. Two people were shot, Jeff Martin and Tracey Nightingale, in the bedroom of a bed and breakfast hotel in Whitby, which Martin ran with his wife. One bullet was found in the brain of the man—it traveled through from the forehead—and one in the neck of the girl, rupturing her spinal column. Very clean shots, no bullets found lodged in furniture, just the two cartridge cases on the floor. Firearm expert reckons they must have been fired at close range, five feet at the most, and the victims must have been taken by surprise, no evidence of a struggle, dermal nitrate tests were negative, powder traces on the man's shoulders and the girl's chest. They were both naked, by the way—"

"What? Slow down a minute, mate. Who shot these two? Have North Yorks arrested anybody?"

"No, but listen. The wife of the man, this Susanne Martin, disappeared immediately after the shootings and hasn't been heard of since."

"It's classic crime of passion stuff, isn't it. And you think this Martin woman—"

"They found a body in the Humber, which they thought might be hers. But Tom, I saw a photograph of her in the paper. She's blonde, short, pretty, blue eyes— exactly as Mrs. Kurowski described Tracey Nightingale. I remember thinking to myself when I saw it, she doesn't look the type to get mixed up in something so sordid, and then when the landlady said—"

"You think Tracey Nightingale is this Martin woman?"

"It can't be coincidence—too many things tie up."

"So she took the alias of the woman she shot" Tom mused.

"Stranger things have happened. The criminal mind…"

"But why kill again? What did she have against those two in the hotel?"

"I don't know…but…something Ruth said…"

"Ruth?"

"I scoffed at the time, but…she may have a point."

"What's Ruth got to do with this?"

"It was her newspaper that carried the article I saw. She seemed to think that there was something that triggered this woman to kill…something physical…a reminder of the first murder…like the hair, the hair of the victim…"

"I'm out of my depth here, you'd better talk to Dr. Plowright on that one." Tom suddenly thought of something, and leaned forward. "What about the other murders, Hampstead Heath, the disco—you told me you thought there was a connection…?"

Graham gave a long exhalation of breath. "I thought there was a connection…with Hackett. Maybe I was wrong, just chasing my own demons. But we've got to find this woman, Tom! And she's in London somewhere."

"No problem, mate. We'll send out a posse. There's only about two million fair-haired girls in the capital. Nah, it'd be like looking for the proverbial needle. Besides, she could easily just flit across the channel or hole up with relatives in the country."

"Her actions so far have been illogical and badly thought out, I don't think she'll cover her tracks too well. I just have this intuition…"

"You and your intuitions." Tom gave a smile that was almost affectionate. "Don't worry, I'm not complaining."

Graham was hardly listening. "I think we can find her, I really do. I'll get that paper from Ruth, then I'll liaise with the press, get them to carry a brief story, description, maybe a photo on the front page or something. A woman in that state can't hide for ever, someone's bound to notice she's acting strangely and report it to us—"

"You, liaising with the press? I never thought I'd see the day!" Tom gave a long laugh, more out of relief and pleasure than amusement. It was a long time since he'd seen Graham so excited by a case.

*   *   *

Coming in the back way, Pat went into the kitchen first and dumped her bag of shopping on the table, then put water on to boil for the pasta. She was pleased with what she had bought from Fiorelli's—some fresh green tagliatelle, wonderfully pungent prosciutto ham, black olives and grated Parmesan cheese in a cone-shaped greaseproof bag. After a quick search in the cupboard, she found some crisps left over from her last dinner party and she took these and the olives into the living room.

Opening the door, she was surprised to see Tracey slumped in the armchair by the fire. Graham's newspapers had been taken out from under the coffee table and scattered on the floor. One newspaper hung from the girl's listless hand. When Pat went up to her and gently called her name, touching her on the shoulder, there was no response. The girl was in a deep sleep. There was something unnatural about a sleep so heavy: Pat thought of the Sleeping Beauty in the fairy tale, who wouldn't wake for a hundred years.

Well, there was no point getting lunch prepared now. It seemed that what Tracey needed most was rest. Pat eased off the girl's shoes and lifted her off the armchair. Fortunately, the girl was light enough for Pat to carry, without too much effort, upstairs to Gemma's bedroom and deposit gently on the bed, laying a blanket over the sleeping figure. She lay on her side, with a look of sleeping innocence and peace.

The phone rang suddenly, and Pat hurried downstairs. "Hello. 2938."

"Hello Pat, it's me."

"Gray?"

"Yes, is that so surprising?"

"Well, no. I just didn't expect you to call, I suppose."

Graham seemed tongue-tied. Contrite even? "Sorry I didn't say goodbye this morning. I had to leave very early and I didn't like to wake you up."

"That's all right."

"I didn't think you would have got much sleep last night."

"Yes, I had plenty thank you."

"That's fine then…I'll be home about eight tonight, so—"

"I'll have dinner ready" she replied curtly. Row or no row, she would continue to observe the rituals.

"Yes, all right, maybe we can see each other tonight and…talk things over a bit, eh?"

"If you like." Pat hadn't been going to tell Graham about the girl staying in Gemma's room. A little spiteful instinct rather relished the idea of springing it on him. But now that he'd rung and he seemed to want to make amends, she changed her mind. To her surprise, he wasn't cross about it at all. He was even unusually sympathetic.

"I don't see why she shouldn't have Gemma's room for a few days, if she's got nowhere else to go. Where did you say she was from?"

"Up North somewhere. One of those seaside towns. She was fast asleep when I got home so I've put her to bed. I hope she's all right. I found an empty pill bottle on the table, so I think she must have taken some tablets."

Pat could hear another phone ringing in Graham's office and a babble of voices. "I've got to go, love. I'll see you later."

"Goodbye Gray." She felt less angry with him but she wasn't going to call him dear.

*   *   *

It was 12 noon when Ruth arrived at Temple Green with the precious newspaper. She told the desk sergeant she had an appointment to see Graham Brunswick, and despite his suspicious look, he ushered her into Graham's office.

Graham cut out the relevant article and scoured it hungrily. Ruth was less surprised than Tom when he suggested that she run an insert about Susanne Martin on the next *Watch Out For Crime*. They discussed the case briefly but it was obvious to Ruth that, once business had been dealt with, Graham was anxious for her to leave. He asked her distractedly if she was spending her day off at home and she replied that she was, not wanting to tell him of her intended visit to his wife. There was one thing, though, that she was determined to ask: "Did you have a word with Pat last night?"

"Ruth, it was very late when I got home."

"But she must have asked questions."

Graham kept his gaze averted from her face and his voice casual. "Yes she asked me some questions but we didn't discuss it much."

"I suppose you're going to do that tonight?" Ruth couldn't keep the sarcasm out of her tone. She hated the bitter sound of it.

"I was intending to, yes."

"Well, Graham" she said icily, daring him to look at her, "You may just find that this time you're too late." With that cryptic comment, she ignored Graham's bemused glance and strode out of the room, pausing with pounding heart outside the door, ready for her next move.

Graham relaxed his body and realized that he'd been holding it taut like a clenched fist. At the back of his head, someone was knocking with a small wooden hammer. As usual, the heating had been turned up too high and the air was stifling. He pulled at his tie, trying to loosen its grip on his throat. The indigestion—which hadn't troubled him for days, ever since his visit to the doctor—had returned with especial vigor.

Reaching into his drawer, he pulled out the vial of vitamin C tablets and dropped one into a glass of water which had been on his desk for a day or two and had caught motes of dust. He stared at the fizzing bubbles rising to the surface of the water, and suddenly it reminded him of something.

He picked up the phone and dialed extension 254.

"Lab."

"Hello Joe, Brunswick here. Have you finished analyzing those tablets I gave you yet?"

"Yes I have, sir. They're Triazolam."

"Triazolam?"

"A tranquilizer, one of the short-acting benzodiazepines."

"Don't blind me with science, please, Joe" begged Graham tersely. "What does this drug do?"

"Doctors prescribe it—to women mostly, to relieve stress, cure insomnia, that sort of thing. Though to my mind it's not such a good idea to go handing these tablets out like smarties, they can cause more harm than good in the long term."

"What sort of harm?"

"Well, particularly with the shorter acting drugs, withdrawal symptoms can be quite severe. In fact, I've heard some rumors that this particular drug is about to be withdrawn from the market—there've been reports of it causing personality deviations as a side effect."

"Deviations? What, you mean the personality actually changes?"

"Not completely changes but the drug certainly can up anxiety levels, cause sleep disturbance, and in some cases induce abnormally aggressive behavior and marked memory impairment, even evidence of psychosis."

"Good God! No wonder they want to withdraw it."

"Nothing's proven as yet. It's still available over the counter at pharmacies."

"I see. That's marvelous Joe, thanks a lot."

Tom's voice came from the doorway: "Coming to the canteen, mate? It's after two o'clock."

"Not just yet. I've got a few things to do first."

"No point in starving yourself."

"I know, but..." He made a harassed gesture with his hands, "the phone hasn't stopped and I really can't think about food at the moment."

Tom said nothing, but gave Graham a look that was half-disbelief half pity, and left. Jane Cherrill gusted in from the ante-room, struggling to put on her cream fur jacket as she walked.

"Just a minute, Jane, could you do something for me before lunch?" said Graham, halting her hasty exit.

"Oh!" Her face visibly fell and she looked pleadingly at Graham, as if she thought she could change his mind.

"I need you to check the N.H.S. patients register for me" said Graham without looking at her. "Find out the G.P. of a Mrs. Susanne Martin from Whitby, North Yorkshire. When you've got his number, ring his surgery, tell him we need all the information he can supply on his patient as soon as possible. He can send a written report to his nearest police station and have them fax it to us. Have you got all that? Hadn't you better write it down?"

"Please sir, couldn't I do it after lunch? I'm meeting someone at—"

"No you *can't*, this is urgent, Jane. In case you'd forgotten, we're dealing with people's lives here, this isn't some nice cozy little estate agents where you clock on at nine every morning and leave at five on the dot at night. Now I want the job done immediately! If you can't stand the pace here, I'll have to find somebody who can."

*   *   *

Pat was singing as she beat the mixture for her scones. She'd put on her Richard Clayderman album in the living room and the notes drifted over to her in the kitchen, enticing her to sing along. It wasn't that she felt happy, exactly, but the burden of wondering had been lifted and her heart was lighter in consequence. She hadn't yet started to think what she would do about her situation.

When the telephone rang, she was overjoyed to hear her daughter's voice. The line was crackly and the pips kept going, but Gemma sounded her usual bubbly, resilient self. Gone was the insecurity of her last phone message, when she'd told her mother how she longed to come home.

"No, really, I'm fine mum. I've had a chat with Julian and I feel much better. I don't know why I was panicking so much before. I guess it was just before my exams and I was in a flap. But it's a much better idea for me to stay here."

"You're sure now? I'm sure I could persuade dad if—"

"Absolutely sure. I think Julian's finally got the message. And…well…I've made friends with somebody else…"

"Another boy, you mean?"

"That's right. He's my swimming instructor, actually."

"Well, I hope he turns out to be nicer than—"

"Oh yeah—he's great! And I'm having a good time."

"Oh good, I'm so glad. Actually, I feel a little guilty, but…"

"What?"

"It's a good thing you don't want to come home just at the moment, because I've let somebody have your room."

"Oh? Who?"

"She's just a young girl like you. I met her at the hostel and she had nowhere else to go."

"Does dad know?"

"Oh yes, I told him today and…to my surprise he was fine about it."

"Well, maybe he's mellowing in his old age."

"Yes maybe" Pat replied, not believing that this was the reason. Whatever her own doubts about the marriage, she felt she had to protect her daughter and shield her from any family traumas. She wasn't going to let Gemma suffer, whatever happened.

Pat spent the rest of the morning distracting herself with physical activity—cooking and cleaning parts of the house that didn't need to be cleaned. It was after she put the finished scones into the oven that she went up to Gemma's room to check on its sleeping occupant. The girl lay curled up like a child, one hand under her head and the other by her mouth. The clock in the hall chimed twice.

*   *   *

Graham came back from a brief visit to the canteen for a sandwich to find the note on his desk. When he read its contents his face darkened and he went straight up to the front desk and accosted the Desk Sergeant: "Who brought this in?"

"I don't know, sir."

"For God's sake, man, you're at the front, you must have seen him. He can't have *flown* into my office. How the hell did this get into my room?" He slapped the paper on to Lumley's desk and the young man gave it an anxious glance.

"I must have been at lunch, sir. Carson was on duty. I can ask—"

"Forget it—there's no time!" Graham was already on the way back to his office. He picked up the phone and dialed a number, then waited for it to ring twenty times just in case she was in the bath. Getting no reply, he slammed down the phone and fought off the fist of fear squeezing his stomach, grabbed his coat off the hook and on his way out of the building snapped at a startled Lumley, "If anybody wants me, I'm in Camden Town."

On his way there in the car, he refused to look at the note lying on the seat beside him but he didn't need to see it to refresh his memory—the words still swam before his eyes: *Her face would be more pretty with a scar. She's at my place for her beauty treatment. From the Facecutter.*

It didn't take him long to reach Charlie's street. Seeing again the battered houses, which had once been proudly maintained but had fallen into disrepair after years of neglect and abandonment, he felt the familiar sickening nausea in his stomach at the thought of the dark underworld Charlie inhabited, a world which produced the kind of mind that could take pleasure only in other people's pain. *Could Ruth really be in there?* he wondered *And how did he entice her? I thought she said she would be careful.* The image of her tied up on one of Charlie's chairs in the midst of some torture—or worse—was too horrible to contemplate, and he thrust it from his mind as he stepped out of the car and moved stealthily to the front door.

Looking through the cracked, curtainless window, he could see nothing but blackness inside. The street seemed suddenly, eerily quiet as he crept up to the entrance. He wished suddenly that he'd thought to tell someone at the station of his exact location, or to bring someone else with him who could provide back-up if he needed it. But it was too late now. And anyway, this was his problem to deal with, his demon to extinguish.

He pushed the door gently with his fingers and it eased open with a creak. Charlie was obviously expecting him.

Inside, the front hallway was empty. A light bulb dangled from a cord above his head. Plaster and old wallpaper were peeling from the walls and he could hear the drip of water as rain leaked through a hole in the roof upstairs. The stench of grime and urine was almost overpowering. *Dear God, the thought of Ruth coming to harm in a place like this!*

He stepped through the door frame where once a door had been into what must at one time have been quite a pleasant front room. In the far corner of the room, a figure huddled, its back to him.

"Where is she, Charlie?" Graham asked quietly.

The figure turned round and saw Graham. "What's that? Where you come from?" Charlie seemed genuinely surprised.

"Where *is* she?" Graham repeated, approaching him.

"Who? Who? Don't know who you mean."

Graham strode up to Charlie and grabbed him by the throat with one hand. He didn't care any more what the solicitor might say. "You little bastard! Do you want me to kill you!" He shook Charlie until the little man went pink in the face, gasped and spluttered. Then he threw him against the wall. "If she's in here, I'll find her."

"She's not here. Nobody here but me" Charlie croaked as Graham stormed out of the room.

There weren't many places in the house to search, the building being almost entirely bare of furniture and only consisting of a few empty rooms. When he'd checked the house he searched the jungle of a garden, and even across the half-toppled fence into the adjacent yard, but he found nothing and nobody.

He went back into the front room, to find Charlie still cowering in a corner, looking even more pathetic than usual. "All right" said Graham. "What is this—some kind of joke?"

Charlie merely shook his head, his face a mask of innocence. "I done nothing."

There was no more Graham could do. Without another word, he turned on his heels and left the room.

As he closed the front door behind him and walked down the steps to the street, he heard laughter behind him. It wasn't quite a maniac's laugh. More a child's giggle—like some delighted three year old who has played a prank on his parents. The laughter went on and on and pursued him all the way to his car.

He shut the car door behind him and cut out the noise. Not even caring if anyone could see him, he leaned his elbows on the dashboard and hid his head in his hands. The pain of heartburn lay heavy on his chest, like the vice of a torturer unwilling to relax his grip. He breathed deeply and tried to relax, but all he could hear was Charlie's mocking laughter in his mind, seeming to taunt him. For several minutes he sat in the same position, unable to move.

He felt like a character in one of those films where snatches of the hero's life flash on to the screen in a random mix. Words and memories came back to him, and he tried to piece them together in his mind, but it was like a jigsaw puzzle where he'd never seen the overall picture. He questioned himself again and again, trying to give an honest reply, trying to mine a gem of truth from the ore of tangled thoughts in his head. Why had he been so sure the killer was Charlie Hackett? Did he have a need to redeem himself so strong that it had blinded him to all reality? Had he ever really been honest with himself about his motives for pursuing Hackett?

And then he gave an enormous sigh and leaned his head back against the seat, staring at the gray interior of his car roof. He knew in his heart of hearts what had happened. It was time to admit it, at least to himself. He'd been a fool. All these weeks, he'd been chasing Charlie Hackett because he'd been living in the nightmare of his past, hoping to prove he was not a failure by catching Hackett this time. And Hackett had preyed on this obsession, knowing all too well how to play with him. *Do you think I am easier to play on than a pipe?* The quote mocked him.

People had told him as a young policeman that too much personal involvement with a case was a dangerous thing, and he knew the truth of that. In the past he'd always kept an objective eye. But this time he'd forgotten all the warnings, his vision so clouded by the cataract of his emotions that he could no longer see clearly. His fear of what Hackett might do to Gemma or to Ruth had been a miasma, a treacherous siren luring him off on a tangent. Pursuing Hackett had distracted him from finding the real killer. So concerned with exorcising the demons from his past, he had completely ignored what was happening here and now.

Graham put his key in the ignition and started up the car. He prayed that it was not too late yet. He knew he'd wasted valuable time but he vowed to do so no longer.

*   *   *

Pat looked at the self-possessed young woman with the earnest stare, sitting opposite her. So this was the girl who'd been claiming Graham's attention for the past nine months, who'd made him change in so many ways. But she was so much younger than him and from a different background entirely: what could they possibly have in common? *Perhaps that's the attraction*—thought Pat bitterly—*he's seeking someone different from himself, and different from me, of course.* The girl was talking to her again, waiting expectantly for an answer. Pat had been so absorbed in her own thoughts, she'd hardly heard. "I'm sorry?" she flustered.

"I said that's a lovely painting above the fireplace—it's a Monet isn't it? One of my favorites. Did *you* choose it, or Graham?"

Pat was nonplused and stood for a few seconds with her mouth open, not knowing what to say. She wasn't used to making polite conversation in this sort of situation.

Ruth noticed the older woman's bewilderment. "I'm sorry if I'm embarrassing you. But we may as well be civilized, Pat, don't you think? I mean, we've probably got a lot in common, we're both in the same boat, really. I don't feel any antagonism towards you—I hope you don't feel any, or at least not too much towards me, now that you've met me." Ruth searched Pat's face with the air of a psychiatrist concerned for her patient's wellbeing.

After a moment's pause, while Pat battled with herself to speak the truth and decide how she really did feel, she replied hesitantly, "No...I...don't feel antagonism exactly. It's a bit of a shock, I admit." Pat straightened herself and patted her neat bun with a prim gesture, before rising. "Since we're being civilized, can I offer you a cup of tea?"

Ruth couldn't help smiling at Pat's obvious desire to change the subject, but she responded with equal politeness. "I'm afraid I don't drink normal tea, I'm allergic to milk. You don't have rosehip or camomile do you?"

"I'm afraid not. Is there anything else...?"

"No—it's all right, really."

"It seems we don't have all that much in common" Pat said, with an attempt at a laugh.

Ruth gazed back at her levelly, refusing to lighten the tone of the conversation. "In the important things, we have a bond. We're both women. We both have a..."

Ruth searched for a tactful way of putting it, "relationship with Graham."

"A very different kind of relationship" replied Pat, rather sadly.

"I'm sure he cares about both of us, in different ways."

Pat sat down again, rather heavily, on the sofa. She was aware of the large bright ring glistening on Ruth's right hand, and she couldn't stop herself wondering if Graham had given it to her. She forced herself to look up and meet Ruth's steady gaze—the sympathetic look she found there made her feel patronized, she didn't need her pity. Good Lord, she'd been with Graham for twenty-five years, she was his wife, surely she had more claims on him than this young girl, for all her beauty and self-confidence.

"He can't have both of us, though, can he?" Pat affirmed. "At least—*you* may be content with that, you have been content with it up to now, but I certainly shouldn't be."

"No, you're right, he can't. He'd like to, of course." For a moment, the women regarded each other with empathy, united by common experience against the man who had betrayed them. "That's why he didn't want you to know" Ruth continued. "He'd never have told you, if it hadn't slipped out by accident. I've thought about coming to see you for some time, actually, but I never had the courage."

Pat responded with a wary smile: she knew that feeling of not daring to face things or people that might turn out unpleasant. She had to admire the girl for taking the bull by the horns. *Could I have done the same, if the tables were turned?* she thought. *The tables wouldn't be turned, I'd never have become involved with a married man in the first place.*

But Pat knew that you can't dictate to your heart where love is concerned.

Ruth was still speaking, in a confessional tone. "But when I found out that you knew, that you'd found out, I felt I must come and see you so that you know who I am, can see me as a human being, and I you. Does that sound stupid?"

Pat shook her head, but was unsure how to respond. "You certainly know how to express yourself" she said, ruefully.

Suddenly, Ruth felt guilty. What had Pat done to deserve this? It wasn't Pat's fault if Graham had tired of her. "I'm sorry" she gushed, "I really am. I didn't mean…I never meant to get involved with your husband. Do you understand? These things just happen sometimes, you say it's something you'll never do, and then you find yourself doing it. And you know people are going to get hurt, including yourself, but you just can't stop. It's like a…drug…an addiction or something. Do you see?" Ruth held out her hands palm upwards, in a gesture of supplication.

Pat could sense the girl's sincerity. She didn't feel angry any more, just sad.

"Yes I do see" she said, simply. "But what can we do?"

CHAPTER NINE

▼

It was silent in the office, now that the typists and day shift officers had gone home, and Graham missed the murmur of voices around him, finding the silence itself distracting. He read over Dr. Freund's report for the third time:

'I have been Mrs. Martin's G.P. for twenty-three years, and have also treated both her parents, Coral and Harold Gray. My records show her medical history to be relatively normal. During childhood, she contracted Rubella at age eight and Pertussis at age ten. She was prone to dizziness and fainting fits, which disappeared during adolescence. These were caused by a form of mild epilepsy, probably inherited from her mother, who also suffered from petit-mal. A course of pheno-barbitone was successful in suppressing the attacks. My patient married Jeff Martin a year and a half ago and I diag-nosed her pregnant last September. She was physically in good health. During her second month of pregnancy, I prescribed a mild tranquilizer, as she was experiencing insomnia. There was also a certain amount of weight loss and slight hypo-glycemia, for which I prescribed an iron tonic. Up to her fourth month of pregnancy, she visited the ante natal clinic regularly once a fortnight and I made routine checks on her

blood pressure, weight and blood sugar levels, as well as taking blood and urine samples and checking abdominal palpitations. She complained of headaches, abdominal pains and vaginal bleeding. As my tests had shown that she had no major physical difficulties with the pregnancy, I believed these symptoms to be nervous-related and prescribed a further course of tranquilizers. As to the mental health of my patient—while not being a specialist in this field and therefore not able to give a professional opinion—I saw no signs of mental instability. Her personality is gentle and restrained. I only dealt with her in other than a medical capacity on one occasion, when she sought advice on entering the nursing profession. I believe that she did indeed study nursing for a while before her marriage but discontinued when her mother became seriously ill. Mrs. Gray was hemiplegic and died of a cerebral infarction last November at the age of sixty-eight. My last contact with Mrs. Martin was on Thursday, December 11th. We were naturally concerned when Mrs. Martin missed her January appointment, and when efforts to contact her failed we informed the local police, who we understand are trying to trace her."

The third reading was no more instructive than the first two had been. The most bizarre thing about it was that the girl seemed so ordinary. Would anyone reading that report suspect that its subject may already have committed three murders and one attempted homicide?

The twirling note of an ambulance siren drew nearer, grew deafeningly loud, then hurried away into the distance. Graham hated that sound, and he suddenly had an idea that the ambulance was racing to another murder, one that he should have prevented. He shook himself and smiled inwardly. It was years since he had held himself personally responsible for every evil that happened on the streets, as he had when a young policeman. He had learned later, that to protect yourself it was necessary to grow a philosophical shell.

A lean figure passed the open door of the office, noticed there was a light on and did a double take. "Well well, Cinders, has everyone else gone to the ball?"

Graham laughed noiselessly and took the opportunity to stretch himself, putting his arms behind his head. "You've seen too many pantomimes."

"What, me? I never go to the theater" replied Tom, coming into the room. "No point if you haven't got kids, is there. What's this?" he asked, fingering the doctor's report with vague interest.

"It's from Susanne Martin's G.P. in Whitby."

"Christ! You want to give this thing a rest, Graham. Do something else for a change. You're getting obsessed." Tom was unexpectedly serious, the usual half-mocking grin gone from his face. "Does it say anything useful?"

"Well…not—"

"Not really, I thought so. Come on mate, let's go down the Star and Garter for a quick one, forget work for a bit." He gave Graham an encouraging slap on the back and moved towards the door.

"No, I can't, I've still got a few things to do here. Maybe I'll pop round in an hour or so."

"Oh yeah? I've heard that one before." Tom looked at him suspiciously. "You'd be better off leaving this and getting a few pints down you. You might need some fortification before you go home. But don't listen to me, I'm only your fairy godmother. Smart's on late duty tonight, so I'll tell him to throw you out at eight o'clock. See you later."

Tom shut the door and left, not giving Graham a chance to respond.

*   *   *

Upstairs in Gemma's bedroom, a small human shape stirred under the bedclothes, as the sound of the wind moaning outside roused her into consciousness.

She was afraid to open her eyes at first, so she lay there for a few moments trying to remember where she was and what had happened before she'd fallen asleep. She couldn't. She couldn't remember anything. Except, her house, Coral Cottage, she remembered that. The blue walls, the yellow flowered curtains, the seagulls (but there were no seagulls). Perhaps if she opened her eyes, she'd find she was at home.

She let her eyes drift open. The light was gray. Twilight. Evening. She sat up slowly, and her eyes adjusted to the light. No, it wasn't her room, not her house. She'd never seen this room before. It had posters of pop stars on the walls, a pile of records in one corner, by a music center. A desk with papers and books on it and a vase of dried flowers. A dressing table with jars of make-up and old lipsticks and a photograph in a silver heart shaped frame. Susanne didn't look at the photograph. She didn't need to look. She knew whose room this was, even though she'd never been there before. It was a teenage girl's room. It was Tracey's room. Tracey must have brought her here while she was asleep. Another joke.

But what had happened before? Before that? It was horrible, this not remembering. Like being in a fog all the time, never able to see properly, but a fog of the mind. Like some sort of nightmare.

She had to get up. Quick. Before they came to get her. She pulled off the bedclothes and stood up on the warm carpeted floor. She didn't even recognize the night dress she had on, a pale green night dress, a color she never wore. Whose was it? Tracey's? She shivered in horror. She wanted to tear it off, but she had to wear something.

I must get down to the kitchen, she thought, *make myself a cup of tea, make myself remember. Remember.* And the wind kept sighing and crying and rattling the window panes, wanting to come in.

*   *   *

Tom's veiled reference to Pat had galled Graham, but before he could brood about it, the telephone rang.

"Hello, is that Detective Inspector Brunswick?" said a light male voice, with distinctively Asian vowels.

"Yes it is."

"I'm ringing because my son took a phone call earlier this evening from one of your men—Detective Constable Fields, I believe—asking if anyone had purchased the drug Triazolam today. I have a small pharmacy in St. John's Wood Road, you see."

Graham was suddenly interested. "Oh yes?" He knew that pharmacy. It was conveniently near his house and because of its long opening hours he often popped in on the way home from work to buy some indigestion tablets or throat pastilles. The vitamin C tablets on his desk bore the chemist's label.

"I believe it is you I should speak to?"

"Yes, yes, did someone buy the drug today?"

"Well yes, that is right, somebody did make a purchase of…let's see now…one bottle of Triazolam containing twenty tablets. This would be at about, oh, twelve noon today."

"Can you remember, could you describe the person?"

"Oh yes, I can remember, . It was a young girl, maybe twenty years old or thereabouts."

"What color hair?"

"Ah…fair I think."

"And how did she speak? Did she have an accent at all?" Graham didn't realize the inappropriateness of this question till after he'd asked it.

"Well, I don't remember that she spoke at all, actually."

"Not at all?"

"Not that I can remember, no."

Graham suppressed a sigh of annoyance. "So I suppose you've no idea where she went after she left you?"

"Oh no, she just bought the pills and left. Is that all the information you require?"

"Yes, thank you very much for ringing, Mr…"

"Patel."

"Mr. Patel. Oh—just one more thing. Can you tell me if Triazolam has any harmful side effects?"

"Well…" He paused to consider. "Every drug has side effects to a greater or lesser degree, and it depends on the individual patient. But this drug is not particularly toxic. Taking one or two tablets a day would not cause any noticeable side effects."

"What about if taken in large doses?"

"There is a warning on the label—"

"If the warning was ignored?"

"Well, in large doses…In a pregnant woman there would be some risk of miscarriage. But this woman was not pregnant."

"What's it generally prescribed for?" asked Graham, wondering if a second opinion would back up Joe's findings.

"Sometimes it is used for cases of mild epilepsy. But mostly it would be prescribed for insomnia or stress."

"And this woman didn't have a prescription from her doctor?"

"She did not. But we are allowed to sell small quantities of the drug over the counter. She had an empty bottle with her which had obviously been obtained on prescription."

"Can Triazolam be addictive?"

"I suppose there is the potential for any drug to become addictive, but that would depend on the personality of the patient."

"Mr. Patel, I want to thank you very much for your help" gushed Graham. "You've been very kind in calling me."

"Not at all, I'm very happy to be of assistance. Good evening to you, Inspector."

"Goodbye." Graham put down the receiver and sat staring at his hands, lost in thought. So the girl was in London, and even in the same area. But how the hell did he locate her? She was so close, almost within his grasp, yet tantalizingly unreachable.

What the chemist had said about a miscarriage made a lot of sense, after Mrs. Kurowski's story about the girl in her hotel. If she'd been popping those pills like no tomorrow, no wonder she'd lost her baby. It seemed like reckless behavior, even unhinged. Perhaps her actions really were totally out of her control. Even if she had committed murder, she was bent on her own destruction too, and that made her more tragic than evil. What a waste of a young life.

Graham couldn't help smiling to himself as he thought that. It was so like something Pat would say. She was always willing to see the good in people and to sympathize with their troubles. Perhaps that was why she was drawn to the hostel and to helping down and outs. Even inviting them home, for heaven's sake! This young girl Susanne Martin, for example, was precisely the type of person that would elicit Pat's sympathy: pretty; young; distressed, possibly—having lost her baby (Pat would no doubt empathize strongly with that)—hooked on sleeping pills to dull the pain...

Something suddenly came back to Graham. Something Pat had said. Hadn't she mentioned the word *tablets*?

Something horrible had been gnawing at his mind all through that telephone call with Pat, and now that he had time to think about it, the possibility of its being true made him feel sick. He picked up the phone with trembling fingers and dialed a familiar number, his heart beating hard as he heard Pat's voice on the other end of the line. She had lost her tone of pent up rage and she sounded calm, almost cheerful.

"Hello. 2938."

Graham couldn't keep the urgency out of his voice. He didn't have time to make conversation. "It's Graham, Pat. Just tell me—the girl you've got staying in Gemma's room, what's her name?"

"What do you want to know that for? You can meet her when you get home."

"Tell me her name!"

"Tracey…something…I don't know her last name, I don't think she told me." replied Pat in a baffled voice.

"Tracey Nightingale."

"What? Do you know her?"

"You could say that. Just…just…don't do anything. Just wait there till I get back." Graham hung up. Pat wouldn't know what he was talking about, of course, but that wasn't important. The nightmare had arrived. And he had to act fast.

Chapter Ten

▼

Graham jerked to a halt at the traffic lights—the fifth in a row that had gone red just as he drove up to them. Why were the bastards always against him when he was in a hurry?

As they changed to green, the chap in the car in front started up his engine, moved a foot ahead, then stalled. Graham bared his teeth, put his fist on the horn, rolled down his window and yelled obscenities. The drivers in the right hand lane glared at him in disgust for making such a fuss, but Graham ignored them, seizing the first opportunity to push into that lane himself and scudding along the road as fast as he could without actually bumping the cars in front.

He continued to swear to himself, in a rage of panic and frustration, oblivious of everything but the need to get home, urgently, at once, before it was too late.

Now all the pieces of the jigsaw had come together and the full horror of what had happened was dawning on him. Susanne Martin was the killer he'd been looking for. And Susanne Martin was at his house, being "sheltered" by Pat. She was a dangerous woman, sick in the head.

She'd killed several times before, complete strangers, with no motive but her own warped imaginings. There was no telling what she might do next.

Why hadn't he listened to Pat before when she told him about the girl at the hostel? Why didn't he ask her name? Why didn't he pick up the clues earlier? Why hadn't he taken more notice of Ruth's crazy notions?

Too late to castigate himself now. *Just get home in time. Pray God, let me be in time!*

*   *   *

In the living room of Graham's house, a fire was blazing cheerfully in the grate. The sky had darkened almost to its evening tones, and a cold wind was blowing around the house, making the windows shake. But the two women didn't notice. Pat hadn't even bothered to draw the curtains, as she usually did at this time of day. She was listening to one of Ruth's anecdotes. Ruth was speaking animatedly between mouthfuls of one of Pat's homemade scones, and laughing at something in her story.

The sound of this laughter reached the small figure clad in a pale green night dress, who hovered outside the half open door. She peered into the brightly lit room from the dark recesses of the hallway, and recognized Pat—the *kind woman* as she referred to her in her thoughts, as she'd forgotten her name—sitting on the sofa, her face in profile. The other person, sitting on an armchair opposite, Susanne could see less distinctly. She had her back turned to the door, and her long black curly hair hung down her back in lavish folds. Susanne knew who it must be. She'd already guessed, of course. That was why the kind woman had invited her here. At Tracey's instruction.

Well, there was only one thing to be done. She had to stop them laughing. They were laughing at her again. She couldn't stand that laughing.

She padded down the hall and opened the first door she came to. The light had been left on, and a few wisps of steam floated from the lip of a kettle that had just been boiled and was left on the table. The kitchen was very neat and tidy, with pine work surfaces and cupboards and a gleaming electric cooker with a black shiny face. On the wall above the sink was a wooden spice rack with rows of jars, uniformly labeled, and a number of hooks with kitchen utensils—a fish slice, a wooden spatula, a spoon with holes, a cheese grater, a large pair of scissors…Susanne eyed the scissors with interest. They had a red plastic handle and quite long down pointing blades. Like her scissors at home.

She had to do it. It was the only way. She had to do it.

She slid the scissors off the hook and held them in her hand. Her mouth had gone dry. Her hands shook. She was frightened. But she had to do it.

*   *   *

Graham reached the corner of his street. *At last!* But he didn't dare breathe a sigh of relief yet. Not till he was inside the house.

He changed down into first gear and drove slowly along, searching for a parking space. *Damn!* That bloody blue Fiat had parked outside his house again.

He couldn't believe it. Not a single solitary space the whole length of the street. He'd just have to double park for once, for now. This was an emergency! He reversed, as quickly as he could, till he was level with his house.

*   *   *

Pat made a move towards the living room door. "Would you mind if I leave you for a few moments, Ruth? I've just got to check upstairs."

"Yes, of course."

"I've got someone staying in Gemma's room at the moment."

"Oh really—a relative?"

"No, a young girl I met at the hostel where I work. She seems to be in trouble, so I thought it couldn't hurt to let her stay for a while. I just want to see if she's still asleep, or would like a cup of tea."

"Go ahead" said Ruth, smiling. "I'll just have a look at your photographs, if that's all right."

Pat disappeared and Ruth moved to the mantelpiece over the fire and fingered a picture of a little girl in a brass frame. Graham was sitting beside her, looking much younger, and every inch the proud dad. If only she'd known him before, when he was young, before he'd met Pat. But it was too late. Ruth already realized the truth, she'd realized it as soon as she met Pat and talked to her. Graham belonged to her. His relationship with Ruth wasn't real, it was a male fantasy, an ego trip. And for her, a bit of adventure, a dangerous flirtation. She would tell him it was all over.

The door creaked open behind her, but Ruth didn't turn round, assuming it was Pat.

"Is she still asleep?" she inquired, still looking at Gemma's photograph. There was no response.

Ruth turned and saw a young girl standing behind her. Her eyes were wild and staring and on her face was an expression of rage mingled with terror. In her hand she held a pair of kitchen scissors, raised as if poised to strike. She screamed one word: "Tracey!"

Ruth stepped back and gasped in horror, as the girl lunged for her.

Graham heard the scream, as he came plunging through the front door. He followed the sound and leapt into the living room, to see the girl standing over a prone body, the bloody scissors in her hand, ready to strike again. She was screaming in a high-pitched wail like a banshee. The words were incomprehensible, as if it was a wild animal screaming.

Graham threw his weight on to the girl, knocking her sideways, and the scissors flew out of her hand and across the floor, leaving a trail of droplets of blood. The girl fought and kicked, still screaming, but Graham held her arms pinioned behind her back.

"Oh my God!" Pat's startled cry, made Graham turn his head towards the doorway. He was amazed to see her standing there. In his mind he'd connected her with the body on the floor. Now, as the body stirred weakly, he saw by the mass of tousled black hair, that it was Ruth lying there, with blood gushing from the wound on her face. *Ruth!* What in heaven's name was she doing here?!

Pat took in the horrific scene, without knowing the significance of its events. She rushed over to the groaning

Ruth and stemmed the flow of blood from her gashed face with the edge of her white blouse. "What happened?" she wailed. Graham ripped off his tie and tied it tightly round Susanne's wrists. Then he got up and rang for an ambulance, too stunned to answer Pat's question.

Susanne lay motionless, no longer needing the tie to restrain her. Her eyes were wide and unblinking, staring at the ceiling above her. She saw the pattern on the ceiling so clearly, it felt as if she had just awoken from a long and dream-filled sleep. The joker had gone. She remembered everything. And she wished she could die.

Chapter Eleven

It was half-past two on a Wednesday afternoon in late December. The air on the street was cold and clear and shoppers walked quickly, huddled into their fur coats or sheepskin jackets, their footsteps making a sharp clack along the pavement. *Jack o' Lantern's* coffee bar had its name written across the beveled windows in gold Victorian lettering. Inside, the decor was tasteful and unfussy—small tables covered with lacy tablecloths, a single flower in a small white vase on each one. At the moment, there weren't many people in the place. *Jack o' Lantern's* was always less crowded at this time of day, once the lunchtime snackers had left and before the evening rush began. A single waitress—clad in black skirt and white apron—waited idly for custom, hovering next to the kitchen door at the back so that she could chat to her companions.

At the table by the window, a middle-aged woman sat. She was wearing a neat blue suit and her silvery ash blonde hair was stylishly bobbed to frame her round, rather fleshy face. She had ordered two coffees, as if waiting for someone, and as she sipped from her own, she gazed out of the window with a comfortable smile. Suddenly, her face lit up and she waved to someone in the street.

A young woman entered the coffee bar and joined her friend by the window. She was tall and rather striking, with a mass of curly black hair which was pulled hastily back from her face into a plain ponytail. She moved with energy and assurance and it was obvious that she had once been very attractive, but some unfortunate accident had left a large ugly scar on one side of her face, which no amount of make-up could disguise.

"Hello Pat, sorry I'm late" she said as she sat down. "Oh, you've ordered for me already—thanks."

"I knew what you'd like" Pat replied, smiling. "How are you? Busy as usual?"

"Of course" Ruth laughed, gulping her coffee gratefully. "I need this, I can tell you."

"I didn't know if you'd have difficulty getting here. With the tube strike."

"Not at all. I didn't realize how close we are to you, actually. It only took ten minutes to get here. Josh gave me a lift in the van."

"Josh—is he your boss?"

"Oh no, I don't have a boss as such. He's one of my colleagues. He's a great guy, always on the go."

"Just like you?"

"Absolutely. I never seem to stop from morning till night. Not that I'm complaining. It's great. You know I like keeping occupied."

"It sounds like you're enjoying your new job."

"I certainly am!" Ruth enthused, her eyes bright. "I don't know why I never did this before—well, yes I do, I was addicted to the money and the glamor of working in television, but I always felt hollow inside. Of course, it's hard work, bloody hard, and sometimes the kids drive me nuts, but I always know I'm doing something worthwhile, you know?"

"That's wonderful. I had a feeling you'd be happy there."

Ruth suddenly grinned. "And how are you?" she asked.

"I'm fine."

"As ever. I like your hair like that, by the way" Ruth commented. "When did you get it done?"

Pat touched the coiffure, as if reassuring herself that it was still in place. "Only the day before yesterday. I think Graham was a bit unsure about it at first but, once he'd got used to it he had to admit it suits me better."

"Men are always suspicious of change, aren't they?" Ruth didn't wait for an answer to this rhetorical remark, but continued: "Shall we order a cake? I've heard they're wonderful here."

"Not for me, thanks. I'm watching my figure. But you go ahead."

"It doesn't matter how much I eat, it just falls off me. Nerves, I suppose. Or metabolism."

"You're lucky" Pat remarked without envy. While Ruth asked for the sweet trolley to be brought round to their table, she inquired: "So, this Josh—is he your new beau?"

Ruth laughed at the old-fashioned word. "Oh good heavens, no. He's just a friend. Think I'm quite happy without a man at the moment."

"Good. As long as you're happy."

"And you—are you happy?" Ruth asked the question very directly, with an earnest and well-meaning gaze.

"I'm very happy" Pat replied. "I really am. Life's very pleasant. Gemma's living with us again now, well it seemed more sensible since she works just round the corner."

"She's working?"

"Oh yes, passed her degree with flying colors and got a job almost immediately—"

"Good for her, in the current climate."

"Exactly. Of course, she wants to move out as soon as she can find a flat on her own."

There was a slight pause. Ruth wondered how Pat would cope when Gemma left home for good, in view of everything Graham had said about how much their daughter meant to them and how she was the cohesive glue that made their marriage stick together. But for some reason she had a feeling that Pat would cope surprisingly well.

Ruth knew that there was one subject they had been skirting around. But it would have to be broached sooner or later, for the sake of their friendship. "How is Graham?" Ruth didn't betray any emotion when she said the name. Anyone listening in would never have guessed that they'd been more than just good friends.

"He's very well" responded Pat with a flicker of pride. "He's been promoted to Superintendent."

"Really? That's great."

"It's done him good, his ego I mean. It'll be more of a desk job now, I expect. But I think that'll suit him better in a way."

"You must be pleased. I mean, you never were too happy about him working in homicide anyway, were you?"

Pat laughed. "You make it sound like one of those American police programs. No, I wasn't happy. It always made me nervous for his safety."

"And you're proud of him, of course?"

"I am. In fact, we're going on holiday for a couple of weeks to celebrate."

"Well" Ruth rubbed the edge of her cup with one finger, "I think that's a good idea."

"We haven't been away together in years."

"About time then. Shall we have another one of these?"

"Not for me, I'm afraid. I don't want to be bulging out of my swimsuit."

Ruth ordered another coffee for herself, then changed the subject. "I saw an article in the Ham and High today. About Susanne Martin."

"Oh yes. Poor girl."

"Did Graham tell you what sentence she got?"

"Yes. Twenty years in Westbury mental asylum." Pat shook her head. "I suppose they think it's preferable to a prison sentence, but…"

"Oh it *is* better. She'll get some help there, not just be left to rot."

"I can't help feeling sorry for her. Just a young girl."

"You always did, didn't you." Ruth smiled.

"I'm sorry, Ruth" said Pat apologetically. "It must be different for you. After what she did…to you."

"No…I don't hate her. I don't blame her. I know she suffered. I'm even sort of…grateful, in a strange way."

Pat looked puzzled. The scar was so noticeable.

"Obviously I'd rather not have had *this*." Ruth fingered her scar with a habitual gesture. "But it forced me to change my life. And it was a good thing in the long run. I'm much happier now, in myself."

Pat shook her head in admiration. "I think you're very brave."

"No, not really. I had to cope with it, so I just did. I think everything in life is meant. I was meant to leave television and take up counseling. I wasn't meant to be with Graham. You were."

The two women smiled at each other for a moment without speaking. There was a bond between them, stronger than friendship, the bond of mutual experience, of a trauma shared. They had nothing in common, except an understanding of each other, and an appreciation of each other's differences. Ruth admired Pat's stability and selflessness, Pat admired Ruth's courage and strength.

A ray of late afternoon sun streamed in through the window and lit up their table, making their faces shine, as if they were on a stage.

*   *   *

"Did you do that?"

"Yes."

"It's a baby Jesus, isn't it? It's very good."

Susanne looked down at the picture she had painted. A child's face—the expression vivacious and full of life—was depicted in glowing colors of red, yellow and orange, surrounded by a sort of golden halo. It hadn't taken her long to do—a couple of hours at most—and the paints had seemed to arrange themselves on the canvas as if she had nothing to do with the picture's creation. It had sprung directly from her soul and imprinted itself on the cloth.

"Do you really like it?"

"I do. You've got a real talent." Claire McDonald leaned over Susanne, her left earring dangling by the girl's head. Claire McDonald was a resident care worker at the asylum: she led the patients in Group Therapy, Music and Drama, and Susanne was her special protege.

Susanne always felt warm when Claire was around. She liked the scent she wore, and the soft Angora cardigans and her earrings, which were always large and colorful—a string of bright beads or a gaily painted bird. Susanne felt more confident when Claire was there to protect her. And she told Claire things she'd never told anybody else before.

"My husband…Jeff…" Susanne replied, forcing herself to speak his name, "didn't like my paintings. I tried to do them sometimes…"

"What did you like to paint?"

"Oh, just the things around me. The sea…the abbey. I liked the abbey. But Jeff said my paintings were terrible. He wouldn't have them in the house."

"He didn't destroy them, did he?"

"No, I hid them in a drawer." Susanne hid a smile behind her hand. "If he'd found them he would have burnt them. He didn't let me paint."

"Well, more fool him."

Susanne smiled up at Claire. "Can I sing again today?"

"Well, we'll have you leading the choir next, won't we, Susie? Yes, of course you can sing again. Do you like carols?"

"Oh yes" she breathed, her eyes bright. "My favorites. I like that one…that children's one…what's it called?…"

"Which one do you mean? *Away in a Manger?*"

"Yes. I love that one."

Claire smiled indulgently and thought to herself what remarkable progress this young girl had made, in just a few weeks. It hadn't taken much to make her trust: just some love and attention. "Just do me one favor, would you, Susie?"

"Yes?"

"Give Arthur his tea. He won't take it from me."

Susanne was the only one who could get on with Arthur. Most people found the old man crotchety and unreasonable, but he and Susanne were the best of friends. She'd painted the picture for him and she was going to give it to him as a Christmas present. It was supposed to be his child, the boy he'd lost in the war and never got over. And maybe it was her child, too.

About the Author

Carmen Lynne is from Yorkshire in England and moved to London as a teenager to pursue an acting career. The little town of Whitby written about in the book, was a favorite vacation spot from her childhood, and a place of atmosphere and mystery. This—her first novel—was written several years ago while living in England. The crime thriller is her favorite genre, and she prefers the exploration of character, to twists and turns of plot. She has written three other novels. For many years an actress, Carmen now works in television and film production, and lives in Los Angeles with her two cats.